I've travelled the world twice over,
Met the famous: saints and sinners,
Poets and artists, kings and queens,
Old stars and hopeful beginners,
I've been where no-one's been before,
Learned secrets from writers and cooks
All with one library ticket
To the wonderful world of books.

© JANICE JAMES.

THE GIRL WITH RED SUSPENDERS

If Detective Inspector Dave Smart's trained eye had missed the flash of her red garter, he would never have discovered Patricia Felton's otherwise demurely clad body — extraordinarily beautiful, even in death. The coroner's verdict confirms Dave's heartfelt conviction that Patricia was murdered, and he becomes embroiled in her last days: her dangerous delving into crime, drugs and vengeance. Dave would have moved heaven and earth to win her had he known her alive — now he'll do the same to apprehend her murderer.

Books by Barbara Whitehead
in the Ulverscroft Large Print Series:

HOUSE OF GREEN DRAGONS
SHADOWS END

BARBARA WHITEHEAD

THE GIRL WITH RED SUSPENDERS

Complete and Unabridged

ULVERSCROFT
Leicester

First published in Great Britain in 1990 by
Constable and Company Limited
London

First Large Print Edition
published August 1994
by arrangement with
Constable and Company Limited
London

British Library CIP Data

Whitehead, Barbara
   The girl with red suspenders.—Large print ed.—
Ulverscroft large print series: mystery
I. Title
823.914 [F]

ISBN 0–7089–3142–1

Published by
F. A. Thorpe (Publishing) Ltd.
Anstey, Leicestershire
Set by Words & Graphics Ltd.
Anstey, Leicestershire
Printed and bound in Great Britain by
T. J. Press (Padstow) Ltd., Padstow, Cornwall

This book is printed on acid-free paper

To Barry, with love

Author's Note

I would like to thank Mr and Mrs P. Eckart for kindly allowing me to set several scenes in the delightful Ship Inn at Acaster Malbis.

Although the story takes place in York, all the interior settings except those in the Ship are imaginary, as are some of the external ones. Also purely imaginary and not based on any real person, living or dead, are all the characters. My fictitious police force still has its headquarters in Clifford Street, although the real police headquarters moved to Fulford long ago.

Prologue

THEY were alone and savouring their loneliness.

"It's not often we can be by ourselves, is it?"

"But you're going away and I don't know how I can bear it."

"One day we'll have our own house and live together all the time and we'll be able to do as we like and not see anyone else."

"We might want to sometimes. You'll want to go sailing, and flying and I'll want to go shopping and eating out and . . ."

"We can do those things and still be alone whenever we want to be."

"We could go up on the moors and take a tent and not see anyone else."

"We could have a country cottage deep in a wood."

"Oh, my darling, why do you have to go away!"

"To make a lot of money so that we

can break away and be on our own."

"All our lives it's been like this. We're no sooner together than we have to part again. Ever since we were six."

"No, seven."

"Yes, you're right, seven. We ought to be used to it by now."

"But we never do get used to it."

"Never."

"It's like a pain every day that we can never forget."

"You could get a job here."

"Harry's gone to a lot of trouble to get me this chance in the City. I can't throw it in his face. We can't get anywhere unless we earn enough to be independent and you aren't going to get much."

"There are other things that matter to me, my work matters. I'm not very bothered about money. You know that."

"I am. And you're as ambitious as they come. So while you're indulging your hobby I'll go and earn a lot of lovely lolly and then we can . . . "

"I'm frightened of what might happen with you away."

"You mean to me. Without Sister taking care of me."

"Yes, I mean that."

"I've always managed before, haven't I?"

"You're very competent, Sebastian."

"I've had to be."

"I'm still frightened, this time. I don't know why."

It was Easter and the weather was warm and in the garden there was the scent of young leaves.

1

THE suspenders were the only speck of colour in a low-toned scene.

Overhead the sky was dark and bellowing as Detective Inspector Smart stood on the end of Lendal Bridge and looked out over the river, the riverside walk and garden on the nearside of it, and the range of buildings on the other side of it, and saw a picture of dun and grey — a dozen different greys — and black and brown. A picture an artist could have painted given only three colours to mix all the shades; ivory black, flake white and raw umber would have done it nicely.

Apart from that tiny touch of scarlet, brighter than arterial blood.

DI Smart wondered afterwards what impelled him to retrace his steps — for he had just started to climb the bridge from the Tanner's Moat end. He was coming off night duty, two hours late due to unforeseen circumstances arising

5

— the little matter of a burglary which was the last in a series, now concluded satisfactorily from the point of view of law and order and less satisfactorily for the team of criminals involved.

At least the late finish to his shift — by now it was eight o'clock — had meant that the cheerful little corner shop was open, and he paused near the bridge end only to put away in the pockets of his thick winter overcoat the things he had bought there.

He put two tubes of Polo mints and three packets of chewing gum in one pocket, and a bag of Maltesers and two Kit-Kats in the other. Having just stopped smoking, he would need something to chew at and nibble during the long deliciously idle Sunday that stretched ahead of him. He intended to spend his day sleeping, reading, eating, watching television, all sitting by the coal-effect gas fire, just as the fancy took him.

If he had not paused he would never have noticed the scrap of scarlet. If he had not been a Detective Inspector he would no doubt have put it down to some colourful piece of dropped litter.

Dave Smart paused irresolute. The thought of his bed and his flat was strong within him — and the longing for them.

He turned.

He went back down the slope. He rounded the end of the bridge wall and turned again, almost 360 degrees, to walk down Tanner's Moat towards the river. The trees shook and shivered in the strong wind; in the grey light of morning an old sheet of newspaper blew along ahead of him as if leading the way. He came to the paved walk by the riverside, before the ornamental gardens began, where in summer the tourists strolled.

All the wooden seats were deserted at this hour on a winter Sunday morning. He went past them towards a black heap on the ground, a heap that from the bridge might have been taken for a couple of half-full dustbin liners, or a pile of black decaying leaves — for anything but what it was.

As he came close there was a feeling round his heart like ice and he wished he had not paused on the bridge, not looked over here at all.

The figure lay sprawled on the ground, such a muddle of disordered black that it was at first glance hard to make out. But there was no doubt about the left leg.

The black skirt was up to hip level revealing a patch of white thigh and the scarlet suspenders, the fragment of colour which had caught his eye. They were pulled taut across the pale flesh, running between the black of the skirt and the black of the stockings.

As he stood motionless looking down, a stronger gust of wind pulled up black sodden leaves from the gutters and brought them plastering themselves against his trousers. They flapped like low-flying bats across the body of the girl. One of them rested like blotting paper on her exposed skin and Inspector Smart bent and picked it off with a shudder of distaste that she should be so desecrated. He almost expected that patch of pale skin to be warm to his touch and indeed it did not seem truly cold; as if it had not yet taken on that marble coldness . . .

Looking up, Smart saw that he was no

longer alone in this grey chill world where only the Open All Hours sweet shop had given a sign of human life. A down-and-out was walking, head bent, along the road towards him, old jacket tied round the waist with orange plastic string. The down-and-out went past, shambling, incurious. His passing snapped Smart out of his inactivity.

He felt in his pocket for a notebook, looked round, and wondered how he could get in touch with the police station without leaving the girl unguarded.

Of course, the sweet shop. He ran back to it; the down-and-out had gone, probably under the bridge.

"Look, I must ring the police with an urgent message," he said to the girl behind the counter. She blinked her eyes and looked at him owlishly as if she had been up all night, but she lifted the hinged flap in the counter and let him through. Ringing the station took only seconds.

He went back immediately to the girl by the riverside, and began to look at her properly.

The legs, the first thing in view, were

in plain black stockings with a band of lace round the tops, and were unusually graceful and pretty. They ended in black court shoes with a medium but slender heel. The tangle of black clothes above the legs was made up of the wide-skirted coat and the dress under it, both black. The body seemed somehow to be a huddle of black, so that until Smart walked round it — past the outflung hand lying like a white petal on the stone flags — he did not really perceive the girl's head.

She was extraordinarily beautiful.

At first he saw only the back of her head — the pale cream-gold curls, the slender white neck. He walked round the top of her head. Her face was in profile against a wide-rimmed black hat which had fallen on to the ground. Pure and haughty, he thought. An outline so pure, those delicate bones and that wonderfully textured skin, that artists must have longed to paint her. The eyes were slightly open — enough to give a blue gaze between the straw-pale lashes. Although the eyebrows were cosmetically darkened, the lips were so pale a pink that they must have been untouched by lipstick. Her whole head was like a cameo in ivory, and she lay outflung, arms wide, one hand still clutching the strap of a black shiny handbag. Her legs were modestly together, one on top of the other, and it was the top leg — her left one, revealed by those shockingly raised skirts — which showed the only thing which seemed at variance with the rest of her. The scarlet suspenders were made of gathered chiffon and topped by a peeping frill of scarlet lace, the metal and rubber of their clips the same identical brilliant red, fastening up the lace-topped stockings.

He took her pulse, gently lifting the slender wrist, but there was no pulse to take.

Smart stood perfectly still.

In a few moments the rest of them would be here. For this tiny space of time he had her all to himself, and could gaze at her.

The clothes were expensive, he knew that. His marriage seemed a long way away now . . . but he remembered enough of what Aileen used to wear to know which women's clothes were expensive, well chosen and good, and which were not. Even now he flinched at the memories; he thought he could remember all Aileen's clothes, her blouses, her skirts, her suspenders . . . He knew she would have touched these fabrics appreciatively and admired the cut, even though he saw them crumpled and disordered.

It was the first time since Aileen's death that another woman had had the power to stir him — and this girl too was dead.

Her skin is not milk, he thought; nor is it cream. Perhaps it is single cream — yes, that's it. How proud she is, even in death. Only just in death, for surely she was not quite cold when I touched her? A little earlier and I might have prevented it, might have been here when . . .

But there was no sign of violence, no blood.

She lay as if tossed down, a rag doll thrown away by a child. Or as if flying, pirouetting on one leg, but somehow in the horizontal plane.

12

There was even a grave joyousness about her.

And the knowledge crept in on Dave Smart that unless he found out who had killed her and in some way avenged her death, he would never sleep soundly in his bed again.

He knew that a bright, new image had for the first time overlain the fading image of his wife and their child, who had been born when his wife was technically dead after a car crash; a child who had followed its mother into death so quickly that he could hardly remember what sex it had been. The drunken driver had got six months.

All that had been five years ago.

He thought he had got over it. He didn't often think about it any more. As he bought his supply of sweet stuff today and anticipated his Sunday's leisure he had had no thought for anything but animal relaxation and self-indulgence.

Perhaps he hadn't thought properly about Aileen for a very long time.

"If I'd met her when she was alive . . . " he thought now, looking down at the girl in red suspenders, "I would have

13

moved heaven and earth. No sooner found than lost. Not that she would ever have looked at me. Too ordinary for her. What hair."

He longed to run his fingers through the pale curls, to touch the fragile hand again. He stood there like a block of wood, and so the patrol car found him.

The two constables parked and walked over. They glanced briefly at the body of the girl and looked away again, as if almost embarrassed. "What a place to die," one of them said, and shivered. They had hardly time to greet Dave, stand around, comment on the cold of the wind and decide to light a fag, before a police car arrived from Clifford Street with plain-clothes men.

They also walked over in an elaborately casual way, saying, "Hi, Dave."

"Suspicious?" asked Detective Inspector John Rollo from the morning shift.

"Young and healthy-looking, no immediate sign of cause," said Smart. "Sunday morning. Probably the result of something happening Saturday night."

"You were just going off duty, mate?"

"Surely was."

14

"You look half dead. And you'll have to come to the station to give your witness statement before you have a bit of kip." John Rollo had strolled closer and now he looked down at the body. He did not speak for a while, then drew the automatic conclusion for a policeman of his experience. "Booze or drugs," he said cheerfully. "Party last night I expect."

"Could well be," said Dave Smart, who was convinced it was nothing of the sort.

"Well, we'll have to take the usual preliminary steps in case, but I don't think you've any reason to worry, mate. This looks like a natural or accidental death to me. Pretty typical case on Saturday night or Sunday morning. Inhaled vomit or whatever. It will be all cleared up at the post-mortem. Waste of resources really, doing all that photography and stuff."

"You may find something useful." Smart was rapidly going off his colleague.

"Oh, don't you worry. We'll do a careful search."

Rollo's manner was casual. It was a foregone conclusion to him. Youngsters these days would fool about and this was the result. Mentally he shrugged his shoulders. A pity and all that — Smart looked quite upset. Have to jolly him along a bit.

There was a screech of brakes to herald the arrival of the police surgeon. He looked pale and tangle-haired as if just aroused from sleep. Dave bristled. This was a man he couldn't stand, though it was hard to say why.

The police surgeon came over and gave a casual nod. He looked at the girl without any change of expression.

"Mysterious death," said John Rollo, with a teasing glance at Dave Smart.

"Really?"

"If you will certify death . . . "

The surgeon nodded. "Better go through the motions, I suppose — but she looks pretty dead."

He took a long look round. Then he squatted down with one knee on the stone flags. He picked up one of the girl's arms to test for post-mortem rigidity, then took out a stethoscope and, pushing his hand into her clothing, listened for the heart. He took out an ophthalmoscope and looked at the optic discs, seeing there the expected 'trucking' of the red cells in the retinal blood vessels.

"Nothing to it," said the police surgeon, glancing up from his kneeling position beside the body. "Just a boozer."

He had done all that was required of him. It was a matter of seconds rather than minutes before he had certified the girl dead. Dave Smart remembered why he didn't like the police surgeon. He was a cocky beggar.

He was greedy as well. "I don't want to be here all day," he said. Pulling the thin form 22s from his pocket he added, "Here, somebody sign this for the attendance allowance."

"You're in a hurry, aren't you?" said Dave.

"I don't turn out at this time on a Sunday for the sake of my health."

DI Rollo signed without comment.

"I'm glad to see the back of him," said Dave as the surgeon drove away.

The police surgeon had only been a demonstration of the way things were.

The girl in red suspenders no longer

belonged to DI Smart. An anonymous body, she belonged now to the mortuary, to the post-mortem, to the pathologist, to the forensic scientist.

The Coroner's Officer appeared a couple of minutes later.

Dave Smart, an onlooker only in the current proceedings, noticed that it was the younger of the two Coroner's Officers who had responded to the Detective Inspector's radio message. The lad looked nervous. He hadn't been on the job long. The sight of the dead girl obviously produced in him a kind of horrified fascination. He could neither look nor not look.

"Handbag, eh?" said cheerful DI Rollo. "Soon identify her, as soon as the boys have taken their pretty pictures. Doesn't look as if there's much to stop us moving her, Simon." He turned to the Coroner's Officer. "We should be ready in less than half an hour. Can you get permission from the Coroner?"

Smart felt as though he could hardly bear to see the routine work — to see everything carried out in such a matter-of-fact and normal way. But he wanted to stay with her, as if he could give her moral support.

Then his colleague said, "You may as well get down to the station, Dave, give your statement. This is the big one, eh? Not often we get to actually find a body ourselves. Bet your adrenalin's flowing."

To his surprise, Dave Smart found that it was. The time when he had felt sleepy was as far away as last year. He turned abruptly from his brooding contemplation of the girl.

"Right, I'll get on there."

Without a backward glance he walked off, retracing the steps he had taken such a short time before. All thought of his lazy Sunday fell from him. He hardly noticed the wind, the lightening sky, the gleam of sun which was reflected on the dull khaki-coloured river.

In his mind's eye was the profile of the girl. Since finding her he had become aware of a change within himself; after the arid years he had found an aim and an object in life, something to search for, his own personal Grail.

One of the police team was about to set up posts and tapes to define the way by which everyone must approach the body to avoid destroying possible evidence. A second was preparing to photograph the girl.

"Don't bother with the posts," said John Rollo, kicking with distaste at a pile of dead leaves. "Nothing to this death. Just a few photos will do."

Most of the leaves were too wet to fly satisfyingly up into the air. They settled down again with a kind of heavy collapse and only a few were carried along by the wind.

They carried on with the bare minimum of routine work.

In less than half an hour they lifted her from where she lay.

2

WPC Jenny Wren (christened Gladys), twenty-four, five feet seven inches, nine stone, single, straight medium-brown hair cut boyishly short, hazel eyes, no distinguishing marks worth mentioning, had parked her car at nine o'clock on the Sunday morning in the Lord Mayor's Walk car-park.

For one thing there was no car-parking space for her at the police station; for another, she expected to be sent out west of the city during the day and parked here she would have a quick get-away instead of being stuck in the traffic.

She shivered slightly as she got out of the car into the cold wind. The strange tingling feeling of early morning was still around. Hers was the first car in the park.

As she turned into the narrow stone-flagged alley-way leading back to Lord Mayor's Walk proper she hummed quietly to herself. Perhaps because she remembered it was Sunday the tune was 'All Things Bright and Beautiful'. Lifting her eyes, she could see, filling up the farther end of the alley-way, the city wall with the Minster rising above it, the lovely tracery of some of the windows of the North Aisle, and part of the long horizontal line of the roof.

A serene city, far from industrial wastelands, race riots, or any of the other kinds of deep trouble in society. The city walls girdled its heart. The soaring Minster was steadfast and grey in the morning light.

Her heels clattered on the stone flags of the alley-way. She looked down at something quarter seen. In front of her was a mess she side-stepped hastily to avoid. She stopped, on the few inches of clear paving.

A pool of crystal liquid. A smashed hypodermic and two broken phials, one with a chemist's label. Debris including a Walkman and two cassettes, smashed also as though the whole lot had crashed down on to the pavement together.

It was the shock of it — in this cathedral city. This prim county town. This hidebound, conventional place. A place, she thought, where people did not need to take drugs to escape their lives.

She bent down, a good police officer, observing things. Observing with her gorge rising because this was the first time she had been face to face with the fact that even in this perfect city there was a rancid underbelly. She had known with her head without realizing it emotionally that there was drug abuse everywhere, and that it must be here too.

She stretched out her hand — and withdrew it. Better not touch. The thought of Aids came into her mind. There was no blood or vomit or anything except this clear liquid which she did not think was urine, but supposed must be something to help an addict get over an addiction. But still better not touch.

Jenny Wren walked on; there was no action to take. The city looked as serene as ever. It was only her perception of it that had changed.

★ ★ ★

The station, when she arrived there, was buzzing.

"What's happened?" she asked.

"Well, if you will arrive at lunchtime . . . "

"You know I'm not due today until nine thirty."

"All right then. DI Smart's found a body. He's giving his witness statement now."

"A body?"

Strangely enough it was not often that a police officer found a body. It was usually a member of the public, walking home perhaps, who noticed a shape in the river water, or a sodden lump on the bank, or that a neighbour had not taken in the milk bottles, or who had heard a scream in the night. Then the police would be called and would go into action, often not alerted until long after the most vital evidence had been dispersed by curious sightseers or rain and wind and time.

"That'll be exciting for him," said Jenny. She tried to remember which DI Smart was. After only a fortnight at the station since her transfer she was finding it difficult to call him to mind.

"Nothing will excite old Dave. He's

24

made of rock. You never see him lose his cool."

"Oh? Which is he, anyway?"

The other WPC stared at her. "You don't know? He's our dear Robert Southwell's side-kick. You know our Bob, I expect?"

Jenny did, because he had interviewed her.

"Is Smart a big bloke?" she queried, trying to bring him to mind.

"Big like the side of a house, black hair a bit curly, reddish face, grey eyes but because they're usually crinkled up they look dark as if they were brown."

"Oh, full marks for observation."

"I just happened to notice one day. Don't worry, there's nothing in it."

"I wasn't worried. Nothing to do with me. Is he married?"

"Yes. Still. His wife died five years ago. But he's never looked at another woman since."

"Faithful type."

"He's all right, our Dave. You'll see him today anyway. They won't let him go for ages. You know it takes for ever to go through all that has to be done."

"I know we spend most of our time doing paperwork," grumbled Jenny.

* * *

Detective Chief Inspector Robert Southwell should not have been on duty that day at all. Nor — on the face of it — had anything happened which necessitated his presence. But the Detective Inspector who had come out to North Street in response to DI Smart's telephone call had, by ten o'clock, decided that he ought to let his superior know. Not summon him, of course. Not for such an ordinary death. Just put him in the picture. Then — if he decided he ought to come in — then that was all right. If not, Monday morning would do just as well.

Bob Southwell might have been away from home, taking his family out for the day — 'and about time too,' Linda, his wife, would have said. Or he might have replied to the telephone call, 'Right, get on with it,' and that would have been that.

As it was in the modern semi-detached house on Ouse Avenue they had all

26

risen late and the four of them were just finishing a very enjoyable Sunday morning breakfast.

Apart from Bob's wife Linda, who was watching him thoughtfully, there were the two children, Susan and Paul.

"Daddy, can I have the supplement to cut up?" asked Paul, who was making a scrap book full of sports cars.

"I want it, Daddy," said Susan. Her scrap book (because she always had to do what Paul was doing) was full of ballet dancers and there were some nice pictures in the supplement today. Mostly they were on the back of the article about sports cars.

"I don't think your mother's read it yet."

"Mummy, when you've read the supplement please can we . . . "

"We'll see. If you promise not to quarrel over it."

Bob had finished the Sunday paper and he had begun to wonder what to do with the rest of his day.

The herbaceous border was what Linda had suggested. Once a year — and today was the ideal day for it — herbaceous

27

borders needed a good clear-out. She did what she could in the garden (Linda was very good at sounding aggrieved when she wanted to) but really digging up great big plants which needed splitting was a bit beyond her.

Bob had protested mildly that he thought on such an unpleasant day it was beyond him as well — when the phone rang.

"I'll come down to the station," he said.

"Bob! You are the limit!"

So he kissed her.

"I really will do that border, my love," he said, "and it might even be this afternoon if the weather picks up a bit. Otherwise one day soon, and let's spend today in front of the fire, with the kids, just enjoying being a family and reading or watching telly or playing silly games."

Which was the sort of day Dave Smart had planned out for himself two hours earlier, except that he would have been spending it alone, and much of it in sleep.

"Well," said Linda, "there's no rush, is

28

there? Have some more coffee before you go. I've just put the percolator on again." It wasn't that she minded being a police wife. But there were other things. Like togetherness.

"Can we come down with you, Daddy?" asked Paul. He knew the answer would be no but it was worth trying.

"What sort of silly games are we going to play?" asked Susan.

★ ★ ★

WPC Jenny Wren had made her trip out of the city and returned before a police constable came into the main office, carrying the black handbag of shiny Italian leather which DI Smart had first seen in the hand of the dead girl.

"We may need it again, but you'll want to notify the girl's family," the pathologist had said on the phone to John Rollo, who now walked into the room behind the constable.

The contents of the handbag were spread out on the nearest desk.

A fine handkerchief of white linen,

hemstitched. A packet of tissues. A lipstick in a fat gold holder. A matching gold compact with machine-tooled decoration. A small spray of very exclusive scent. (Expensive Christmas presents, thought Jenny, looking up from her work.) A slim purse matching the handbag, rounded by a few coins. A matching wallet, the kind with more places for credit cards than any ten people could possibly want. A diary of the Filofax type, in black leather. A key-ring with a gold bauble and a short gold chain, bearing a latch key and a car key. A Lillet in a small polythene bag. A foil tape of headache tablets with one gone. A slim paperback book.

Jenny's superior turned and beckoned Jenny over. Jenny picked up the paper-back while her superior picked up the diary. The title of the book was the kind she found hard to remember, but it was on sociology, she knew that much. She'd failed to make head or tail of such things when she was at police college and doubted if she'd have much more success now.

Glancing over her superior's shoulder

she admired the neat pointed writing on the personal pages of the diary.

Patricia Feltame, The Grange, Murtwick, York.

"A job for a WPC, I think," said DI Rollo.

"Trip for you, Jenny," said her superior. "Someone will have to go out and break the news to her family, tactfully, and make sure they're all right before leaving. I think you'll do it well. We'll need one of them to come down and formally identify her. Tell them that their daughter has been found dead but that we don't know the cause of death yet."

"I don't know where Murtwick is."

"Not far away. Come here and look at the map. You can even see The Grange, it's marked. They won't be short of a bob or two."

★ ★ ★

After nearly two miles of suburbs where the city had run out to join its surrounding villages, Jenny was driving through a flat, drab, agricultural country-side. Apart from the dun-coloured pasture

31

fields there was newly turned ground, some of it probably winter-sown with grain crops. The hedges were nearly bare and the taller trees were giving up their remaining leaves to the wind. Except as a relief to suburban streets, she saw little to recommend it.

The farmhouses were brick-built, mostly tall and Victorian, with large complexes of grain silos and the most utilitarian farm buildings possible. She began to lose hope that The Grange would have anything better to offer.

There were at least trees. She turned in at the drive entrance and went down between the swaying branches and tall ivy-clad boles of what she guessed might be ashes, because they certainly weren't oaks, elms or sycamores. Then there was a turning circle of still-green grass in front of a refreshingly long and low building of old clamp bricks, obviously expensively modernized. It had a porch supported by mass-made Ionic columns and windows of the most modern double-glazed imitation Georgian variety, where the glazing bars seem to be between the two layers of glass. In an unexpected patch of sun the house glowed like a well-tended cat.

Jenny rang the door bell and waited. It would not have surprised her if it had been opened by an aproned maid.

Mrs Feltame was in her fifties, a largish woman although not as tall as Jenny. She had hair that visited the salon once a week, a colour-matched pale blue jersey and skirt, and a smart spotted blouse showing at collar and cuffs.

"Yes?" she said.

"Mrs Feltame? I've called about Patricia. Are we right in thinking that she is your daughter?"

"Yes?"

"Mrs Feltame, may I come in?"

The sitting-room into which Mrs Feltame led Jenny had ivory walls and a beige carpet, but the predominating colour was a delicate aqua, from rugs and curtains and palely from paintwork. The vases in deeper blue-green were filled with flowers — mainly chrysanthemums — in creams and very pale yellow. It was lovely, but the kind of room in which Jenny felt that she had mud on her shoes and hairs on her skirt, and was a blot on the landscape in general. She reminded herself that here was a mother, who had shortly to learn that her daughter was dead, and that grief was the same whatever the home.

"I'm sorry, but I have bad news for you about your daughter," she said.

The other woman was still impassive, presenting a front behind which Jenny could not see.

"Was she living here with you?"

"Yes. My husband is abroad for some time and Patricia came to live at home while he was away, so that I should not be alone." Walking to the door, Mrs Feltame called out in the direction of a clattering kitchen noise, "Coffee for two, please, Mrs Briggs."

Jenny felt faintly surpised. She could not imagine Mrs Feltame caring whether she was alone or not. She gave the impression of being one who 'liked her own company', as the curious expression is.

"Patricia was not at home last night, I think?" she questioned gently.

"I really don't know. Saturday. I don't think I saw her all day. Oh yes, after breakfast. I breakfast in my room, you see. She did come in and tell me that she was going into York and didn't know when she'd be back. So I wasn't surprised when I hadn't seen her by eleven o'clock. I always go to bed at eleven. I haven't seen her this morning but I expected that she was still asleep. Mrs Briggs," went on Mrs Feltame to the woman who had just come in with the tray and two cups, "have you seen Patricia this morning?"

"Her bed's not been slept in," was the short reply.

Jenny waited until she was alone again with Mrs Feltame.

"I'm afraid that I have bad news for you," she repeated, thinking that she had not been properly understood before. "Patricia has met with an accident."

"How are you so sure that it is Patricia?" asked Mrs Feltame, without apparent emotion.

"Her diary gave her name and address."

Jenny felt that she ought to go on to give more details. "She had her handbag with her; it was black leather, with a few personal possessions, including a diary."

"Her handbag could have been stolen."

"Yes." Jenny felt at a disadvantage. She had not seen the body and if she asked Mrs Feltame for a photograph of her daughter could not know if the girl was the same as the corpse. "I'm afraid, Mrs Feltame, that the girl who had the handbag was dead," she said very gently.

There was in response a stiffening of an already rigid back, and a firming of already firm features. Mrs Feltame gazed at her blankly. Jenny returned her gaze in silence, unable to say anything else.

"It will be a mistake, of course," said Mrs Feltame.

"We will need someone to identify the dead girl."

"Sebastian will have to go."

Jenny wondered who he was.

"I couldn't be expected to go to see some dead girl to prove to you that she is not Patricia," went on Mrs Feltame. "Her brother will have to do it."

"Sebastian is Patricia's brother?"

"They are twins. But Sebastian isn't here either at the moment. I'll have to get in touch with him."

The uncomfortable tête-à-tête was interrupted by a ring at the door bell.

36

Mrs Feltame rose impatiently and went out to answer it. Jenny took a quick gulp of her coffee; it was extremely good, but then, Mrs Feltame was not likely to have anything that was not.

On her return Mrs Feltame preceded a large man who immediately dwarfed everything in the room. There was something about his solid, almost ponderous walk, and his massive bulk, which made Jenny guess instinctively who and what he was.

"Detective Inspector — what did you say your name was?" Mrs Feltame said to him; "Smart — that's it — I expect you two know each other."

"I'm new at the station," responded Jenny, jumping to her feet. "WPC Wren, Detective Inspector. I came to break the news to Mrs Feltame that we believe her daughter has met with an accident. She has suggested that the handbag might have been stolen, and that therefore the girl might have been someone else and not Patricia Feltame."

DI Smart turned courteously to Mrs Feltame. "Have you a photograph of your daughter?" he asked.

"I'll bring one." She went out of the room.

Jenny Wren and Dave Smart exchanged glances. They stood in silence until a few seconds later Mrs Feltame reappeared bearing a large framed photograph.

"Patricia has some weird friends," she said. "A photographer is one. He has made a lot of studies of her."

Dave Smart took the photograph. As he looked down at it Jenny felt as though a shock wave had hit the room, yet apart from a slight movement of the mouth he stood still and apparently impassive. He looked at it, now quite motionless, for what seemed like hours.

"Well?" said Mrs Feltame sharply.

"Mrs Feltame," and his voice had a curious cracked timbre, "I must ask you if I can borrow this photograph for our use at the station. I must tell you, with very deep regret, that this is the girl who was found this morning."

"Found?" For the first time Mrs Feltame's composure split a little.

"She is dead, Mrs Feltame," and Dave Smart's voice was as gentle as the touch of fur.

3

JENNY had to stay for a little while at The Grange and then, if Sebastian Feltame could not be contacted, bring Mrs Feltame down to the station to identify the body and make a statement.

At the moment Jenny was standing in the faint sun, near the porch with the Ionic columns, talking to Dave Smart. He had passed her the photograph, yet somehow she felt that he did not want her hands to touch it.

It was not a single image, but a composite of three heads, in the manner of old painters when they were doing preliminary studies for a portrait. One was full face, one the left profile, one the right; a sculptor could have modelled a bust from it. The three were arranged artistically so that they made a satisfying composition. It was not this aspect of the photograph that held Jenny's attention, but the sheer beauty of the girl portrayed.

She had that look which can be taken

for arrogance but is the effect of a certain sort of fair, delicate-boned beauty in a girl brought up with every luxury. Her hair seemed to swirl out round her head in soft locks which curled round naturally at the ends. The profiles were striking, like outlines on coins, but the full face was more so because the effect of keen intelligence was added, in the gaze of the light eyes and the waiting look, as if the girl was intently listening to a fascinating conversation and thinking out her own contribution.

"She's stunning," said Jenny.

"That's the right word. Only the wrong tense."

"Is there anything you want me to do?"

"Ask Mrs Feltame to lock or seal in some way the door to her daughter's room. Explain that in order to discover how she died we may need to examine it. Drive the importance of that home. She's the sort of woman who would be in there, messing around. In fact I should have fastened it myself."

"I'll do it," said Jenny. "The death must be suspicious, then?"

"We don't know yet. It's not obvious how she died. Shall we say, that's suspicious. Her clothes were dry so she hadn't drowned. There were no marks or injuries to be seen, not as she was, dressed. There'll have to be a PM. She looked like a healthy girl, and she was just there, dead."

"You didn't formulate any theory?" asked Jenny.

"No. Rollo did. He thinks it's just a typical Sunday morning death. Over the country there must be quite a few through the year — young people. Drink, or perhaps drugs, or a rough house, and there you are."

"If it had been a hit-and-run driver," volunteered Jenny, "she might have internal injuries which don't show."

"It's a theory. I suppose it's possible to be damaged internally without breaking the skin, sufficiently to die. Then the driver might have got rid of the body before running — just moved it a little way off the road. Yes, that's certainly a theory."

"But you don't think that's what happened?"

DI Smart looked at her heavily.

"You know what I think happened? What I thought as soon as I saw her? I think she was murdered. It is fanciful. Not the sort of thought that one is supposed to have on seeing a body . . . but it seemed in my head as if she was crying out, 'Avenge me!'"

He laughed, a nervous sort of laugh for a large man. Then he realized that what he had said could make him the joke of the police station. He should have kept his big mouth shut. Was Jenny the sort who would retail the remark? He really looked at her for the first time. She seemed a nice sort of girl, and gazed seriously at him without any trace of a smirk.

"And you're going to," she said.

"If I possibly can."

She handed the photograph back to him. "You'd better get on with it then."

"I'll probably see you later," he said more happily, taking the photograph and going to his car.

Jenny faced the unpleasant task of dealing with Mrs Feltame.

★ ★ ★

A middle-aged woman with a bush of wiry hair under a knitted hat was walking in the blowing wind under an unexpectedly sunny sky. She was by the open river with its winter-desolate gardens and had just left the morning service at All Saints North Street.

She had enjoyed herself. The church was one of the most interesting in the city. It had a good deal of very ancient stained glass, a ceiling with carved angels, and a beautifully proportioned spire.

Now she was relishing the morning, and decided to make a detour from the direct route and walk a long way home. There was a path as far as the lattice ironwork of Scarborough Bridge, which was built for trains but also had a footway. There she would cross over the river.

She walked along North Street and all unknowing passed the paving stones where not long before DI Smart had found the body of Patricia Feltame. There was nothing now to show that anything out of the ordinary had occurred.

Walking on sensible flat-heeled shoes through the arch under the flank of Lendal Bridge the woman came out into the open area leading to the boat house of the rowing club, then the Esplanade car-park, and at last to Scarborough Bridge.

The wind ripping through the trees was tearing off fresh leaves and filling the air with them. They hurtled towards her like many tiny golden discus, and the blue air in the temporary sunshine made her think of Greece, and athletes, and ancient Olympic Games, and the straight handsomeness of the group of rowers who just then passed carrying their slender craft reinforced the theme.

A broken-down old wino had also passed so it did not surprise her to see by the riverside another dark, helpless-looking figure. What a pity that this wreckage of lives could not, it seemed, be avoided.

As she walked closer the figure by the river did not move. There was plenty of time to observe him.

There were moments when the woman was glad that she had left youth behind.

The longer she looked at the young man by the river the more she felt that she ought to speak to him and see if there was anything she could do to help, and if she had been younger she would have hesitated. When you were still personable men always thought you were making a pass at them if you behaved in a natural way — particularly a caring way. But being middle-aged, and having put some weight on, and not really worrying how you dressed — all these things made a difference.

Even so, it was not easy.

The young man was sitting on the edge of the footpath, where there was an abrupt slope down to the water. When the river was low a second footpath was seen lower down, but now it was running full and fast, and the thick soup-coloured strength of it covered the lower path.

The man looked young, in his twenties it seemed at first. But closer it could be seen how ravaged his face was. The profile was lined in the way no young face should be. He was shivering. His clothing was smeared with mud and powdered with dust as though he was sleeping rough. It was the look of abandonment to tragedy that had drawn the passer-by towards him.

She stood next to him for a few seconds and he took no notice of her.

"Do you need any kind of help?"

He did not seem to hear. She repeated the question.

Then waited. It seemed stupid to ask again.

At last he stirred, and turned his head, and looked at her.

She felt her heart crumple, her whole being fall, fail, tumble inside, and wished there was something to hold on to. Standing there four-square sturdily on her feet, she felt overwhelmed by pity, so overwhelmed she could not speak.

After a while, in which she deliberately thought of other things, of the golden leaves, of the rowers who were now skimming by on the river, impervious apparently to wind and cold, of the blessed blueness of the sky, he replied, grudgingly.

He did not need anything. He did not want anything. He wished she would go away. He spat a curse at her and called her a word which she knew and wished she didn't.

The golden leaves blew down to join the black sodden ones on the pavement.

★ ★ ★

By the time she had walked on as far as Scarborough Bridge the woman knew that she could not leave it like that. She turned and went back, but the young man was nowhere to be seen.

Disconsolately the woman wandered along retracing her steps, once more through the arch under the flank of decorative statue-bedecked Lendal Bridge, past the flagstones, past the flower beds of the gardens.

Then she met Canon Oglethorpe leaving All Saints with his surplice rolled up under his arm.

"Looking for something?" He knew her very well, but for the moment couldn't for the life of him remember her name.

There was a young man I spoke to. I'm sure he's on drugs. I wanted to help him, and I don't know where he's gone."

"We'll look together. Those sort of

people often congregate round the shelter at this end of the gardens."

She blessed the old man's instant acceptance of her desire to help. Together they went to the shelter, built like a curved triangle, and on the side of it nearest to the river they found the young man.

"Got anywhere to sleep?" Samuel Oglethorpe asked in a friendly way.

"Sleep?"

Macbeth hath murdered sleep . . .

"I don't think they'll take him in at the Shelter under the influence like this — it isn't the sort of thing they're meant for — but there's a new little refuge started and nobody knows about them yet so they aren't full and might be able to cope. Let's try to get him there. You're quite right, he can't be left."

They heaved him up and half carried him along.

"Frog marching, eh?" shouted the young man. "I'm gonna throw myself in the river. You aren't gonna stop me."

"We're only taking you to somewhere safe," said Oglethorpe in his surprisingly beautiful voice. Men in their seventies

48

did not usually sound so clear and resonant, even though he could not in any way compare to his friend Canon Grindal whose voice sounded like musical chords.

"The party's over," said the young man. His limbs flopped in all directions.

The three struggled onwards. The woman had long since stopped enjoying the wild autumnal weather. The young man became aggressive and began to fight them.

"It's not far now," panted Oglethorpe.

As quickly as he had become aggressive Sebastian Feltame seemed to pass out. Luckily they were almost at the small makeshift refuge.

The warden promised to do what he could. "Though they're pretty hopeless at this stage," he said.

"You know, my dear," said the Canon as they turned away, "I'm not sure that you ought to get yourself into things like this. These people can be dangerous. He could have hurt you. Drug addicts can have the strength of ten men. It really is stupid. You would have been far better notifying the proper authorities."

The woman had the horrible feeling that he was right. She had felt frightened. She had had to fight the longing to run away and leave the young man to throw himself into the river if he wanted to. His eyes had been peculiar as if they saw some other world and in that world she might seem to be a monster. His face would haunt her dreams. She left the Canon and went the quick way home.

* * *

There had been no passer-by to intervene when, seven or so hours earlier, Patricia Feltame had parked her car in the Esplanade car-park and walked under the arch of Lendal Bridge.

She struggled to remember what she had done with her useful flat driving shoes and tried as she walked to keep the slender heels she was wearing out of the roughnesses of the paving. Then she leaned against the rusticated stone wall of the Electricity building, sheltered from the wind, melting into the darkness of early dawn and tree shadows.

Patricia was half crazed with emotional

exhaustion and lack of sleep, keyed up with tension, desperate almost to madness. Her eyes were fixed on the windblown river and road, watching the empty choppy water and the empty tarmac for the first sign of something coming; watching, watching . . .

4

THERE was that feeling in the station. It was hard to describe, but every policeman knows it. It was the feeling which comes when something special has happened, or is happening. The Queen is coming, or it's the university Rag Day, or a crime case has occurred which everyone instinctively feels has the hallmark. The hallmark which marks it as different to everyday crime, the hallmark which makes it distinctive — a crime for the history books.

Bob Southwell felt it the moment he walked over the threshold. "A body?" he had said on the telephone. "Dave Smart found a body?" And here he was at last — wanting to know more about it; wanting to know who, what, where and why.

"Dave here?" he asked.

"Yes, sir. I'll ask him to come through to you."

Bob found there was something different, too, about his Detective Inspector. Dave Smart walked in differently; his bright glance from those screwed-up eyes that were grey — and only looked brown because of the way they were always crinkled, as if against the sun — his glance was different. He was holding a large framed photograph in his hands, and a thin file of papers.

"This is your case, I hear," said Bob humorously. "No need for me at all."

"I found the body, sir. An apparently healthy young female, no injuries to be seen, no obvious cause of death. In fact she hardly looked dead, when I first saw her. I was just going off duty at eight o'clock. Delayed by the Bristow case."

"Sorted out?"

"Eventually."

"Right." Bob settled in his chair. "Tell me."

Detective Chief Inspector Robert Southwell and his Detective Inspector David Smart had taken to one another when DCI Southwell had moved to York on promotion and they had first worked together. Neither of them had found any reason since to stop liking the other.

Bob enjoyed his post, but there were times when he cursed his administrative work and the time he spent at his desk and wished that he could work more often shoulder to shoulder with Dave on actually doing the nitty gritty of enquiries — the very thing he had been bored with not so long before.

He leaned back now in his chair, teetering on the back legs and doing the old Marley-tiled floor a bit of no good, long and light in the body and leg, long in the jaw, large in the spectacles, wide-browed and thin-haired, keen. That was the word for him, his staff had long decided. Keen as a knife blade, that was their DCI. He could be cutting, too. He wasn't as soft and purry as an old kitchen cat, not by a long chalk.

Dave told him the facts. He could not tell him the way he felt about this girl, the feeling he had had of being a ship which has passed in the night and missed its chance, the feeling that she cried out to him, 'Avenge me!'

"You feel possessive about her, don't you?" asked Bob.

54

Dave's head shot back and he looked, startled, at his superior. For once those crinkled-up eyes were wide open and anyone could have seen that they were really grey. Bob stretched out his hand for the photograph. Stunned, Dave yielded it up.

"Yes." Bob studied the black and white print, which still gave the impression of the girl's colouring. "I can see why you're smitten."

"How can you be smitten with anything that's dead?" asked Dave angrily, for that was the problem that had been exercising him.

"People fall in love with the bust of Nefertiti," said Bob, "and she's been dead for considerably longer. People have been fascinated for several centuries by Mary Queen of Scots. Don't worry, Dave, you're not likely to go in for necrophilia as a hobby just because you found a body which, for once, was not repulsive but beautiful. Bodies often are beautiful — read a few Victorian novels and see how the appearance of the dead is eulogized. We aren't usually so lucky. The bashed-in look, the throttled expression, the cyanosed, the bloodied, the agonized — those we're used to. The beautiful is not a frequent mode in police circles."

Dave's aspect lightened.

"No reason why you shouldn't be in charge of the investigation," said Bob.

"That's what I want."

"Sure."

"Don't want to upset anyone, though."

Unspoken was the knowledge in both their minds that the officer officially in charge at present was John Rollo, and that he wasn't going to like being displaced.

"I'll have a word."

The case didn't need two Detective Inspectors, but it should be possible to sort it out amicably.

"Rollo and you on good terms, aren't you?"

"OK, boss."

Dave sounded guarded. They'd got on well up to pres. But after this morning, Dave Smart wasn't so sure any more. He wasn't sure because of John Rollo's reactions to the dead body of Patricia Feltame.

Bob got up and went over to a chart on the wall. "As it happens," he said, "John's got leave booked, starting Thursday. So it makes some sense for him to hand over to you. But it will take time to rearrange schedules. You'll have to work your normal shifts for now."

"John asked me to go out and see the girl's family, although I'm officially off duty," put in Dave. He knew why John had asked him — to get him out of the way. Dave supposed he had been looking over everyone's shoulder a bit too obviously. Well, he knew he had.

"As I see it at present," Bob went on carefully, "this could well be an accidental death, in which case it will be cleared up in no time and that will be that. Fuss over."

"Yes, Bob."

"If it isn't accidental, where does that get us?"

"The suggestion has been made that it was a hit-and-run driver, internal injuries only, threw her over the bridge, say — no, she couldn't have landed where she did — carried her the short distance to where she was found — "

"Seems possible. The PM will check that theory. And if it's wrong, as I said before — where does that leave us?"

"Murder."

"Which is what you've thought all along?"

"It's what I've been sure of all along."

"Not suicide?"

"I don't believe so."

"File?" said Bob.

Dave produced the file — still slim as yet, very slim.

Bob studied the list of the contents of the handbag, the report Dave had made on his arrival back from The Grange, Murtwick, Dave's witness statement, and the other papers.

"About that hit and run theory — it seems unlikely judging from this. Stockings not laddered, no obvious clothing damage. Car key, I notice. Hardly the sort of girl who waits for buses. Where's the car? First job, find it."

"Right."

"Second job, examine the diary, try to find out what she was doing last night, and what her pattern of life was, generally."

"Right."

"Find out her job."

"We know that, from her mother."

"Yes?"

"Social worker."

"I don't believe it."

"It does seem unlikely. Her mother seemed to think it was beneath her."

"She looks the Sloane Ranger type. A little light relief in an estate agent's office for upmarket housing, a secretary to a very important captain of industry, a career girl in the diplomatic service, an antique shop perhaps. Hardly going round slummy dwellings trying to persuade mothers to feed their children properly or fathers to keep their hands off them, or struggling with the problems of today's teenagers."

"I agree. She doesn't look like the type that usually goes in for social work — not that there is a type, exactly, only that she isn't it. It tells us that she must have had something else besides the beauty you keep going on about."

("Hardly mentioned it," murmured Bob.)

"Compassion, a sense of responsibility

for society. I think she'd be practical, too. She'd think, don't just feel sorry, *do* something about life."

"The more loss, then. Though we can't afford to lose beauty from this world either." Bob suddenly tired of the discussion. He pushed his chair away from the desk on its two back legs with a screeching sound. "I leave it to you, Dave. I'll be in at six tomorrow morning. I'll have a word on my way out, and tomorrow I'll see what can be done about reorganizing rotas to get you put just on this — work what hours the job requires — eight a.m. to eight p.m. if that suits you. Until that's organized you'll have to stay on your scheduled shifts, as I already said."

"Right, boss."

"Don't forget that until we get a result from the pm we're only speculating. Find out where she was last night and who with if at all possible. You can get in touch with me during the rest of today if you want, but I'd rather you didn't. I have an appointment with a herbaceous border."

The idea of the garden had gained

considerably in charm.

"Not a very good day for gardening," commented Dave Smart.

"True. But it will do me good. It will take my mind off our work a bit to wrestle with earth and roots and get cold and possibly wet. It's an old neglected border planted up by the previous occupants of our house and during the summer Linda marked which plants she wanted to keep and which wanted splitting and which are going out altogether. She's got great plans for it. All I'm needed to supply is the hard graft."

Dave wished he had a wife to boss him about in a garden. And he had a new mental image of her, superimposed on the old one of Aileen. A slim blonde girl with blue eyes and a skin like single cream. Somehow he was sure she would be good with plants, even though her hands were so delicate. If she had planted anything he felt it would have grown. Perhaps she had planted something — many things. He must find out what.

Bob turned at the door. "I'll tell you one thing, Dave, to get you thinking," he said. "That handbag. It wasn't her day-to-day one. Unless she'd cleaned it out specially because she was going on a date. Women's handbags are more random than that. Where are the old check-out tickets — bits of paper with shopping lists — screwed-up tissues — ball point that leaks — that sort of thing? It's all too neat and glamorous. Find her other one, or her waste-paper basket, when you get round to it."

Bob set out on his journey home in a different frame of mind to that in which he had left it. Linda, warm, desirable, with that serious expression when she talked about her plants, her comely rounded face and dark hair, above all, her *aliveness* — their two lovely children — the comfort and relaxation of home — all glowed ten thousand times brighter than they had when, eagerly on the scent of murder, he had left them an hour earlier.

He felt sorry for Dave. True, Dave had no beastly herbaceous border to tackle. But the girls Dave loved were dead. A herbaceous border was a small price to pay.

* * *

Patricia Feltame had never been able to garden at her parents' house — they employed a gardener and he was jealous of his preserves. 'When we've got our own home,' Sebastian had said.

'Roses?' 'Lots of roses.' 'I'll plant silver-leaved plants and foxgloves and silver birch and honeysuckle leaning in at the windows . . . ' 'Just for us?' 'Just for us.'

* * *

Patricia Feltame's car. That was the first thing.

There was nothing for it but to ask her mother. The car key shared that gold chain and bauble with the latch key, no useful tab with the maker's name. There had been no clue to the type of car among the contents of the handbag. Reluctantly he picked up the telephone and dialled the number for The Grange at Murtwick.

The voice that answered didn't sound like Mrs Feltame, so he asked for her.

63

"I'll see if she is available," said the voice. Mrs Feltame's came on next, rather harsh, controlled.

"Detective Inspector?" she said brusquely. "I'm coming down, as you requested, Detective Inspector."

"Yes, ma'am." Dave Smart couldn't have said the last time he'd used that form of address. "Thank you for your co-operation. I rang to ask if you could tell me the registration number of your daughter's car?"

"I've no idea. It's an old Metro." Her voice conveyed what she thought of Metros.

"What colour, ma'am?"

"White."

"How old is old?"

"It must be at least three years."

"Do you know in what town your daughter bought it?"

"Here in York."

"Thank you, very much."

Not quite what he expected until he thought about it. A social worker could hardly visit all sorts of places in — say — a Lancia or a Porsche, which would have seemed more natural for Patricia

— he could quite see what her mother meant. A Metro would be just about the right image, as acceptable as the all-black garb she favoured. With the information he had he would be able to ring Swansea, and ask them to help if they could. Given the town of registration, the year, and the name and address of the owner to use as a check, they should be able to find the exact number for him — he hoped.

The uniformed branch and the traffic wardens were asked to keep a look-out for the car, using the description he had at present, and the matter could rest there until with the actual number they could check out the car-parks and so on.

A priority job was to contact the Social Services and find out what her job was, etcetera. As it was Sunday and already afternoon Dave decided that that could wait until Monday morning first thing.

Her diary, Bob Southwell had said.

It was not the kind of diary in which young ladies pour out their hearts, but he had not thought that it would be. It was an engagement diary, with brief entries, mostly a name and a time, often only initials. Sometimes there was a place mentioned.

He was amused to see that she had conscientiously filled in many of the personal details asked for on the front page, National Insurance number, and so on. He wondered how many people bothered. Somehow he found that infinitely touching. Then he had a brainwave. He turned back to the page. Yes, she'd written in the registration number of her car. That problem was solved. Triumphantly he circulated the new information.

Every now and then there was the name 'Seb' or the initial 'S' and he remembered that she had a twin brother called Sebastian, and made a note to interview him.

There were no entries for the Saturday. I think I ought to talk to this Sebastian right now, thought DI Smart. He wondered what the present position was with Mrs Feltame. Had that new young WPC brought her in yet? Yes, was the answer to that. They were in the building.

Jenny Wren had brought the mother

to the station with some difficulty. At present she was trying to persuade her to drink a cup of station coffee, with the realization that it was infinitely inferior to the product drunk at The Grange. The Coroner's Officer was with them, waiting until Mrs Feltame was ready to do the identification.

DI Smart entered unobtrusively, amazing Jenny, who hadn't realized that he could.

"I would like to talk to your son, Mrs Feltame," he said. She lifted a face ravaged by tears.

"So would I," she exclaimed in a tart voice.

"Excuse us a moment," said WPC Wren, and gestured Smart from the room. Once they were out of hearing distance she could put him in the picture.

"She flatly refused to come to the station at first, and I was about to decide that a statement would be just as good taken at her home and to have the identification done by someone else, when she said she'd ring her son. It seems he's been a good athlete. He went in for skiing and bob-sleighing, the sports you'd expect in someone of his background. He's not a bad cricketer, either, so I'm told. Pilot's licence, of course. She has lots of photographs of him, all in sporting gear. Very much *jeunesse dorée*."

"You what?" said Dave.

"She rang his office. He's now gone in for a career in the City. Sounds pretty cushy. Anyway, he's stopped working there. She didn't know. He finished last month and hasn't been seen since."

"Didn't tell his mother?"

"Too right."

"When did she see him last?"

"Six months ago. The way she talked of him, I thought he must be around all the time, but that isn't the case. She must be a lonely woman, Inspector Smart, because her daughter doesn't seem to have meant as much to her as this son. He was everything, I think. The husband hardly gets a look in. Oh, she has photographs of him too — very high-powered appearance. It didn't seem to occur to her to ring him first, although he's the dead girl's father."

"You suggested it, I suppose?"

"Oh yes. 'There's the time difference,'

she said. As though he wouldn't want her to ring him whatever the hour of day or night, on a matter like this."

"I expect she is stunned, people don't think straight. The son seems to have had a better relationship with his sister than he does with his mother. Patricia was seeing him regularly. There are a lot of entries in her diary for 'Seb' or 'S' which is probably the same."

"His office had no address for him. Mrs Feltame wanted him to do the identifying, but as he's not available and her husband's abroad, I'd no alternative in the end but to more or less force her to do it — hence the coffee. I'm having to nerve her up to go to the mortuary. The Coroner's Officer is waiting."

"One thing," Dave Smart said. "She looks pretty distraught. She must have really cared very much for her daughter, although you think she didn't."

"She didn't shed a tear until she found that Sebastian had gone missing."

"Oh. Well. But I suppose it suddenly hit her."

Jenny liked Dave Smart the better for his efforts to be charitable, not realizing that he couldn't think ill of Patricia's mother, hard and arrogant though she seemed to be. Had she been one of Macbeth's witches he would have found some excuse for any behaviour on her part. It stood to reason, he thought, that no one could lose a daughter like Patricia Feltame without being shattered for life.

★ ★ ★

A few minutes later Jenny and Mrs Feltame drove off in the still-strong wind to the mortuary.

The body they were shown was shrouded in a sheet to the chin. Jenny gave the beautiful head no more than the quickest of looks. Yes, she thought to herself. That's the girl in the photograph. That's the girl DI Smart was so affected by. She's lovely. Men always go for that. Jenny felt no special reaction; she could see that Patricia's beauty had had a spiritual quality, but she felt untouched.

What concerned her was the atmosphere of the mortuary, the chill of the bodies there, the smells which could not be totally quenched. Also she was in charge of Mrs Feltame. She was more bothered about how she was reacting to things.

"She took after her father, you know." Mrs Feltame turned to Jenny. "She didn't take after me at all. All those silly ideas." The voice was still harsh, but the shock of seeing her daughter had had a profound effect. She was speaking more colloquially. Jenny took her arm with sympathy.

"Come away now," she said.

"It ought to be nice having a daughter," Mrs Feltame went on in a complaining tone. "You ought to be able to do things together, go shopping and things like that. She ought to come out to bridge parties with you. Not always be fretting about people who aren't anything to do with her. People who ought to help themselves and not need helping. And if she wasn't worrying about other people she was always off out with her own friends or with Sebastian. You might as well not have a daughter."

"I'm sure you enjoyed each other's company very much," murmured Jenny.

"She never chose to give me her company," said the mother acidly.

Jenny wondered when the tears would come. She knew that this was a common enough reaction to death, the voicing of complaints about the dead, who no longer had the opportunity to change themselves and be the way their loved ones wanted them to be.

It was a little clearer why Mrs Feltame felt as she did about Patricia. Jenny guessed that Mrs Feltame had made demands — which would inevitably have been resisted. That the mother had tried to extort from the daughter the subservient companionship which the daughter could never give her. That in the end she had withdrawn, and written off the girl, and resented her. Now she resented the fact that Patricia was dead.

Jenny felt the arm she was holding tremble. She opened the door on to the cold and wind and helped Mrs Feltame into the car with care. "I'll take you home," she said softly, "as soon as you've made your statement at the police station."

Then Mrs Feltame, shaken by her ordeal, windblown in the few yards she had walked in the open air between car and buildings, and with the tracks of tears down her maquillage, gave a statement detailing all she knew of Patricia's recent life and friends. After that Jenny took her home, and did her best to be calm and comforting.

At the last moment as Jenny was leaving The Grange Mrs Feltame asked her if she would take the responsibility of telephoning Mr Feltame and telling him of his daughter's death.

"She said that she was too upset to do it," Jenny told Dave Smart.

"Understandable."

"So I'm going to ring him now and to hell with what the time is in America."

Dave decided to stay in the room while she did it.

He perched on one side of the desk (Jenny half expected it to tip up, but police desks are made of stern stuff) as she picked up the telephone and with her other hand flipped the pages of the directory, checking the dial code she had been given.

She dialled and they were both silent, imagining the distance the threads of wire were going, wondering where it was that some telephone was ringing.

The call was answered by a hotel switchboard operator.

Jenny was using a new handset, and to his surprise Dave found that he could hear the voice almost as clearly as if he had been pressing the instrument to his ear himself. There was an American accent, but not a marked one. Jenny asked for Mr Feltame.

"He'll be asleep. Do you know what time of night it is here?" snapped the operator.

"I'd like to speak to him, please," Jenny replied politely but obstinately. "This is the British police and this is a very important matter."

A sleepy but firm voice answered the ring in the hotel bedroom.

"Feltame," it said.

Jenny explained gently and as gradually as she could what had happened.

"I want to speak to the officer in charge," said the crisp, no longer sleepy voice on the other end of the line, after Jenny had told the story into a stunned silence. She leaned across the desk to Dave and handed him the phone.

Dave uttered a few words of conventional sympathy.

"Tell me the facts again, I haven't taken them in," demanded Patricia's father.

Dave explained once more that she had been found dead and that so far they didn't know what was the cause of death. That there was no immediate question of a burial, until the cause was established.

"Do everything, regardless of expense," commanded the father. Dave courteously said that expense didn't come into it.

"What's Sebastian doing in all this?" asked his father.

Dave put him in the picture there too.

"Oh my God," said Mr Feltame. "As soon as I can wind things up here I'll be over. Something's going on."

Dave was inclined to agree with him.

"Now I really am going," said Jenny Wren. "I only came in on a Sunday morning for that special job I had to do, and look at the time. I hope I get paid overtime for this lot."

"If you don't like it you shouldn't

have joined," said Dave offhandedly. His head was bent, looking at the file in his hand.

Jenny glared at him indignantly. Are you a machine, Detective Inspector Smart? she felt like saying. Only she didn't. She had been proud and flattered to be working with him as they had done today, she admitted to herself. She'd seen how the other half live, too. She wondered whether she would have any more contact with the case of the girl with red suspenders, and with Dave Smart. Seeing that he wasn't going to look up, she left the room to go home.

"Thank you, Jenny," said Dave as she passed through the door.

★ ★ ★

The file on the death of Patricia Feltame was growing thicker by the minute. Dave Smart had been awake for twenty-four hours, and it would soon be time for his next shift. No concessions would be made for the fact that he had never really been off duty. Police officers were not supposed to sleep when things like this happened to them. Nor, at the moment, did he feel in need of it.

The pathologist rang in.

John Rollo, who had also worked long past the end of his shift, beckoned Dave over.

"You may as well take this if you're now the Officer in the Case," he said, a little tartly. "The pathologist."

Dave took the handset with a conciliatory air. "Who is it?" he asked Rollo. "Brian?"

"Brian's on holiday. It's the senior registrar from the hospital, doing the weekend duty. Martin Smith."

"We've finished our post-mortem," Martin told Dave Smart. Dave closed his eyes. He had deliberately not been thinking of the PM, which had been due to take place straight after the identification of the girl. He could have been present at it — instead, someone else less concerned had been there. He knew that he could not have borne to see her body thus despoiled. A dead carcass it was, no longer holding the spirit of the girl with red suspenders, but to see it cut apart would have been impossible.

Martin, the man who had done the job, was breezy.

"No injuries?" asked Dave cautiously, knowing he had seen none.

"None."

"So that disposes of the hit-and-run driver theory."

"She had no internal bruising, or external either. All her organs were perfectly healthy. She ate well on Saturday evening and drank a little, I base that opinion on the slight smell of alcohol from the organs. There were no injection marks so it doesn't look as if she was on drugs. I've taken blood and urine samples and sent them for testing."

"Pregnant?" asked Dave, his throat suddenly dry.

"Not pregnant. She was not a virgin, although how one is to tell these days when they start using tampons at the age of thirteen goodness only knows."

A patchy mist had formed in front of Dave Smart's eyes and he blinked it away impatiently. Tiredness. Don't let it affect you, Dave. You're a police officer. Just because she was wearing

78

red suspenders of a very dainty and provocative kind doesn't mean she was promiscuous and you never thought she was. It's hearing this man bring these details straight out like that, and not bearing to think what had happened to her body, to her privacy. Did she wear them just to please herself? Not a virgin, though. Did she put them on deliberately, that Saturday night — not just to make her feel good, but to use . . . to tempt someone, for a reason . . .

"What time of death?"

"As far as one can say in these things about two hours before you found her — say about six — but it could have been earlier."

"So what happens now? You're giving me nothing to go on in this enquiry."

"I can tell you what I did find, and what I think it means."

Dave cast his eyes to heaven and prayed to be given strength.

"There was a subarachnoid haemorrhage."

"Which indicates?"

"Something young people do die of. A small aneurysm. There is bleeding around the base of the brain — I haven't found the actual aneurysm, but then you often don't."

"You're saying this is a natural event?"

"Happens from time to time."

"And that's all?" Dave's voice betrayed his feelings.

"Can't give you what I haven't got," said Martin huffily. "We're just plain old obvious cause of death men. Heart attacks, suicides, or heads bashed in. We've done all the tests I can think of, and will await the results of those. We've found nothing even suggestive of violent crime, that's what I'm telling you and that's all I can do. There was nothing under her fingernails. There were no ladders in her stockings. An apparently healthy unmarked body. I say, death from natural causes, probably following on a party the night before."

"It would help if we knew what she'd had for that meal," said Dave Smart humbly. "So far her last hours are completely unaccounted for."

"I'll make a note of your request for that — looked like the usual meat and two veg., but we've saved samples for Wetherby along with the blood and urine," replied the pathologist.

Sitting back in his chair, Dave Smart felt that there was one thing that pleased him about the result of the pm. Patricia had died at least two hours before he found her, looking like a pile of discarded rubbish on the paving. The haunting thought of her seeming not-quite-coldness — the lurking worry in case there had been a chance of saving her and he hadn't done whatever it was — was now dispelled. There had been nothing he could have done except what he did.

Now, the next thing. Wasn't that Baron Corvo's motto? It wasn't a bad one.

What could he do — stuck on night duty — when all the enquiries he wanted to make would have to wait until morning? What was his next thing? Inevitably there would be the normal work which always cropped up on a shift, but so far there was not much sign of a busy night. Sunday night was one of the better ones. So far no suicides or mysterious break-ins or anything else requiring more than routine police work. The other detectives on duty were quietly getting on, catching up with their paper work, writing reports, and drinking coffee. Downstairs the uniformed branch would be listening to the radio messages, if any, responding, answering the telephone. Outside the wind had dropped since sunset, and a grey, damp night had settled over the city. He could hear a light fingering of rain against the window, and could see in his mind's eye how the old building would be turning a darker colour as the rain soaked its surface, how the empty streets would gleam in the lights as their surfaces turned greasy and treacherous. A normal, quiet, Sunday night. So — about this case?

Dave Smart did not for a moment believe that Patricia Feltame had died of natural causes. He did not stop to think that if he was wrong, he could well be blamed for wasting his time and that of others on further enquiries into a death which did not merit the expenditure of resources.

She was a social worker, he remembered. That meant that she might well have been involved in court cases, or been in contact with the police in other ways to do with her work. He could do a few computer checks to see if her name cropped up at all.

He could go through various tall files which were not recorded on the computer, and look at the names of the social workers involved, to see if she was one. She had only been in the job six months, her mother said — but then hadn't she mentioned June? That made it less than six months. A convenient time limit, anyhow. If not too much cropped up this shift he might get quite a lot of checking done of that kind. Of course it might be quicker simply to ask the Social Services in the morning about her workload for the time she'd been with them, but would they be ready to divulge that? Always better to do your own research if you can.

So DI Smart prepared to spend his night shift.

Over the Atlantic Charles Feltame prepared to come home.

5

OVERNIGHT the wind had dropped, and the city drew breath. The last days had been like a combat with the cleansing strength of the tearing westerly. Combed clean of everything which could be blown away and at the same time litter-strewn by flying debris, the old buildings needed time to recover themselves.

Dave Smart was standing with his overcoat collar turned up and the drops of light rain settling on his dark wavy hair, outside the door of the social workers' office when it opened on Monday morning. His hands were shoved deep into his pockets. At that point he had been forty-one hours without sleep. He was not yet feeling the lack of it; as his colleague had said, the flow of adrenalin had kept him going — was still keeping him going. His eyes were acquiring red rims, and towards the end of the night the print before them had blurred a little;

but he felt as fresh and well as he ever had. He had no thoughts to spare for himself, anyhow.

Behind him a few other people had gathered — a man and wife, both in their twenties, with four children in, under, and round a pram, an old man whose coat had worn threadbare on the folds.

"I believe Miss Patricia Feltame works here," Smart said to the girl at the enquiry desk.

"She does, but she's not in yet," was the answer.

"I'm afraid she won't be coming in. Can I see her supervisor?"

There was something in David's tone, calm and normal though he tried to make it, which alerted the girl to the fact that all was not well.

"You mean the area officer. I'll see if he's available."

She rang through. "Who shall I say?" she asked Dave, and he produced his identification.

"Detective Inspector Smart," she explained over the phone, and Dave realized that there was a tiny *frisson* in the air from the moment that she knew he was from the police. "You can go up," she said, and directed him to the area officer's room.

His mind had been so fixed on Patricia Feltame that he had not thought of the effect of the arrival of an unexpected Detective Inspector at her place of work.

Both organizations were working for a peaceful and harmonious society, yet it was often thought that they were in opposition. People condemned the police for being too harsh and brutal at the same time as condemning the social workers for being too soft. He realized that these attitudes were bound to colour his reception, but the matter which concerned him was more important than anything else right now. He had a job to do.

The area officer's door was already open.

"Yes?" said the man. "Can I help you?"

He was of medium height, just taking off his own coat, shaking away the rain, and hanging it on a wooden hanger behind his office door. About forty, Dave

Smart guessed. With the sort of face that has been everywhere and seen everything.

"I've come about Miss Patricia Feltame. I'm afraid she won't be in for work this morning."

"Oh? Nothing wrong, I hope?"

The area officer was looking carefully at him. Under the dripping overcoat Dave was neatly and conventionally dressed in a sports jacket, cavalry twill trousers, white shirt with a faint fawn check and a plain hand-woven brown tie. There was nothing about the detective to raise alarm, although Dave Smart's general massiveness and self-confidence had been misconstrued before now. "Sit down," his host added.

"Something is very wrong." Dave paused, to allow for realization.

People naturally suspect the worst.

"An accident?"

"Possibly . . . I'm afraid that she was found dead yesterday morning."

The area officer held on to the edge of his desk. He didn't say anything for quite a while.

"You say it was an accident? She was a healthy, energetic girl. Very sensible. I wouldn't have thought she was accident prone at all."

"I don't suppose she was. I did not say it was an accident. The fact is, we are enquiring into her death. That's why I'm here. She was found dead and it appears that the cause may have been natural, but we have not ascertained all the facts."

"Will you be holding a post-mortem?"

"That's already been done. We are awaiting the results of tests. Meanwhile we are treating this as a suspicious death which may possibly be murder." Dave had said that before he remembered that officially he had no justification whatever.

The word murder has strange effects on people. There are the pruriently and/or morbidly inclined, who perk up enormously at the very idea. Then there are those whose work leads them into unusual and difficult situations which may be threatening, and to whom it is a spectre which would not be treated lightly.

As the area officer did not say anything, Dave read his thoughts from the expressions which flitted across his face, and replied to them.

"You do see," and his tone was very quiet, "that I must enquire into the circumstances of her life, hoping that something will help us understand her death. So far I know very little. Her diary had no engagements for Saturday night. Her mother did not know what she intended to do that day. Of course she was not at work, but it is possible that she mentioned her plans for Saturday to her friends and colleagues. We have not yet contacted any of her friends and I am hoping that her colleagues here may be able to tell me something."

"They'll be glad to help in any way they can."

The area officer was still looking shell-shocked.

Dave Smart produced his identification, as he had to the girl at the enquiry desk.

"Would you like to check with the police station that this is a genuine investigation, and that I am empowered to make enquiries?" he asked.

The area officer felt this was unnecessary, but it gave him something to do and

Smart seemed to expect it. The act of telephoning the police station helped him to a realization of the ramifications of the situation. He was assured that the nightmare was true and that Patricia Feltame was really dead.

"What do you want to know?" he asked more briskly.

"First, as I've said, I want to talk to her colleagues. Secondly I would like to get the background of her working life — know something about her general routine. Thirdly, I would like to know what she has been working on recently — what people or groups of people she has been dealing with — "

"You realize that most of our work is confidential."

"Yes. So, often, is police work. Can we start with non-problem aspects, and when — and if — I need to ask about confidential matters, we can discuss that then."

The area officer stood up. "I'll go and break the news," he said. "Meanwhile, her personal file need no longer be confidential. I'm willing to show you that if you like, while you wait."

Dave was pleased. He opened the buff cardboard folder almost reverentially. It gave him Patricia Feltame's curriculum vitae; the name of her expensive private school, and the grades she had achieved in O and A level examinations. He saw without much surprise that academically she had outshone him. Then her university career, ending with a degree in botany — and he smiled wryly to himself, remembering that he had been convinced she would be good with plants and gardening.

After her degree she had done a postgraduate year in social work at a university in North Wales. Then a year with a voluntary society in Bradford, working with children. Then her application for a vacancy in York had been accepted, and she had been in her present post for four months.

He glanced at the most recent papers in the file. Patricia had started off well in her new job. She had shown initiative and common sense, two qualities which do not always go together.

* * *

91

"They're naturally very much upset," said the area officer on his return. "But the team she worked with are in the common room now, waiting to talk to you. Luckily no one had gone out yet, but I'd be grateful if you didn't keep them too long. They have a lot of urgent work. Even more if they are to be one short."

Dave felt irritated. The girl was dead. She had lain there on the pavement in the bitter wind. His heart was sore in his body for her. He wished he was a film cop and could say, "This is a murder enquiry we have here, mister," in a thick accent, instead of having to be a polite English detective and say, "I realize that you people have a heavy workload."

Of course they must go on with their work. Death cannot stop life. The area officer's words were only a standard reaction to the fact of death, he knew that. He was reacting too personally himself.

The common room was the kind of place in which no one spends much time. Its colouring was mostly grey to match the rain outside and the furnishings were too standardized to be interesting, in tones of orange which were meant to be cheerful. There was a coffee machine in one corner with a notice on it, 'Out of order', and a tray in another corner on a tiny sink unit; the tray held a kettle, a teapot and an array of different mugs.

There were six people in the room, evenly divided between men and women, young on average. It's a new profession, thought Dave.

"This is the team Pat was part of." The area officer waved a hand towards them. "Usually we have five social workers and two welfare assistants on a team, under one supervisor. That's myself, in this case. I've told them why you're here and what you want to ask about, so I'll leave you to get on with it."

Dave sat down facing the tight defensive circle. One girl had been crying and still had her handkerchief to her eyes. They all looked stunned.

"You know why I'm here," he said, repeating the area officer, anxious to give them time to get over the shock. "As it happened I was the person who found Patricia, so I can tell you anything you want to know about that. But what I don't know is what sort of person she was . . . " Oh, yes, I do! a voice screamed in his head. Be rational! he silently shrieked back. It is the need for sleep playing tricks. Get a hold of yourself! And he went on talking without any noticeable pause. " . . . what her working life was like, and so on. Particularly I need to find out what she did in her last hours, and so far no one has been able to tell me anything about her programme for Saturday night. I'm hoping that one of you might have an idea. Now, do you mind if I take a note or two? I know it's inhibiting to have someone with a pen and paper but otherwise I might forget."

The group had calmed down as he spoke. They began to talk now, apparently anxious to help. One of them could be her killer. One of them could know her killer. One of them could have been there.

"She was a super girl," a young man with a beard said devoutly. "They threw away the mould after making her."

They all nodded vigorously.

"She was popular with all of you, then? You're not just saying that because she isn't going to be here any longer?"

"We're not just saying that." An older woman was contemptuous. "She was just a lovely, sweet, gentle girl, who cared about other people. There couldn't have been anyone easier to get on with."

"She was easy to get on with," repeated the young dark girl who was still crying a little. "But sweet and gentle doesn't give the right idea of her at all, Sue. She would stand up to anybody. There was nothing soft about her. If she thought it was right, there wasn't anything she wouldn't do. She was daring and determined and brave."

They were all looking interested and alert now, discussing their colleague's character.

"So, she had plenty of backbone?"

"That's what I'm saying."

"Energetic?"

"She was a damn hard worker," said the bearded young man. "Never left anything for tomorrow she could possibly do today."

95

"Which of you worked closest with her?"

"Well, we didn't," the older woman called Sue said. "Joanne and I are the welfare assistants. We spend most of our time in routine visits to the elderly. We report back, and the social workers ask us to visit this person or that, but we don't have as much working contact as they do with each other."

"Sometimes more than one of us is involved in a case," supplemented a quiet-looking man who looked as though he ought to have a pipe in his mouth.

Dave guessed none of them smoked. There were no ashtrays in the room. Their job would attract the kind of people who didn't. "But normally you each have your own cases for which you are responsible?" he asked.

"That's right."

"Now, you two welfare assistants. You both knew Patricia and liked her?" They both nodded as if they meant it.

"Had either of you talked to her about her plans for Saturday night?" They shook their heads.

"I didn't see her at all on Friday,"

volunteered Joanne.

"I saw her," said Sue. "She was in the office when I came, but my business was with Frances, and I only heard Pat talking to you, Kevin, about a case. She was more likely to talk to you, Frances, about the weekend, and that sort of thing." She looked at the crying girl as she spoke.

"Had you seen her much at all this week?"

The two welfare assistants shook their heads.

"She was a super girl but I never said anything to her except about work," one said, and the other nodded.

"Perhaps at this stage neither of you two can help me much. Would you like to go now and leave me to talk to the others? I'm sure you all need to get on, so I'll let you all go A.S.A.P. But, Sue and Joanne, if you happen to think of anything at all you think I ought to know, will you tell me right away? Give me your names and addresses on this page in my notebook." They wrote down their names as he suggested. He handed them both a card with his name, rank and telephone number on it, and added, "If I'm not there, leave your name and I'll get back to you as soon as I can."

The two welfare assistants nodded and left the room. They were both slightly older than the others who remained.

Dave looked at the four social workers in front of him. There was the dark weeping girl named Frances, the bearded man called Kevin, the quiet clean-shaven one whose mouth was just right for a pipe, and a thin lanky man with what might become a moustache if he went on growing it, who was leaning back in his chair with his hands deep in his pockets.

The team as a whole was evenly divided between sexes now that it was minus Patricia Feltame, but as the welfare assistants were out visiting most of the time the social workers were weighted on the male side, which Dave guessed was rather unusual. From previous contacts he'd had with the profession he would have expected there to be more women than men.

"Frances," he said, "perhaps you're the most likely to have talked to Patricia

98

about plans for Saturday night."

"I don't know why you think that," snapped the lanky man. "I asked her to a party I was giving at my place, so I certainly talked to her about Saturday."

"Did she come?"

"No, she didn't. Said she had to do something for her brother — go somewhere or see someone for him."

"Oh yes. We'll come back to her brother in a minute. You didn't see her, then, after she said she couldn't come to the party? She didn't change her mind, or come on to join it after going somewhere else first?"

"No. We didn't see her at all."

"Right. Now, Frances?"

"I did see her Saturday. We had lunch together in town. A pub lunch, actually, at Thomas's. I asked her to help me choose curtain material for my bedroom — I have a little flat on Sycamore Terrace and the landlord said I could redecorate so I've been busy with that for the last month every spare minute. Pat came round and helped one weekend."

"Good. Did you choose your material before or after lunch?"

"After. She'd been shopping for herself in the morning. She bought a frock at Laura Ashley, she showed me the fabric, pulling it out of the top of the carrier bag."

"What was it like?" asked Dave, before reminding himself that the question was not at all relevant to the enquiry.

"Oh, a very subtle flower print — delicate pastel shades on cream."

"Not the kind of thing she normally wore, then? She seems to have gone in for black?"

"She liked black." Frances was all in black herself. "But this was for a bridge party she'd promised to go to with her mother, and for wearing at home. Everyone likes a change occasionally."

"And then you chose the curtains?"

"Yes. We went to Habitat. I found just what I wanted."

"Good. And then what?"

"And then we split up and I went home to make the curtains."

"Can you tell me what time that was? And where did Patricia go?"

Frances screwed her face up, trying to think. "It was about three o'clock. She

100

did say something. I asked her what she was doing next and she said, 'I'm going home to change. I've got to be in York this evening,' but she didn't say why."

"Did she mention her plans for Saturday to either of you?" Dave asked the other two young men, but they shook their heads.

"Right. Now, her brother. Had any of you met him?"

There was more shaking of heads.

"Did she mention him much?"

"Occasionally," said Frances, and the thin lanky one broke in, "Mostly we talk about work. It needs a lot of consultation at times. We don't have much time for gossiping."

"No. But any stray remark might be helpful. You see, her brother appears to be missing. He left his job a month or so ago. His mother didn't know that, nor has she seen him since. Patricia had though, because her engagement diary has his name several times quite recently. Either 'Seb' or 'S'. I'm presuming 'S' is for her brother, also 'Seb'. Any comments?"

"I don't know of any other relatives or friends of hers whose name starts with S," answered Frances, which was exactly the kind of answer Dave liked.

"Anyone else any comments?"

They hadn't.

"Perhaps we've gone as far as we can with this," said Dave. "I'd like to see her desk, if I may — where she worked."

"You'd better ask the boss about that," said the thin lanky man.

"Before we split up, would you mind giving me your names and addresses, in case I need to get in touch? I'll give you all my card so that you can ring me if you think of anything which might be useful, however small or apparently insignificant."

Dave passed round another sheet from his notebook and a ball point, and they all wrote obediently.

"You realize that we've a real problem on our hands with her death, don't you?"

Dave remembered that he'd already mentioned murder once. Might as well be hung for a sheep as a lamb.

"It looks like murder, and we have to find out who the murderer is. One of you may have heard something, seen

102

something, which didn't seem important but which might be vital. Get in touch if you think of anything at all . . . " He paused and they got up, sensing that the meeting was over. "Thank you for your co-operation," Dave added as they filed out of the door.

Frances turned to give him a tearful smile. "Just find out what happened, that's all," she said.

* * *

The area officer looked doubtful when Dave asked to see Patricia Feltame's desk. He could guess what was coming. Seeing a desk led on by natural progression to seeing what was inside it, and he wasn't at all sure about that.

"Look, I'm a detective," said Dave. "Not uniformed branch. If there's any-thing to the detriment of one of the people you're helping . . . "

"You'd have to pass information on," said the area officer. "If because we'd shown you confidential files, you discovered something you thought was irregular, you'd have to pass it on."

"I suppose so. What I need to know is — has she had any case where threats have been made to her — who she saw in the days immediately preceding her death?"

"It's easy to tell you're police," said the other. "Anyone else would have said 'just before', not 'immediately preceding'."

"Fair comment," said Dave.

"Come on. I'll show you her desk."

The rest of the team had gone back to work, and as the two men entered the office everything went quiet. They had obviously been discussing what had happened. Frances was crying again.

Dave smiled round at them but no one smiled back. He wasn't smiling because he was cheerful — it was meant as a gesture of reassurance. He wasn't altogether sure how it had been taken.

"What was the normal daily routine?" he asked.

"We arrive in the morning, look in the in-tray to see what's turned up, if anything. The post has usually been sorted and delivered by the time we get here. If there is nothing new and urgent, we check in the desk diary for jobs scheduled to be done that day. Then there's always the pending tray, and often I come in with something to discuss with the team."

"I see."

"After that morning round-up of tasks, we often — in fact always — need to go out on case work. We group visits in one area together so as to cut down on travelling, and come back into the office from time to time to write up what has happened, check if we are needed anywhere urgently — that kind of thing."

"I get the picture," said Dave.

"Here's Pat's desk diary. You see how she's got various jobs and visits scheduled, to be fitted into today."

"Could I have a photocopy of last week's entries?"

"I'll have to ask higher authorities about that."

"Right. Will you do that?"

"Yes, I will. To revert to your former query — had she had any threats — the answer, as far as I know, is no — agreed, everyone?"

"No hassle at present on Pat's cases," said Kevin, the bearded man. "I got threatened last week — a man was going to beat me up if I took his kids away. I wasn't going to, anyway. Only see they got fed occasionally, something apart from crisps and coke."

Dave and the area officer left the office. They stood on the landing a minute, talking.

"If you can get authority to give me names and addresses of those people Patricia went to see during her last week," Dave said, "it would be of immense help. I can undertake not to go visiting them in an official capacity — at least not at this stage. What I would do is wander around a bit, get to know what kind of people they are, and where she went on her visits. If necessary — and it may not be — I would ask if I could visit them in company with whoever takes over from Patricia, if it would help to ask them anything."

"I'll see what I can do."

★ ★ ★

Dave decided enough was enough. He radioed the station that he was going home. He was already four hours past the end of his shift. He really ought to go back, hand in the radio, sign off — all the rest of it. For once, he wasn't going to.

The rain was half-hearted. It came down limply as though it could hardly be bothered. The autumn light was too gentle and washed-out to make it seem really like day, even though it was by now mid-morning. Cars squished past with their lights on, soaking Dave with water from the gutters, as he made for home.

There was only one thought in his head, but he was no longer thinking in words. He could only think now in pictures, pictures of a fine pure profile, pictures of a pretty leg with a streak of red and a black leaf adhering to bare flesh, pictures of a huddle of disordered clothing that at first sight didn't look human at all. His head felt as if it was bursting. His eyes had been dipped in fire and had taken to burning like living coals.

As he neared the small block of flats where he lived he stumbled and had to catch hold of the railings to steady himself. The world revolved. The stairs to the first floor turned into a corkscrew. He fumbled putting his key in his own front door. He thought vaguely about a drink and something to eat but the need no sooner surfaced than it was overwhelmed by a greater. He walked into the bedroom, kicked off his shoes without undoing the laces, and stepped out of his clothes leaving them muddled together on a chair.

Then he thought of something. He summoned up a last shred of will-power, and made his mind focus briefly. He radioed the station again. "Can you get the pubs and clubs circulated with Patricia Feltame's photograph? Ask them if they saw her Saturday night?" he asked. "It wants doing today."

Without waiting for the response he switched off and put the radio down, and fell into bed.

6

DAVE woke at seven on the Monday evening to the sound of rain beating against the window and saw a pale blonde girl walking across his bedroom. More accurately, he saw her head, in ivory profile, as she moved from right to left. The hair was drifting out behind in locks. Everything below the slender neck was dark — black. He stared, but even as he looked his vision cleared from sleep and the girl was there no longer.

He lay back, trying to collect his thoughts. It was ridiculous to think that she had been present. Even more ridiculous to think that she was a ghost. He must have been dreaming about her, his subconscious visual image persisting through those seconds of waking. Everything was quiet; now was the time to try to think things over.

There were a lot of things that weren't surfacing about the girl in red suspenders.

Outwardly she seemed conventional, shrouded in her black clothing, but underneath was the streak of daring, of unconventionality; symbolized in one way by her choice of a career so much at variance with her background, and in another by that ribbon of gathered red chiffon trimmed with lace.

A well-off family, private education, everything that money could buy; why had she turned, after her degree in botany, to social work? A conscience? Political ideas picked up at university, contrary to those she must have been brought up with? Just an old-fashioned desire to do good? A feeling of responsibility towards the society she lived in? Certainly her choice was contrary to her mother's wishes. Dave didn't yet know about her father.

She had been a good and responsible employee, friendly but not taking her work colleagues completely into her confidence or into her private life. Still, she had only been with them four months; it was early days. Dave doubted whether he was going to get much enlightenment from interviewing her cases: mothers struggling with small incomes and no idea about nutrition or budgeting, or fathers accused of whatever, or snotty-nosed kids, or spotty teenagers.

She was a twin; that fact was much more likely to be central to her inner life, and Sebastian had vanished. Yet she had seen him, according to her diary, only a couple of days before.

Dave decided that his job must be to find Sebastian. Before doing that he would need a photograph and more information. A visit to The Grange was indicated. While he was there, it would be as well to search both Patricia's room and also Sebastian's.

It was at that point that he became aware of a small sound outside his front door, followed by a hesitant ring of the bell.

He got out of bed and into a dressing-gown, and went to answer it.

Leaning against the wall as though she was not sure whether she ought to be there or not was the weeping dark girl, Frances, who had worked with Patricia. As Dave opened the door and she turned to face him he saw that her eyes were red and her nose pink, and that tears were still not far away. They both spoke at once — Dave to apologize for his state of undress, Frances to apologize for bothering him.

"No bother," he said, opening the door and waving her in. "If you'll excuse me for five minutes I'll make myself decent."

She stalked in tentatively, like a wary sparrow.

"Do sit down," went on Dave, indicating the living-room with a flip of his hand.

"Can't I make you a coffee, if you've just got up?" she asked.

"I'd be very grateful. I'm on nights, you see. Evening is morning to me at present."

Frances found that it was obvious in the tiny kitchen how to manage. On a shelf was a range of tins and packets, holding tea, coffee, cocoa, sugar and so on. Underneath the shelf a row of cup hooks had been fixed and a line of mugs was hanging on them. Nearby on the worktop stood a Russell Hobbs standard kettle. Immediately under the worktop was a drawer and when she opened it she found the cutlery and could take out a couple of spoons.

Dave felt very uncomfortable as he dressed. He had really wanted a bath or at least a shower but didn't feel he could keep Frances waiting that long. He felt that he disliked having only a flimsy unlockable door between him and this unknown girl while he was in a vulnerable naked state, then wondered why.

Frances was young and not unattractive. Any red-blooded man should have been titillated by the situation. Why did he feel irritated? Perhaps he detected in her a capacity to do unexpected things in a random way, and half thought she might walk in on him, even sit on the open bed and proffer him a mug of coffee. It would have been a situation where he would not have felt in command.

He rushed into his clothes with such speed that he walked into the living-room with his tie half under his ear and without bothering to button his jacket. Frances had installed herself nicely. The two mugs of coffee were standing on his coffee table and she was leaning back in a comfortable chair near the tiny balcony. The whole day had been dark and gloomy, the kind of day which is hardly any lighter at noon than at midnight. It was the sort of weather when everyone's spirits are depressed without them realizing why.

Now, the light from the room streamed through the window and lit up the window-boxes and the hanging net of nuts for the birds. Frances had her head twisted round to look out.

"What a nice flat," she said, turning towards him.

"Thank you. And thank you for making the coffee." He sat down and tried to feel at ease with her.

"Policemen must be pretty well paid for you to afford this place," she said, and he was irritated again.

Don't be like that with a potentially important witness, Dave Smart, he told himself. The flats were nice — brick built, fairly traditional, quite well planned internally, with a row of mountain ash trees outside. He'd become fond of those trees. One of the few trees you can plant with safety fairly near to a building, and interesting at all times of year. The flats were one of the local success stories among a lot of new building in the ancient city which was not nearly as satisfactory. Why shouldn't the girl comment politely on them?

He explained, unnecessarily. "When my wife died the mortgage on our semi was paid off by the insurance we had taken out, and the house's value had risen considerably, of course, since we bought it. I didn't want to stay there — all the responsibility of the garden and so on — and these flats were just being built. They've gone up in value a good deal since I bought this. It suits me."

They both drank coffee.

"What have you come to tell me?" he asked, thinking of all the things he meant to do. He had slept longer than he intended — it was already past seven o'clock at night — he had to be on duty at ten. He wondered if Bob Southwell had got the rotas changed. Sometimes it meant juggling with a lot of men's hours, to give one man the freedom to devote himself to an enquiry. If the rotas had been rearranged, tonight he'd wanted to start at six, get a good evening in and then go to bed about midnight — that ought to have worked his internal clock round quite nicely so that he could start at eight in the morning. Well. He'd have to see.

"I just wanted to talk some more about Pat," said Frances.

"Have you remembered anything?"

"Not really. I remembered that when she first came to us she used to mention her brother a lot. She seemed immensely proud of him. He is a sportsman, you know."

"And works in the City, I understand."

"Yes, I believe he's very high-powered. But before he became a businessman he thought of going into teaching, games, because of being good at them. I believe he taught unqualified for a while in a minor public school. She said that it was the way he got so involved with the problems of his pupils that first made her interested in the fate of children in our society."

"I see. That might be useful information." Although to himself Dave doubted it.

"She used to enthuse about how good he had been at helping the boys, and he led campaigns against this and that. Smoking he's dead against, I remember, and he'd managed to get quite a few to stop it. I think Pat was sorry he'd not carried on with teaching. He's tremendously good-looking. She showed me photographs of him. I hoped to meet him, but I have only done so once."

"I thought that this morning you all said none of you had met him?"

"Well, I remembered that I had."

"When was this meeting?"

"About August, I would guess. I was having lunch in town and so were they. I didn't see them until they got up to leave and walked near my table. Pat introduced me briefly but they didn't stop."

"And was he as good-looking as his photographs?"

"Oh yes, better. But a bit withdrawn, I thought. Not friendly, only polite. He was shadowed round the eyes as if the skin was transparent. A bit gaunt. I wondered if he'd been ill. He didn't have that healthy glow I'd expected, and that he had in his photos."

"I wonder why?"

"Oh, I asked her. She said yes, he hadn't been too well."

"How was he dressed?"

"Odd you should ask that. I expected him to be in — sporty clothes — but he was dressed rather like Pat, all in black, with a big hat like hers. It accentuated the likeness between them."

Dave remembered Patricia's big hat, for it had obviously fallen off when she collapsed to the ground — or was put there — on the river bank. It had lain beneath her head so that her cheek had rested on it, black like most of her clothing, with a wide brim. He could imagine that a man and a woman, twins, brother and sister, the same age with the same colouring, both in black with wide-brimmed hats, would look a good deal alike however many differences there might be between them.

"They were a pigeon pair, so they can't have been identical," said Dave.

"They were a lot alike, all the same. Their colouring and general look. He was taller."

"Thanks for coming," he said, intending

118

that Frances should take it as a hint and go.

"But she stopped talking about him at about that time," went on Frances. "He cropped up less and less in her conversation. I was surprised when you said that there were all those entries in her diary about him."

Dave's thoughts had gone on to his intended journey to The Grange.

"Will you excuse me a minute?" he said, and decided to use the phone at his elbow to get in touch with the police station. As soon as he was through to the right person he asked, "Is that WPC on duty who was working on this case the other day — what's her name . . . "

"WPC Jenny Wren," came the answer.

"That's right, how could I forget? I could do with an assistant and she knows the people involved, is she in the station?"

"Yes, she's on two till ten today."

Dave Smart rapidly made arrangements for Jenny Wren to go out to The Grange with him. "Ask her to call here, will you?" he said. "It's on her way. She can park in my parking space and we'll go on in my car. And has the Chief made any alterations in the rota? He has? Oh, that's great. So I'm free to fix my own hours? Right."

He leaned back in relief, and had almost forgotten Frances and the air of difficulty she had brought with her. But there she was, waiting patiently for him to finish his phone call, and looking quite established in the chair.

"Sorry about that," he said. "I shall have to go out in a minute. How interesting that Patricia stopped talking about her brother soon after you met him in August. Perhaps he had some sort of problem — we know he'd left his job. He may have been looking for the next and she may have worried for him — some people keep their worries to themselves."

"Probably that was it," replied Frances.

She was in no hurry to go. She was still in the flat when WPC Jenny Wren ran trimly up the stairs and rang the bell.

★ ★ ★

Jenny had been pleased to be asked for, and to be working with DI Smart again on this enquiry. She'd felt full of *joie de vivre* all of a sudden, even at that late stage of her shift — always the point where she began to flag a little, before a brief second break picked her up a bit. Odd that she should feel so deflated when he opened his door to her, and there in front of him was that dark girl in the rather draggly longish black skirt. Somehow she wasn't getting quite the impression she had anticipated. She hadn't expected Dave Smart to have women in his flat and to be almost shoving them out, and to be looking himself so far from tidy, with his tie all anyhow.

"Come in a sec," he said.

She thought, You needn't think it's going to be a relay! but stepped inside without saying anything at all, and stood looking very correct in the hallway.

"Sorry to keep you," said Dave, and began rushing about collecting what he needed.

Through the open door she could not help seeing that his bed was unmade and that things were higgledy-piggledy. She glimpsed two mugs standing companionably together on the coffee table.

The previous morning Jenny had not known who Dave Smart was. She reminded herself of that. Why should she feel let down by someone she was only just getting to know? Why should she feel this unreasoning jealousy — yes, she faced the fact that that was what she felt. She sensed an affinity to him, and knew that she would like him to pay her a little attention.

"Right," said Dave, coming to her in the hall. "Let's go."

She led the way without a word.

* * *

"What kind of illness would make your family stop talking about you?" he asked her as he drove along.

"Aids."

"Yes. It's the first thing that comes to mind, isn't it? It would explain everything. The reason he didn't tell his mother he was leaving his job — the

necessity for him leaving in the first place
— the lying low since."

"Who are we talking about?" asked
Jenny.

"Sebastian Feltame, who do you think?"

"Any hint of homosexual tendencies?"

"None as far as I know. In looks he
was a lot like his sister. Feminine type,
I wonder?"

"Not from a photograph I saw. Not
that one need be homosexual any longer
to get it."

"Are we jumping to conclusions?" said
Dave Smart.

Jenny refused to be thrilled by the
matey way he had said 'we'.

"There are plenty of other possibilities,"
he went on. "Venereal disease. At one
time, TB. I don't think people feel the
same about it now, but it used to be
frightening. That's the reason, isn't it
— fear — when an illness is concealed.
Or alternatively that getting the disease
in the first place indicates irregular social
or sexual behaviour."

"Unacceptable social behaviour can
lead to other things. Drink and drugs."

"Both of those might also lead to

someone lying low and not being talked about, while they took a cure."

"Exactly."

"So we may have hit on the reason for Sebastian leaving his job — concealing his plight from his mother, whatever the nature of the plight was, and being succoured in secret by his sister."

"If that's how it is, he'll be getting medical treatment somewhere."

"Perhaps under a false name?"

"Almost certainly."

"I wonder."

"Find the gentleman, not find the lady."

"It might explain his mysterious absence, but it does nothing to explain his sister's death."

"He'll be waiting somewhere in a nursing home for her to show up with the bunch of grapes."

"He'll have to wait a long time."

Dave Smart thought the discussion had been useful. They went on talking in a desultory way on the journey, but there was something different about Jenny. She'd seemed so pleasant before, unaffected and friendly. Tonight she was a frosty little article. As soon as any subject came to a natural break she was silent, and made no effort to originate conversation herself. After a couple more minutes he switched on the radio.

At least the rain had stopped. The headlights scythed through the rapidly deepening night, revealing the stark trunks of the hedgerow trees, and then the avenue of ashes which led to The Grange, with their evergreen clothing of ivy. As he turned the car into the drive Dave thanked Providence for providing his native land with the holly and the ivy, both so cheerful in the winter. The light sweeping over a holly tree had been reflected, twinkling back at him from the shining leaves.

He turned again to his companion.

"I asked for you, Jenny, because you've already done a good job with Mrs Feltame," he said. "I'm going to search Patricia's room, and Sebastian's, and Mum might not like it. I want you to smooth her over, and give me a hand."

"That's a tall order."

"Nonsense. Just the sort of thing you're good at."

"What are we looking for?"

"Anything. Anything unexpected or revealing about the life style of either of them. Anything personal — documents, letters. Anything out of place."

They drew up at the porch with the Ionic columns.

★ ★ ★

Jenny Wren had put Mrs Feltame down as a heartless piece, but when she saw the ravaged face in the soft indirect lighting which was characteristic of the Feltame décor, she changed her mind and felt sorry for the older woman. Even if she was sorrowing over Sebastian's disappearance and not Patricia's death, at least she could feel, and was feeling, and that, Jenny thought, was what a mother ought to do.

Mrs Feltame flinched when Dave gently put his request to search the twins' bedrooms.

"I suppose you must," she said, still in the cold voice which had repelled Jenny so much before. "My husband has been in touch, and he asked me to give you every co-operation."

And if he hadn't, you wouldn't, I suppose, thought Jenny.

Mrs Feltame showed them upstairs and then turned on her heel and went down again, after giving them the keys to the two doors. They were old-fashioned panelled doors, eighteenth-century probably, and the locks with their brass escutcheons were obviously of the same vintage.

"I'll search Patricia's room, you take Seb's," said Dave brusquely.

"Wouldn't it make more sense if I did Pat's room?" asked Jenny. "Being a woman I might notice different things."

Dave Smart looked at her as if she hadn't spoken. He had not heard her. His whole concentration was drawn like a needle to the task in hand.

Jenny looked round, to escape that piercing look which did not even see her. They were standing on the long landing. It was wide in places, narrow in others; the walls, a continuation of the hall, were plain in colour, but the general effect was one of informal and countrified richness. The wide parts of the landing were furnished with chairs, bookcases, and charming displays of pictures. The carpet was fitted into every last inch and was a tiny pattern of turquoise and sage green.

The two bedroom doors in question were side by side.

The Dave of two days ago and the present Dave were two different beings. He was living now in a state of exaltation, above normal behaviour and emotion, and turned from Jenny to open the door of Patricia's room.

He might have been entering the room of his mistress.

There was something even here, where he had expected to find a concentration of her personality, which was formal. There was nothing out of place, everything looked as though it had been spring-cleaned yesterday. Of course, thought Dave, they have staff, and Mrs Feltame no doubt does some housework herself, and they will have all the latest gadgets, every assistance that money can buy.

It was a beautiful room, but so, he had become convinced, was every room in The Grange. It must be Mrs Feltame's passion, this house of hers.

Although one wall was all fitted wardrobes, the chest of drawers were free-standing, antique, dark and well-polished. Opening the wardrobes Dave surveyed the ranks of hanging garments, the plethora of black, the occasional outbreaks of other colours. Beginning at the left and working to the right, he began systematically to go through them, checking all the pockets, looking at the floor beneath them. He opened the cupboard with the hats and looked into the crown of each and ran his fingers round the lining ribbon. He tipped up every shoe and felt in the toe and looked at the heel.

"Why are you doing that?" asked Jenny. She had come in quietly behind him.

"Why? I always do, I suppose. If there's time, and we're as stumped as we are at present."

"What do you expect to find in pockets and shoes?"

"You ought to know that."

"I'm not detective trained," she said tartly.

Ignoring her tone, he explained patiently.

"Here's a girl we know nothing about. Oh yes, on the surface it's all clear. But we don't know a darn thing about her really. She might have left something in a pocket — a ticket from a car-park, a screwed-up sales slip, a shopping list, a note. Something that might have helped us find out where she was likely to be and what she was likely to be doing on Saturday night."

"But why her shoes?" asked Jenny.

"People sometimes put things into their shoes — a cloakroom ticket, for instance — that might tell us something. An unusual scratch pattern, mud or dust, not that there is any of that here, anything might be useful. Are there any sports shoes, for instance? If we could build up a picture of her normal leisure pursuits, apart from meeting her brother, it would help."

"You'd get further faster by checking her office." Jenny nodded towards an open door.

Dave knew it had not been open when he started to examine the clothes. He looked inside the door. The room was minute. It was an old dressing-room, he guessed, or even a powder closet, in a house of this age. It had been made into a tiny private study. There were bookshelves, a built-in desk and upright chair, a portable typewriter. On the desk was a photograph he guessed was Sebastian.

"Did you open this door?"

"Yes. I came in to ask how thorough we were to be. You never heard me cross the room, you were so busy examining shoes."

Dave felt like retorting, how could he hear her when the carpet was so thick? Somehow the way she had said 'examining shoes' made him sound like a shoe fetishist. He'd felt rather like one, handling Patricia Feltame's shoes, running his fingers over the smooth elegant leather, that was the worst of it.

"You must search as thoroughly as I'm doing," he said, and turned back to his task. He was not going into the study until he'd finished here. But it took some time to get back his pitch of concentration, when he had felt that he was in some way communing with

131

the dead girl, finding out her character and her ways.

He hardly liked — and yet he longed — to look through the drawers of the chests, which were full of lingerie — silks and satins. He thought of the red suspenders. There was certainly nothing here from Marks and Spencer. He remembered Aileen's pleasure in buying pretty undies for herself. She would have liked to be able to afford to wear beautiful things like this all the time. He shut off one side of his mind and lifted things quickly and ran his fingers over the bottoms of drawers, lifting the lining papers and looking underneath. He finished the task with a redder face than usual.

Then he went down on his knees and looked under the bed. He turned back the mattress and peered under the pillows.

In her study he discovered little that seemed relevant. It was a surprising place. Here was this glamorous girl and the heart of her home life seemed to be this tiny room, immaculately tidy, with its desk and its files and its typewriter.

He skimmed through the files rapidly. They were very methodical, and it was obvious that she was carrying out some course of study. He guessed, knowing that she had a degree in botany, that she wanted a further qualification in social work. Perhaps she was hoping to finish with a PhD. Children were what she was interested in, children and their problems. The botany books were relegated to an upper shelf out of reach, and the psychology of childhood and case histories took up the nearer shelves.

Even letters from her friends were punched with two holes and filed. These might shed a little light on her life, but they didn't. Like most social letters they were about the activities of the writers, with only brief enquiries about Patricia's existence. Her brother Seb seemed to be of greater interest to her friends, and in young women he supposed this was natural. He made a list of names and addresses.

Surely there would be some evidence of the other side of her personality — or did she keep it deeply hidden? He wondered what she read for leisure, and went to examine the books on her bedside shelf.

To his surprise they were children's classics:

The Secret Garden, Wind in the Willows, The Treasure Seekers, The Borrowers, Swallows and Amazons. Well, it was odd what some people wanted to read when they woke up in the night. Obviously that was the time when Patricia Feltame escaped back into the world of her childhood. There must have been something secure in that world which was missing for her now, some lack she could not forget, something from which with all her sophistication she could not break free.

Soon Dave Smart left the room and went to look for Jenny. She had finished with Seb's room and gone downstairs, and he ran her to earth in the shining kitchen, sitting at the table and sharing a coffee with Mrs Briggs.

"Well?" he said.

"I'll report in the car." She got up hastily.

"No rush. Good evening, Mrs Briggs. You must be feeling very concerned about all this. Have you been with the family long?"

"Ten years," was the reply.

Dave thought that in that case Mrs Feltame must be a good employer.

"Will you have a coffee?"

"Tea, if you don't mind. Somehow I've got to go to sleep again at midnight tonight."

Dave took one of the tall stools. He felt sure that Mrs Feltame would approve. She would wish police, like servants, to be entertained below stairs. While he drank his tea he tried to draw Mrs Briggs into conversation.

"Boyfriends?" he asked of Patricia.

"There's the county set, at least they think they are. Take her out hunting and to point-to-points and hunt balls and all that. There are a couple of those young men who are keen on her." Realizing afresh that that was all over, Mrs Briggs overflowed with tears, but controlled herself quickly. "Her mother thinks — thought — she ought to marry one of them and settle down in a big house and have children."

"I suppose most mothers think that."

135

"But that wasn't what Patricia wanted. She was like her father, you see."

"Is he interested in welfare?"

"No, I don't mean that. I mean work is what matters to him, and it was what mattered to Patricia, really. Her brain was marvellous. The things she knew! And the way she looked at things, it wasn't like anyone else I know. She was always ferreting out the reasons for how things are."

"So she wasn't serious about these two young men who took her to hunt balls?"

"Oh, she liked them. She might have married one if it hadn't meant giving up work. In that class you can't have a career as well."

"I should have thought you could these days."

"Tell the Detective Inspector about Sebastian," put in Jenny.

"Oh, he's a lovely boy! But I think he's in some sort of trouble. He rang Patricia up a while back. I answer the switchboard."

Mrs Briggs waved to the kitchen wall and Dave noticed a small, efficient office-type telephone arrangement.

"He said, 'Briggsey, I've left that beastly place, Heatham. I'm at Pete's Hotel. Is Pat in?' I said, 'What are you talking about, Sebastian?' and he said, 'Hasn't she told you?' and I said, 'Told me what?' and he said, 'It's all right, Briggsey. I expect she didn't want mother to know. I'm here in York at Pete's Hotel. Don't tell mother.' I said, 'All right, I won't.' Then I put him through to Patricia's bedroom extension and as soon as she lifted the phone I put this one down. I could tell that he was upset, and there's been something wrong ever since."

"Have you seen him lately?"

"No. Not since he was home at Easter."

"Look, Mrs Briggs. It's like this. Patricia's dead, Sebastian's missing, you *must* tell us anything you can. Either now or if you remember anything in the future. Now when did you have this conversation?"

"It was about a week ago. Of course I was wondering what it was all about, I was going to ask Patricia, but a few minutes later she left the house."

"In the car?"

"Yes."

"And if you think of anything else?"

"I'll tell you," said Mrs Briggs, and burst into tears again.

★ ★ ★

In the car Dave passed the photographs of Sebastian which Mrs Feltame had given to him, to Jenny; then asked her about Seb's room.

"Just exactly what you would expect," she said. "The room of a rich playboy."

"He had a job."

"I don't suppose he's done anything we would call work in his life."

"Maybe not, but he must be good at what he does do."

"Anyway, I'll be making a written report for the file. A lot of nice clothes and a lot of sports equipment. A few paperback books, mainly thrillers. That's it, in a nutshell. Not nearly so much as you had to check through. But I was thorough. I did look in the toes of his shoes, and checked to see if the heels were hollow and concealing micro-dots."

"Were they?"

"No. I don't suppose he's ever done anything wrong or underhand in his life. Wouldn't need to."

"But if he'd been born in different circumstances you think he would?"

"Yes."

"Why?"

"I suppose . . . "

"Yes? Spit it out."

"Because underneath all that sporty image I think he's still Mummy's little boy, and that type think they should have all they want. I did bring this away with me." She put a small piece of paper on top of the dashboard.

"What's that?"

"A receipt for a gun, taken in for some kind of repair. I brought it because it's dated after he went missing."

"Where did you find it?"

"In the top drawer of a chest of drawers on the hankies."

"Which is where one would expect, do you think?"

"Yes. It's an obvious place to put something one wanted to remember about."

"Any sign of girlfriends?"

"No. Not even a packet of condoms."

"I expect he had girls, though."

"Oh yes. They'd be round him like flies. The room was only used at holiday times, remember. If he still has a desk or locker at work it might yield more. And where did he live when he was in London?"

"His office won't tell us much, now he's left. He would have taken all his personal possessions with him."

"Probably had a good clear-out and threw most things away."

"Yes, of course he would. Still, I think we'll send a request down to the Met and ask them to check. As he's missing that would be quite reasonable. We need to know about his London home, as well."

"About Patricia . . . " Jenny said.

"Yes?"

"Her mother talked about her weird friends. She made that sort of remark more than once."

"You're right. When she gave us the triple photograph."

"So far no one's shown up who is at all weird."

"Mrs Feltame thought being a photographer was weird."

"Pretty low weird threshold," concluded Jenny.

She began to feel tired. It had seemed a long shift since two. Now, driving back to York, sitting beside Dave in the darkness, she felt herself sliding into a dreamy state, not having to concentrate on the road. She had forgotten that prickle of jealousy, and couldn't help feeling at ease with Dave Smart. Just now she felt comfortable and relaxed. She could have fallen asleep and not cared about losing waking control of herself.

"Do I feel safe with him?" she wondered. Safe? What did that mean? He was a good driver, calm, competent, with excellent anticipation, and drove as if it was as natural as walking and he didn't have to think about it. Certainly in that respect she felt safe. The engine purred on. Monk Bar rose in front of them, one of the medieval stone gateways into the walled city. They slid through and along narrow winding Goodramgate. The streets were quiet at this time on a Monday evening.

Dave had forgotten her presence beside him, although later the sense of it came back to him when he was driving alone and to his surprise he would miss her. Just now he was driving automatically and thinking about Patricia Feltame.

7

AS Dave Smart and Jenny Wren made their smooth return journey to the police station their superior was thinking about bed.

DCI Bob Southwell had spent his Sunday afternoon wrestling with the herbaceous border and his Sunday evening exhausted. Now he had had the whole of Monday to recuperate, and he was feeling more like his normal self. The house was quiet, the children asleep. The television programme was not very interesting. He looked across at his wife Linda, who was knitting a cardigan for their son Paul.

"I think it's time we had a dinner party," said Linda.

Bob Southwell groaned.

Linda reflected that husbands were all alike.

"There's no need at all to groan. It's quite painless for you. I do all the work."

"I have to put up with it, though, don't

I? After a day's work I have to spend my evening being polite and friendly to people and have strangers invading my home and I have to stand there grinning idiotically and serving drinks."

"I don't see any need for you to grin idiotically at all. You have a most delightful smile," replied Linda affectionately.

Bob said something to himself about women's wiles but all the same he couldn't help feeling as if he had been stroked the right way, and the delightful smile would insist on appearing.

"Your smile isn't so bad either," he said.

"Now let's stop being a mutual admiration society and decide who we're going to invite."

"Do we have to invite anybody? Look, the kids are both asleep, why don't we go upstairs and . . . "

"I thought of Tom Churchyard for one. He's always been so pleasant and helpful, it would be a little acknowledgement."

Bob began to feel more cheerful about the proposed jollifications. If their friend and neighbour, Tom, was there, the atmosphere would be much easier and more friendly than if the guests were all a load of strangers.

"All right, I agree to Tom. Do we need to have anyone else? Three's company, or something. Though just now I would suggest that two might make music . . . "

"You were telling me about your new WPC, saying that you'd like me to make her feel welcome into the community if I got the chance."

"Do you think it's a good idea to ask my staff? Particularly rather junior ones?"

"I wondered if she would suit Tom."

"Oh, well. Matchmaking, is it? Why don't you have them both to afternoon tea when I'm safely out of the way and let them get on with it? Which reminds me, why don't we . . . "

"You were wondering how you could make Mr Sugden welcome."

Bob was silent. This was a palpable hit. He had been wondering. Richard Sugden was a retired Chief Constable who had just moved into the neighbourhood, and the local force had been notified, with the idea that they were to make him feel that he had come among friends.

"Oh, all right, I give in. Though whether asking him to meet our next-door neighbour and a young WPC is quite up to his mark I don't know."

"Should we include someone of a higher calibre? Who do we know? A university lecturer, for instance? A Minster canon?"

"Canon Grindal, or Canon Oglethorpe? They're the only two we know at all well."

"Canon Oglethorpe's a pet, but he is getting on a bit. He's very set in his ways, and you know he can never remember the name of the person he's talking to. It wouldn't matter in the least if we were on our own, but we really need to ask someone who'll make the party go."

"Besides, he and Sugden would probably start to talk about prisons and that's going to be no fun for Tom. Oglethorpe had that long spell as a prison chaplain, and Sugden has some views he's outspoken about."

"Sounds like a load of laughs for everyone. But Canon Grindal and Lucy are dears. Lucy's so warm, such a comfortable person, and I don't suppose they have much of a social life. I'd love to have them."

"As it happens I heard they're just going on holiday. It isn't often they take one, I think, but this year Lucy's persuaded George to have a sunshine break before winter sets in."

"Where are they going?" cried Linda. She somehow felt that York would not be the same at all without Lucy and her father bumbling about at the centre of things.

"Ibiza, I believe."

"That doesn't sound a bit like them. Canon Grindal won't find anyone to rescue in a place like that."

"I wouldn't put it past him. There is bound to be someone who ought to be reading Luke. However, they won't be here for your party."

"So — Tom, Mr Sugden, your WPC — did you say her name was Wren? What's her first name?"

"Gladys, but usually known as Jenny."

"Would be, wouldn't she? That's only three. Not enough."

"How many do you think we can cram into our dining-room?"

"We can seat eight round the table; two of us, three of them — that's five so far. Three more people to find. One male, two females."

"What about Julia Bransby?"

"Perfect, darling. The very person. She'll do nicely for Mr Sugden."

"Old enough, do you think?"

"Not really. What will she be, forty?"

"Her son's seventeen. She looks thirty-five. I'd guess thirty-eight or nine."

"And Mr Sugden's sixty-odd . . . Do you think they'll suit?"

"Oh yes. She's mature and talks interestingly. He's still got all his buttons. They'll get along."

"You don't think we ought to get an astrologer's advice on whether their birth dates are compatible?" Linda looked mischievous.

"I knew you were setting up a marriage bureau! Jenny Wren for poor unsuspecting Tom and Julia for Sugden. Talking of marriage, it is ordained for . . . "

"We weren't," said Linda firmly.

"We're only planning a pleasant evening among friends."

"Another two people to find? One man and one woman? When we've found them can we go to bed?"

"It's only a quarter to ten."

"All the better."

"It will be our first dinner party in our new home, Bob!"

"A rather special occasion?"

"It is to me."

"Perhaps two more names will come to us. If not, we can make do with six."

"I would have liked eight."

"I've the awful feeling that this is a try-out for many dinner parties to come."

"Well . . . Let's fix the date, then."

"Then can we go to bed?"

"All right."

"Tomorrow night. Now that's settled." Bob jumped up and extended his hand to pull Linda from her chair.

"I can't be ready for tomorrow night!"

"I'm ready any time," Bob murmured into her hair.

"Darling . . . Will you leave it to me to find an evening that suits everyone?"

"Yes, dearest. Do you know you've the most . . . "

Bob vetoed Linda's suggestion of a cup of tea.

★ ★ ★

By the time Dave Smart and Jenny Wren arrived back from the Feltames' house and checked in, it was almost time for Jenny to knock off at the end of her shift, but Dave Smart had planned to stay up until midnight and then try to wake in the morning at eight. She said goodnight and left him to it.

He sat down heavily at his desk. Past ten o'clock. There in front of him were the results of the day's teamwork, carried out while he had been sleeping.

Patricia Feltame's car had been located. It was parked in the Esplanade car-park not far from where her body had been found. After consultation with the uniformed branch, who found it, a team had gone over it for fingerprints etcetera, on the steering wheel and foot controls and generally. Then a police trailer had taken the car to where it could be gone over again if necessary.

So far so good, thought Dave. There had been no obvious clues on the vehicle. Probably nothing helpful at all would be found. But negative results were often as useful as positive ones and if it was clean that told them something in itself.

Also the choice of car-park must be significant. If Patricia Feltame had parked before her evening meal, then the restaurant would probably be fairly close by. On the other hand, if she had driven somewhere after the meal, she may have parked later in that car-park for some other reason. It certainly was not a good choice for her return journey — Lord Mayor's Walk carpark or the new multi-storey by the Foss would have been better.

The other main task that had been carried out was the routine patient checking by as many policemen as could be spared of the popular eating places in the city.

York has many more cafés, hotels serving meals, and restaurants than most cities of its size, because for twelve months of the year it is a mecca for tourists. There are meals being served non-stop, of many different types and at many different prices. Out in the countryside wayside pubs put on elaborate meals and sometimes very indifferent ones. It doesn't seem to matter which. If anything, the indifferent meals seem to be the most popular and to have the best reputation.

There was one thing Dave Smart felt sure about. Patricia had not gone to a cheap eating place that evening. She would not have bothered to take her best go-to-meeting handbag, with that expensive perfume spray in it, or — he flinched a little — or to put on her red suspenders, and those stockings topped with black lace, if she was going to stand up at a bar and eat chicken in a basket.

Although the police team had been most careful and thorough, so far they had not found out where Patricia had been. They had taken copies of her photograph with them and showed them to half the bar staff in York and what felt like half the waiters and waitresses. Although she was such a striking girl, not many people had recognized her. Those who did remember her as a customer said that it was on other occasions, not on the previous Saturday night.

Her old handbag — that's it. Bob said, find her old handbag. We didn't find it. Also the waste-paper basket had been emptied and the dustmen had been, thought Dave Smart.

He remembered that phone call and Sebastian's conversation with Mrs Briggs, and how she had next heard Patricia run down the stairs and out to the car — out to meet her brother.

"I must go to Pete's Hotel first thing," he decided. "There's something else, too."

On his desk was the key-ring which had been found in Patricia Feltame's handbag, with the car key on it. He picked it up idly. The key was ordinary enough but the key-ring was something else. He looked at it more closely. A gilt bauble, he had thought on first seeing it, but now he recognised its quality. It was a hollow sphere with a wooden ball inside it, and it smelt of something. He put it to his nose. Fragrance. An expensive one, he thought. The wooden ball must have been soaked in it at some time. The hollow sphere was of gold — there was a tiny hallmark on the smooth place where the short chain was attached. It was pierced and fretted so much that it had become a sphere of network, prettily designed.

Sitting there with it in his fingers Dave felt very much in touch with the dead girl, as he had felt in touch with her when he stood by her body, on the stone flags by the river. He put the sphere to his nose again, and rubbed his fingertips over the crisp edges of the goldwork.

He thought of the phone call. Patricia would have known at once that it was her brother Sebastian. She was probably just out of the bath and would be wrapped in the white towelling robe with her fair hair screwed up in a towel twisted turban-shape. He imagined the conversation that might have ensued.

"You're not supposed to call here . . . mother might have been in the kitchen and picked up the phone."

"What, at this time in the morning? She won't be up. No, Briggsey answered and I asked her to put me through to your extension."

"Extension phones aren't safe, Seb."

"It's all right. Briggsey won't say anything."

"They're still not safe. Look, where are you?"

"I'm at Pete's Hotel."

At this Patricia, Dave thought, would have groaned. "I thought you didn't sound as if you were at the Home."

"F . . . the Home."

"What have you done?"

"Just walked out. The place was like a prison."

"Look, Seb, you promised . . . "

"I'm not going to be treated like that."

"I checked the place out, Seb, to make sure they didn't believe in the short sharp shock treatment, and that it would be OK for you. We went to see it together. You said you were agreeable to going."

"It was awful, it was so awful."

"You didn't give them long enough. You promised me, Seb."

Silence.

"Look, I'll come down to see you. Just

stay where you are, OK?"

"I'm not going anywhere, little sister."

"It doesn't suit you to talk like that . . . don't ring here again."

"Nothing like family for making a boy feel wanted."

Dave thought Patricia would have banged down the phone. He thought of her walking across the thick carpet, slim pink feet bare. Standing at the window where Dave had once stood, she might have looked over the autumnal garden. The colourful leaves on the shrubs had mostly dropped and faded. All that could now be seen were the dark evergreens and the twiggy outlines of what had been summer's lushness. In his drowsy mind's eye Patricia's fingers on the curtain were tight, digging into the expensive fabric.

Quickly she would have brushed out her drying hair and smoothed underclothes on to her firm body, then white shirt blouse, black cashmere sweater, black trousers; black wool socks into flat black shoes; black trenchcoat, broadbrimmed black hat. Hair waving out like pale spun gold.

Her movements he was sure would

have been adroit and economical, graceful as a dancer's, her distress tight contained, only discernible in the puckered forehead.

* * *

In the few minutes since the telephone call her bitter disillusion had burned the room into her brain. Never again would it give her delight or pleasure. Every item it contained would be saturated with the sensations of the last few minutes and would bring back the taste to her mouth of fear and of loss of hope.

She was a girl of courage. In the time it took her to drive into York and park the car and walk to Pete's Hotel she had determined that the fight was not over yet.

Left alone by the maid on the landing Patricia tapped briskly on the panels of the door. Once inside she ripped off her hat and threw it on to the bed.

"You're the bloody limit!" she cried.

"Oh, look, Pat . . ."

"You promised. Didn't you promise? What use are your promises?"

"Not much, sis. I'm sorry."

"You're sorry! It is ruining our lives and it would ruin mother's life if she knew. If you've stopped caring about me don't you care about her, after the way she's always idolized you?"

Sebastian put his arms round her and her head sank to his shoulder.

"Nothing can make any difference to you and me, sister."

"I thought that, once."

"And mother — well, I know I am her favourite, if that's what you mean. But why bring it up now?"

"Oh! Favourite! That doesn't matter. I accepted that longer ago than I can remember. Mummy's boy and Daddy's girl. It doesn't matter." Her voice had dropped to a whisper.

"Dad always liked you best."

She broke away. "Seb! I'm only trying to bring it home to you that mother loves you, idolizes you, and that knowing what you are now would break her heart."

"I've missed you so, sis. It was good of you to come down when I wanted you. I really did want to try that place. Of course I don't want to hurt mother. I'm going to beat it, sis. I'm not an addict, you know. It's not my master. I'm in charge." He put his arm round her shoulders again.

"In charge!"

"Of my destiny. Of my habit. That's all it is, sis. Only a habit. You can change your habits any time you want."

"One of the great fallacies of the world."

Patricia turned from him and bending her head to her hand she bit her knuckle, hard. Tears were in her eyes. Her outburst ended, she was afraid she was going to break down and weep. Over and over inside her head beat the words, this is my brother and I love him.

"Of course you can. You just say to yourself, 'Tomorrow I'm going to stop,' and you stop."

"And is that what you're going to do?"

"Yes. And I don't need any psychiatric hospital to help me do it."

"My love — Seb, my darling . . . " Her voice dropped to a special note. "Let's just face facts, shall we? A: it wasn't a psychiatric hospital. It was a small private clinic, exclusive, feepaying, very large fees, to which you said you were willing and committed to going, right?"

"I didn't know what it was like before I went, did I?" asked Sebastian with sweet reasonableness.

"B: you are an addict. C: to know that would break mother's heart as it is breaking mine. D: you are never to ring me at home again, or she might find out."

"You're feeling loyal to her, aren't you? But we'd have walked out without a qualm."

"Birds leave the nest but she doesn't deserve this." Patricia sat on the bed, looking exhausted.

"I'm sorry to grieve you, sis, really I am."

He took her hand and began playing with it, drawing out the fingers in turn. Before he reached the one which was damp and marked by her teeth, she pulled the hand away from him.

"OK, OK," she said.

"It really wasn't nice there at all."

"Seb. You are a grown man, showing brilliance in your new career and you've been an athlete of world class. You do

160

not need to sound like a child."

"And you don't need to sound like a social worker. What was I to do?"

"Stop in until you were cured, then take darn good care never to take the stuff again."

"That's what I meant to do, of course. There was this awful man, he was a sadist, he gave you all the worst cures he could think of, he just loved to see me suffer. I couldn't take it any more."

"You've disintegrated, that's what it is. By God, if I could get my hands on the creature who started you on that stuff. You knew the cure would be hell. You said you were ready to go through with it."

"I am ready to go through with it."

"It's a good job these old walls are thick. I wouldn't like anyone to have heard us. They are nice people here."

"They've been good to me." Maudlin tears stood in Seb's eyes.

"Value that. Hang on to their good opinion. It is not to be forfeited lightly."

"They bring me anything up, day or night. Food or drink."

For a while there was silence between

the twins. Patricia looked up at her brother. He leaned against the mantelpiece. They exchanged a long, considering, intimate look.

* * *

Dave was still sitting in the police station as the clock crept towards the witching hour. His head had sunk on to his chest. As the door opened he came to with a start and sat up straight. He looked down and saw his fist still clutching the golden keyring, so he pushed it quickly into his pocket, as a stranger entered the room.

8

IT had taken Charles Feltame thirty seconds and two short cool questions to make the journey from the street door to the office where Dave Smart was sitting. That's what being a tycoon means, I suppose, Dave thought afterwards. They speak, you jump.

The older man looked as if he had had a rough passage from America; his face had that curious grey look induced by fatigue. He was wearing a lightweight suit of fine thin fabric with a suggestion of sheen, carrying an expensive air-travel suitcase and had an immaculate raincoat folded over his arm. Altogether he looked what he was, a businessman on the international scene, suddenly brought under extreme stress by a personal loss.

"Detective Inspector Smart?" he asked, putting out his hand. "We spoke on the telephone."

"Mr Feltame?" Dave stood up and shook hands with him.

"Found out what happened to my girl yet?"

"We're working on it."

Charles Feltame sat down and looked at Dave across the desk. "Tell me," he said.

Putting all human feeling out of his voice Dave gave an account of what had happened since Sunday afternoon. As he went over the events Dave studied her father. He saw more likeness to Pat than he had noticed in her mother. The alert listening look was like the look Patricia had in the triple photograph. The fairly narrow jawbone was more like Patricia's than Mrs Feltame's square one, which had been inherited by her son. Above all, the clear blue eyes, with a piercing glance, had a good deal of Patricia about them, though hers would have been softer, Dave thought.

Dave reflected that the other man was keeping himself under very tight control. He appeared calm, but the tell-tale signs of tension were there, and the marks of the aftermath of violent grief.

"I'm going to help, you know that,

don't you?" said Charles Feltame quietly.

"It is easy for the public to obstruct when they mean to help." Dave sounded cautious.

"My daughter has been murdered and whoever did it is going to be brought to justice and I'm damn well going to help bring that about."

"I can't control your actions. I can only ask you not to hinder."

The two men looked at one another.

"Who is your superior?" Charles Feltame looked round.

"Detective Chief Inspector Robert Southwell."

"And his chief?"

"Detective Superintendent Joseph Birch."

"Either of them available?"

"Well, not at midnight . . . "

"We'd better get hold of them then," Feltame said grimly. "There doesn't seem to be much action on this case."

"If I might suggest, sir, that it would only antagonize them and not expedite anything, to be woken up in the middle of the night."

"What time does everyone I haven't met come on duty, then?"

Dave told him.

"And you?"

"I'll be on duty twenty-four hours a day until we clear this up, Mr Feltame. You can ring me any time you want to, day or night. Here's my home phone number."

"Tell me where not to put my foot in. Tell me where I can be useful," said Charles Feltame.

"Talk to your wife and to Patricia's friends. We don't know yet where she was or what she was doing in the twelve hours before her death. Look for your son."

"Report back to you?"

"That would be very co-operative of you, sir."

Dave knew that in any other situation it would be he who was humble, he who gave the deference. Charles Feltame was that kind of man. Dave respected him for the way he was acting now.

"I'll do that. And I'll do something else. I'm going to get you the backing you need," Charles Feltame said after a pause. "I know. You don't have to tell me. Detective Inspectors are not much

166

better than bottlewashers. I'll see to it, Inspector Smart."

Dave was only five minutes behind him in leaving the station.

* * *

Tuesday morning. It was high time Dave Smart went to Pete's Hotel.

The place was dingy and old-fashioned in a comfortable way which made it the In place among York residents. No tourist would have looked twice at the shabby interior as glimpsed from the street. Those in the know went in at any time of day and were served in the friendly upstairs bar with bacon sandwiches and whatever else was going on the day's menu.

Crowded above stairs were unmodernized bedrooms, looked after by the ancient staff who invariably stayed on until they dropped.

Dave stood for a moment looking at the narrow green-painted frontage, before climbing the two steps and pushing open the door. Inside it was dimly lit, a narrow thickly carpeted entrance. He went along to where the quarter-circle reception desk took up most of the middle of the hallway.

Half-past eight saw him interviewing the chambermaid, Maureen, who was seventy if she was a day, and who was wearing a small semi-transparent starched apron with a bib in the old style over her black dress, and a little white circlet of a cap on her head. It didn't take long to discover that she helped out everywhere, on the reception desk if she happened to be passing and no one was in attendance, waiting on table if needed, as well as vacuuming and dusting through upstairs.

"A lovely couple," she said sentimentally when questioned.

"You make them sound like lovers," was Dave's comment.

"Well, they were, in a way, weren't they? They cared so much for each other. It isn't many brothers and sisters do that. Couldn't care less, most of them. But he had a special voice when he spoke to her. Even their quarrels sounded like newly weds, and we've had a few of those here in our time. A lovely couple, like I said.

So good-looking. Awful what happened. A doomed pair, that's what Doris said — you know, Doris the kitchen-maid. A doomed pair."

The chambermaid contemplated this fatalistic remark of Doris's with a kind of bleak enjoyment.

"Sebastian Feltame isn't staying here now, then?"

"Oh no. He left. The boss wasn't so keen on him when he discovered what was really the matter. Not that he would have thrown him out. Mr Feltame just went."

"You know Miss Feltame is dead?"

"I know. That's why Doris said what she did. It was in last night's *Press*, wasn't it? Isn't it awful? Him missing, too. If anyone knew the whereabouts, to get in touch with the police."

"Do you know his whereabouts, Maureen?"

"I don't, sorry, love."

"Tell me all you can."

Maureen settled down to enjoy herself.

"The first time I met her, I came to the desk because she rang the bell, and she said, 'I believe you have a

169

Mr Feltame staying here,' and I said, 'Oh, are you his sister? He said he was expecting you. Poor young man. We're all ever so sorry.' Then she smiled — a funny sort of smile I thought, as if she didn't really mean it. Then she said ever so quietly, 'He's told you, then?' and I said that those psychiatric hospitals, they have something to answer for. Just like Russia. They lock people up when there's nothing wrong with them at all, and she said they meant well."

"I'm sure they aren't like Russia," said Dave.

"Mr Feltame said they were like prison, and she said he'd told her that as well. Then I told her that the boss said Mr Feltame could come here any time he wanted because we're just one big happy family, and she said that was good of him. Mr Feltame was so mopy, really seemed ill, and for a few days he didn't go out anywhere, but his sister kept coming to see him and cheer him up. Then he did go out, and he came back all happy but when she came there

170

was one hell of a row and you could hear them shouting and the landlord heard it and said this can't go on, this is a respectable hotel, this is, and we're not having anything to do with drugs, if he'd known he was a drug addict he'd never have let him in."

"What sort of drugs?" asked Dave.

"Oh! Really nasty things like you read about in the papers, what do they call them, heroin and cocaine and stuff like that. Miss Feltame came out of the room looking all upset and our boss said to her that she'd have to find somewhere else for her brother and she said couldn't he keep him on for a little bit and she'd see it was worth his while. That time he'd been out, he'd managed to buy some more drugs, you see, that's what it was all about. But it was only the next day that Mr Feltame walked out and we've never seen him from that day to this . . . "

"Can I see his room?" asked Dave.

Not that he could learn anything from it in the way of material evidence. A hotel room is cleaned daily and this one had probably been used several times since Sebastian's occupancy, but one never knew. He followed Maureen's rheumaticky knees and veiny legs upstairs.

The threadbare carpet of the landing was clean, yet the place had something dusty about it, and was redolent of the fifties. It had not been briskly updated, like The Grange. Dave almost felt as if he was in a time warp.

The dowdy room boasted only a cracked handbasin in one corner, the single bed, and a wardrobe and chest of drawers that had almost certainly been there since 1946. It was small, bare, uninteresting, yet Dave could see how it had been a bolthole and a refuge. He could almost sense the brother and sister, arguing, moving about, sometimes speaking tenderly. His heart ached for the two of them, discussing their dilemma, the brother weak and wilful, the sister strong — but secret. Why had she kept it all so secret? There must have been someone in whom she had confided.

"Thank you, Maureen."

There didn't seem much point in asking further questions. A nice smile and the thank-you were what Maureen got out of Dave Smart, and she felt well rewarded; she could hardly wait to tell Doris. Such lovely wavy black hair, he had, that Inspector, sort of crispy . . .

★ ★ ★

By now it was past nine o'clock and much lighter. At present it wasn't raining, but there was the thick feeling of dampness in the air, as if it could condense into droplets at any time.

Smart went back to the office where Patricia had worked. "Sorry to bother you again . . . "

This time he was shown straight into the room where the team were busy on their morning round-up of work to be done. Patricia's desk was still unused. Someone had cleared the top and the cleaners had dusted and polished it. There was a tiny vase with a few flowers in the centre; he wondered who had been sentimental enough to do that, and guessed at Frances.

173

There was an extra person present.

"Hi, Dave," said the probation officer.

"Morning, Steve."

The presence of the probation officer made a bridge between the team of social workers and the policeman. Everyone now gathered round Dave quite naturally, and Dave found himself speaking easily and informally.

"Can I be in on this?" asked Steve.

"By all means ... I'm investigating the death of one of the social workers, Steve, a girl called Patricia Feltame. Now, I want to ask you all again about last Saturday night. Bill, you're sure you didn't see her? A party is on the cards; the police surgeon was strong for that idea. The only party we've come across yet where she might have been is yours."

"No dice," said the lanky man. "As I told you, I asked her, she didn't come."

"Can you check round among your friends and associates to see if there was any other party she might have gone to? Look. Confidentially. I know you can all keep this confidential. Her twin brother

174

had become a drug addict, right? She was trying to help him."

He could feel their shock, and knew at once that they had guessed nothing about it.

"If she had only said . . . " This was Jim, the one with the beard.

"Bloody Hell," said Frances.

"Why didn't she tell us?" said the other male social worker. "The first thing she should have done was to tell us and discuss the problem, gaining different angles on it, so that she could take an objective point of view."

"She'd got him into a private clinic for a cure but he'd left and come to York and holed up for a while in Pete's Hotel. He was without a supply, but from what I hear he might have found one."

"Why hadn't he gone home?" asked someone.

"We don't know. Look, I'll leave you now. But keep in touch." Turning to the probation officer, "See you, Steve."

"We'll have a think," said Bill, who seemed to be the natural leader of the social work team.

Dave Smart had not brought a car

because he usually found he could get about York more quickly without one. Heading back towards the police station on Clifford Street he remembered that he had in his pocket the receipt Jenny had found in Sebastian's room — a receipt for a gun. He could easily call at the place.

He was used to the ways of craftsmen in this city. Once they might have been accessible and visible in the many little shops which went back centuries. Now rates and other expenses had made such exposure impossible for most of them. They were to be found up alleys, in attics, in scruffy old-fashioned premises which somehow managed to survive in holes and corners which the fashionable stores didn't want — yet.

Dave remembered with regret that it had been the policy of the City Council to encourage craftsmen and that they had planned to have the Shambles as a street of good-quality handworkers. Very few now survived there. Oh well, he supposed it hadn't made commercial sense, whatever other kind of sense it made.

The workshop was on the first floor, up a flight of unpainted stairs, next to a beauty salon and an interior designer. Before reaching the door Dave could smell a mixed aroma of rich tobacco, leather, oil, and metal. He noted the security precautions of the establishment. On the door was a notice, 'James Gotobedde, Repairer and Restorer of Antique Firearms and Other Weapons. Sales can be Arranged.'

Inside he could have turned back two centuries. The rows of engraving tools carefully ranged in size order above a worn workbench, the mess of oily rags which looked purposeful rather than accidental, the display of antique guns on the wall or propped up against it, all looked as though they would have been the same two hundred years before. There was also a pike and halberd crossed at the top of the wall, and a pair of bayonets lower down.

The figure which turned and came to greet him did not look modern either. Middle-aged, thin, dark hair above a yellowed face like wrinkled parchment. Bony hands with prominent veins.

"I can do without any more visits from the fuzz," said the man.

"Do you get many?" asked Dave in a mildly interested manner.

"Working with guns you do. Have you got permits for this, have you got licences for that. Anyone would think we were engaged in gun-running instead of repair and restoration."

"CID." Dave showed his identification.

"Doesn't take much penetration to see that," replied the man.

"James Gotobedde?" enquired Dave.

"That's me."

Dave produced the scrap of paper Jenny Wren had found in Sebastian Feltame's drawer. "Can you tell me anything about this?"

James Gotobedde reached out for an elegant gun which he laid down on the counter between them. "This is the gentleman. Antique piece. If you take it I'll want a receipt."

"That's all right. You hang on to it. I only want to know if it was brought in by this lady," and Dave showed the photograph of Patricia.

"Yes. That's her."

"I understand it's her brother's gun?"

"Yes."

"Thank you, Mr Gotobedde."

"Is that it?"

"Thank you, yes. Just checking."

"It was a bequest from his grandfather, the young lady told me," the man volunteered. "They wanted it checked over and in working order. It's ready whenever they would like to collect it."

Smart had hardly walked out of the workshop before Gotobedde picked up the telephone.

"You're going to get me into trouble, you are," he said aggressively. "First it was going to be nailing the lad, nothing else. Then organize the party. Then the sister came shoving her bloody oar in. Now I've got CID round. I wish I'd done nothing for you at all. Just get them off my back, will you?"

"I thought you were well in with the police," came the reply.

"Oh aye, some of them," retorted James Gotobedde. "Just you tell your boss I'm standing no more of this." Then he slammed down the phone.

★ ★ ★

"Will DI Smart report to the Superintendent's office immediately, please, if not sooner?"

Jenny Wren looked up from her work as she heard Dave Smart being given this message as he walked through the general office. He was looking tired, she thought. Hardly surprising. What was surprising was that she caught his eye as he went towards the stairs, and he gave her a friendly wink and a smile.

It was all right, then. He wasn't in any kind of trouble. She went back to typing the report she was dealing with in a little glow of happiness, and refused to ask herself why.

Dave didn't ask himself how Charles Feltame had got in on a police meeting of a disciplinary or at least an investigative nature, but he was there. And the atmosphere was enough to tell Dave that what was happening was not friendly.

Bob Southwell gestured him to a chair.

Behind the desk was Superintendent Birch, looking angry. In front of the desk was DI John Rollo.

"Let's just go over this again, John," said Birch in a silky voice.

"It looked like an ordinary enough death," said John uncomfortably. "Sunday morning. Probably the result of something happening Saturday night, which is what Dave Smart said to me."

"Hardly a profound observation," said Birch.

"What I mean is, sir, I agreed with what I thought Dave meant. A Saturday night party or booze-up. Everyone drunk. A youngster finishes up dead. Could be alcoholic poisoning, inhaling vomit, playing with drugs, a punch-up, anything. Hardly unusual."

"As I understand it, DI Smart had formed the impression it was murder?"

"We take the same procedure in any case," said Rollo virtuously.

"But you didn't, did you?" Superintendent Birch's voice was cutting. "We've heard the statement of the scene-of-crime officers. You told them not to bother with the posts and tape, and that just a few photos would do."

"Didn't want to waste ratepayers' money, sir," said Rollo. It was obvious to everyone that he was sweating.

Birch looked at him speechlessly for a minute. What was the point of making an example of him? He sighed. "All right, John. You're off on holiday, aren't you? Get along with you, then. And for God's sake, in future don't worry about the ratepayers' money, don't be slipshod, yeh?"

"So," Birch said when Rollo had gone, "Rollo did not take all the measures he should have done. There was no proper examination of the ground. Nine times out of ten it wouldn't have mattered at all. Even in this case there may well have been nothing to discover. The police surgeon certified death, but appears to have noticed nothing else."

He turned to face Charles Feltame. "That's all the police surgeon is supposed to do, of course. But we do like them to observe all they can, and often they can give us a good written report which saves a lot of trouble. This man in this particular case did carefully check that life was extinct. Apart from that he did as little as possible. It is hardly an indictable offence."

DCI Southwell put in a word. "We still can't be sure that this is murder, if you don't mind me saying so, Mr Feltame. DI Smart here was going on a hunch. You are going on your emotional reaction. What we need is evidence."

Birch picked up and unfolded the preliminary report on the PM.

"Did a top man carry it out?" asked Feltame.

Dave Smart wondered how he'd got such a nose for the weak points of everything that had been done. He supposed that was what made a tycoon different from ordinary mortals.

"The pathologist from our local hospital," said Birch.

"Whose job was it to call him in?"

"Rollo did that. Nothing wrong, of course, with the local man. Quite experienced. However . . . " Birch was frowning down at the report. "In this case it wasn't Brian who did the job. It was Martin Smith."

"What's wrong with him?" snapped Feltame.

"Nothing. Nothing at all. He's one of the senior registrars."

The three policemen all thought the same thought simultaneously. Martin Smith likes to do the odd weekend PM for extra pocket money.

"Nothing wrong with him," repeated Superintendent Birch. "He is perhaps not quite as perceptive as our friend Brian, who is older and very keen. But a good sound man. He took samples which are still being tested."

"In the case of most routine deaths the local hospital pathologist does the PM," explained Bob Southwell. "Road accidents, suicides with the convenient empty bottle and note. It is only in the more suspicious cases that we call in the services of a forensic pathologist. They do all homicides."

"Perhaps you'd better call one in now," said Charles Feltame drily. "It seems to me that this case has been undervalued right along. My daughter died more than forty-eight hours ago."

Forty-eight hours of missed clues, of cold trails.

"We are doing everything that can be done," Birch assured him. "May I offer you a coffee, sir?"

"No thanks. I'll go and pursue my own investigation." Charles Feltame glared round the room. Every line of him was energy. "First I'll have a word with our friend Smart, if that's all right."

Leaving D.S. Birch in his office Charles Feltame, DCI Southwell and DI Smart adjourned to Dave's desk.

"How's progress?" asked Feltame, adding to Bob Southwell, "This is a good man you've got here."

"No prints on the car except Patricia's," said Dave. "The tyres were pretty muddy. Seems to indicate she'd driven in the country recently. Her new dress she'd bought that morning was still on the back seat in its carrier. She hadn't taken it into the house when she went home to change for the evening. Nothing appears to be touched. We think she had been the only person in the car."

"Fair enough," said Bob.

"So far we don't know where she ate or who with. The uniformed branch are still working on that. Mrs Feltame was out visiting friends so didn't see Patricia, but Mrs Briggs, who seems to notice these things fairly accurately, says that she left the house at half-past seven. Let us estimate that she started eating about eight; assuming the meal went on until nine-thirty, or even ten, there are still several hours unaccounted for."

"She hadn't noted any engagement in her diary," commented Bob. "But her workmate, Bill, says that Patricia was meeting someone connected with her brother."

"The drug addict," said Charles Feltame bitterly.

"Tell us about your son."

"Clever, good-looking, his mother's darling, idolized by his sister, you know all that already," said Feltame.

"Good at his job?"

"Brilliant, so they tell me. A friend put him in the way of this job, with one of the top firms in the country. Investment consultants and stockbrokers, you know the sort of thing. He was doing well there. I'd have had him working with me, only . . ."

"Only?"

Feltame was quiet for a minute and then shrugged. "Maybe we didn't hit it off," he said at last. "Certainly he'd have known what I would think about drugs."

"I gather it's the thing among the yuppies to snort coke," put in Dave. "Incidentally, we've traced his car."

"They get away for a long time with taking coke at parties," said Bob. "It doesn't get hold of them like . . . Where was the car?"

"In the hands of its new owner."

"Sebastian sold his car?" Charles Feltame sounded astonished.

"Surely has."

"His Porsche?"

"Yup."

"Bought another one?"

"Not as far as we know."

"Sold it to finance his habit?" suggested Bob. "I hear it can cost as much as a thousand pounds a day."

"Tch!" exclaimed Charles Feltame. "It's almost unbelievable!"

He was wearing different clothes today. The transatlantic image had gone. The dark charcoal grey woollen suit, the winter warm, the rolled umbrella, the hat, were superlatively English.

"I'm going to go round Pat's friends

during the rest of the morning," he said. "After that, am I allowed to invite your Inspector to lunch?" He spoke to Bob Southwell.

"Certainly." Bob's face was impassive. Take the tea lady if you want, he seemed to imply, then added, "I will be arranging another post-mortem, with the best forensic pathologist in Yorkshire."

Dave was acutely uncomfortable. It wasn't done to single out a more junior officer in the way you might behave to the Chief Constable.

"I'll pick you up," Charles Feltame said to him. "Twelve o'clock all right?"

"Yes, sir. Thank you."

"Hmmm," said Bob when they were alone. "Blue-eyed boy, eh? Don't let it go to your head."

Dave wanted to say that Charles Feltame had no right to behave like this, as if a wealthy businessman could swing the police force any way he wanted.

"We're not divorced from the world," Bob added as if reading Dave's mind. "It doesn't hurt to let him think he's wielding a bit of influence. He's doing useful leg work and saving us, and you look as if you could do with an hour off and a square meal. Mind," and his tone sharpened, in the way it could when you were least expecting it, "an hour, mind."

"Yes, boss," replied Dave.

★ ★ ★

Charles Feltame drove a mile from the centre to a newish hotel with a reputation as the haunt of the business community. The dining-room was narrow, but the round tables were a fair distance apart.

Dave was afraid that with his bulk he would knock something over as he threaded his way through to the table selected, but no one would have guessed from looking at his impassive exterior that he didn't lunch here every day of his life.

Charles Feltame sighed expansively. "This is the way I'm used to doing business," he said. "It feels like home. There are people I know about. Here, I can't believe that Patricia is dead, and that helps."

They ordered. Dave chose a large steak

and all the trimmings and a pint of beer, Charles decided on several elaborate dishes with foreign names and a bottle of something extremely expensive.

Dave wondered if at such a time he himself could have cared so much about food, but then he realized that it meant no more to Charles Feltame than eating steak and chips did to him — fuel without which it was not possible to function efficiently.

"Here's a list of the people I saw this morning." Charles passed him a neatly typed page. "You'd already interviewed her workmates. These you might call her social set. She's been dropping steadily out of their ken for several years now I think. They're hardly the sort that go to university or take an interest in social work. But childhood friendships die hard and her mother and I are friendly with the parents of most of these."

"How is Mrs Feltame?" asked Dave.

"Still stunned," the lady's husband replied curtly. "Her life centres on her home, as you may have guessed — that and Sebastian."

"Has she ever travelled with you?" asked Dave.

"The first ten years of our marriage I was travelling the world and she was with me. Then I held a post back in England for a few years."

"Did the children travel too?"

"Well, no. It would have been impossible, really, we were often moving on every few days. My wife came home for the birth, just in time, they were nearly born in transit. Then we got a good nanny for them and they stayed at home. Much better. When I was posted home again they were seven and it was time Sebastian went away to school. High time. I remember they had got a bit out of hand — we had some tantrums because they were going to be separated."

"Mrs Feltame could travel with you now, I suppose," ventured Dave.

"She's grown tired of it. She enjoys entertaining for me when I'm in England. But she was a poor traveller and that tendency has become more pronounced as she's grown older. I'm not away for very long as a rule — it looked like being

191

six months this time, rather the upper limit."

"Your wife provides the gracious background," commented Dave, and Charles Feltame gave him a sharp look.

"Exactly. She isn't a brilliant woman. You may have thought her over-formal. But she is a splendid hostess to our own circle and runs the home beautifully. I would say ours is a successful marriage."

Dave made no comment. He looked down at the typed list and mentally compared it to the one he had compiled of Patricia's correspondents. A lot of the names tallied, if he was remembering aright.

After a moment — "Ah! Here's an old friend of mine. Join us, Harry," said Charles Feltame.

Definitely another businessman, thought Dave. Tall, wellgroomed, well-clothed, clean hands. A man of Charles Feltame's own age.

"Harry Brate," Feltame introduced him. "Detective Inspector David Smart, of our local force, Harry. He's in charge of the investigation of Patricia's death." For a moment there was a tremor in the voice he kept so much under control.

Harry Brate shook Dave's hand, and Dave wondered why he had taken such an instant dislike to the man.

"Appalled to hear the news." Harry Brate rested a hand briefly on Charles Feltame's shoulder. "I've known Patricia and Sebastian all their lives," he explained to Dave. "I got Seb his job in the City. Until recently we were doing business with him."

"Why did you stop?" asked Charles.

"A spot of bother, you know, Charles."

"Tell me."

Harry Brate looked uncomfortable. Ordering his food took him out of the situation for a moment. Then he said quietly, "Well, you know, Seb was being a naughty boy. We had to dissociate ourselves. A pity."

Dave had decided what it was about Harry Brate he didn't like. Although the man's largish head was tanned by the weather, his hands were pale. He had a habit of gesturing with them in an odd way, as though there on his lap or hovering over the table they spelled out some mysterious meaning of their own. The hand Dave had shaken had been cold, even slightly clammy. He shuddered.

"Goose walking over my grave," he explained.

"Harry knows everything that's going on in York," Charles said to Dave, then to Harry, "Dave is trying to trace Pat's last hours." His tone was surprisingly conversational. "We don't know yet where she had dinner the night before she died, or who with."

"But that's easy," Harry Brate said.

He leaned forward and his hands made one of their strange gestures.

"Last Saturday night Patricia had dinner with me."

9

IT was all Dave Smart could do not to hit him.

Was it for Harry Brate that Patricia had put on her red suspenders, for this man old enough to be her father, with his ruddy country head and his uncanny pale hands? Had he as much as touched her with them . . . ?

That strangely impassive face looked at both of them.

"Didn't you know?" Harry asked, as if his information was the most ordinary thing in the world.

"How come?" asked Charles Feltame.

"She was worried about Seb. We happened to meet in the street and she told me she was worried. She seemed to need a bit of guidance, someone to talk to . . . I invited her to dinner at my place."

"At your home?" Dave wanted to be sure he was jumping to the right conclusions.

"No. At my place. My restaurant. I'm not normally interested in catering but I do have a controlling financial stake in this particular place, so I dine there quite often."

"Why should she turn to you?"

"No need to sound aggressive, Dave," put in Charles Feltame. "It seems quite reasonable to me. I was in America, Pat didn't want to have me bothered, or to upset her mother unnecessarily. Harry here has known her all his life. He's had business dealings with Seb. You have business dealings with just about everybody, don't you, Harry? Pat thought with his help she could sort Seb out."

"Something like that," said Harry.

Dave sighed and leaned his elbows on the table. The steak had been too good. He tried to bring his mind into focus.

"Let's go over this, as it seems at present, but some of it is supposition. Sebastian Feltame is good at his job but gets the push from his firm. He's already on drugs. That can cost as much as a thousand pounds a day. He sells his car. His sister persuades him to enter a private clinic from which he later runs away. He holes up in a York hotel, then finds a new drug source and leaves. She's looking for him. She meets Mr Brate in the street and wants to discuss the matter. He askes her to dinner."

"Last Saturday night," said Harry.

"And she is never seen alive again," concluded Dave, gazing straight at Harry Brate.

Harry's hands did a negative kind of sketch. "I knew I should have seen her to her car and made her drive straight home," he said penitently. Was it only Dave's imagination that those hands with a mind of their own were not in the least penitent.

"What was she planning to do?"

"She was all for going round the lowest dives in York trying to find the man who had sold Seb his new drugs. She wanted to break the drug traffic here. I told her it was ridiculous. I told her it was dangerous. 'Leave it, Pat,' I told her. 'That's not your job. You can't lead a one-woman vigilante crusade.' 'I've got to find Seb,' she told me. 'I've got to do something to these fiends who've got him caught on the hard stuff.' Crack it was, but you know that, don't you? Very addictive. Three doses hook a person, they say. She shouldn't have tried to do what she was doing. I told her."

"Would you mind me writing down the facts, Mr Brate?" Dave sounded totally calm.

"Of course."

If he had added 'dear boy' I really would have hit him, thought Dave Smart; and that's the way he does talk.

"First, sir, the name of this restaurant."

"The Black Mamba. Just off Wumpie-gate."

Dave knew it. Verging on the night club, its doors did not open until seven at night and closed at some hour in the morning. The tiny dance floor, the subdued lighting, the couple of musicians who occasionally broke into jazz, it was all very unlike the usual York eating place. He hadn't been in himself, but he had heard that it was very art deco, round mirrors, rainbows on the black walls, orange tables with black napkins, awkward-to-hold forks with only three prongs, the beat of the drum insistent as the saxophone wailed, people still smoking cigarettes and that through long imitation-amber holders supplied by the management.

"Hardly your sort of spot, Harry." Charles Feltame sounded amused.

"I didn't want it. I happened to accept this controlling interest in settlement of a bad debt, that's all. I'm going to offload it, don't you worry. But the meals aren't bad. It's easier than asking my housekeeper to stay on at night, or trying to cook an egg myself, or buying those — what do you call thems — a takeaway."

"There are plenty of restaurants."

"You know how it is," Harry Brate said easily. "Even if I didn't want the investment, and I didn't want it, bad for my image, don't you think? I've got it, and you've got to keep an eye on these things or they don't do well. The best manure is the farmer's boot. It'll be for sale next year. Meanwhile, as I said, the chef is good."

"You can't resist property, can you, Harry?" said Charles.

"Real estate, as they say in America. Yes, I do tend to get involved with it."

Dave was fuming inwardly. He was darn sure that the uniformed boys had checked the Black Mamba.

"We're very glad to know where Miss Feltame was," he said primly. "Can you tell me, sir, what time you met, and what time she left you?"

"Met — oh, about a quarter to eight. Left — oh, shortly before ten. I saw her out and asked if I could escort her to her car, but a very independent woman, your daughter, Charles. I stood and watched her for a moment as she walked off. I'm afraid I wasn't much help to her in her quest. But just talking to someone helps sometimes."

"Mr Brate, I shall have to ask you to come to the station to make an official statement," said Dave.

* * *

Bob Southwell hadn't relished his interview with the senior registrar. It is not easy to convey to someone who has done a PM that you want a second opinion, particularly when there isn't really any new evidence to make it obligatory. He'd drifted in at first as if he'd only come for a chat.

"I'd just like to go over this with you if that's all right," he'd said, producing the report.

For a few minutes they'd discussed it.

"This bleeding round the base of the brain," said Bob. "Did you identify the cause?"

"Well, not positively," replied Martin Smith. "As I said, the usual thing is a Berry aneurysm. I've mentioned that it is associated with the Circle of Willis. I've said that. Give me the report a minute and I'll find it for you."

"No, no . . . " Bob shook his head airily. "No need at all. Did you look at the vertebrals, Dr Smith?"

"Well . . . no . . . "

"Actually, we are having second thoughts about this. Do you mind if we get someone along to have another look? The father is kicking up rather a fuss, you see. It seems a good idea to double check."

Martin Smith could hardly say he didn't like it, so he had smiled and put as good a face as he could on the matter.

201

"If you could arrange to be present, Dr Smith?"

When Bob got back to the police station he had to ring the forensic pathologist. The man he had chosen was Dr Banarjee, a Parsee with the most exquisite manners.

"You realize that I can only come, Mr Southwell," he said in his faintly nasal tone, "if it is absolutely all right with the local people. I would not at all wish to be casting aspersions."

"Dr Smith has agreed and will be present to be of any assistance he can," assured Bob.

"If it is absolutely all right with Dr Smith and with the Coroner — if my respected colleague would welcome the reassurance of my perhaps wider experience — then I would be delighted to be of any assistance I can."

That settled, Bob decided he'd better put Dave Smart in the picture before he went home. He went in search of him. Dave was staring out of the window and whistling under his breath. He didn't look happy; he looked depressed and headachy. Bob stood near him for a few seconds before attracting his attention, listening to the faint whistling. He knew the tune but for a moment he couldn't place it. French, he thought. Yes, that was it. *Aupres de ma blonde, qu'il fait bon, fait bon, fait bon* . . . Near my blonde sweetheart, it's so good, so good, so good . . . a rather cheerful little tune, but not the way Dave was whistling it.

"Enjoy your lunch?" he said at last.

Dave spun round. "No, I didn't."

"Oh."

"The food was good. It was the company."

"Feltame seemed to think a lot of you."

"Not him. This business chum of his, Harry Brate."

"I've heard the name . . . "

"He gave Patricia Feltame dinner the night before she died. At the Black Mamba. He about owns the place."

It was Bob's turn to whistle. "I wouldn't want anyone to take a daughter of mine there."

"That's what I thought. But Charles Feltame didn't take it like that. He can't see anything wrong in anything his old buddy does. And I thought he was perceptive."

"Hadn't we questioned the staff at the Black Mamba?"

"Yes, and they said she hadn't been in. But I went there myself this afternoon. They're not open until night but I managed to contact the manager. He was full of excuses. First he said that the waiter who served them was not on duty when our man went round, then he said that they thought we were asking about customers, not friends of the boss. In other words, they're about as straight as a corkscrew and wouldn't recognize the truth if it bit them in the face."

"But she left there at what time?"

"A little before ten, Brate says. He says he watched her walk away, and wishes he'd escorted her back to her car."

"Do you believe him?"

"Oh, yes."

"You're very positive," Bob said.

"If Brate had anything to do with anything violent or illegal it wouldn't be directly, you can bet your bottom dollar on that. It surprises me that he admits to owning the major share in the Black Mamba. He says that he used to have business dealings with Sebastian Feltame, but stopped before Sebastian got the sack. Dropped him like a hot brick at the first hint of trouble, more likely."

"You didn't like him, did you?"

"No, I didn't."

"At least you know a bit more. What did she do after dinner, that's the question."

"Brate says that she was out to lead a one-woman vigilante mission to clean up the York drug traffic, and that she was going to tour the dives where the stuff's usually for sale."

Bob's fine eyebrows went up towards his thinning hair. If it had been a bit lower down they would have lost themselves in it.

"Foolish," was all he said.

"Do you know what he was on? Crack."

"Crack hasn't reached us yet, has it? So far we've only had the original form of cocaine, not this newer doctored version."

"It seems as if it has reached us, since

he got a fresh supply."

"I'd thought he'd be on heroin."

"Perhaps he's at the point of not caring as long as it was something. But I don't think so, somehow."

"You were saying — apropos of Sebastian Feltame — that these London yuppies snort coke all the time, and I agree with you; that's how it sounds from what we hear. I suppose crack's the next thing."

"The decisive step on the downward path," replied Dave. "Ordinary cocaine you can use for eighteen months or so — maybe even longer if you are careful — and still be in reasonable shape, but with this 'crack' version of it one dose can be enough to hook them."

"Three goes certainly will," agreed Bob, "and it's incredibly difficult to get off it, almost impossible."

"I've asked Mr Brate to come in and give an official statement. As the last person, so far, to see her alive we need to check him out for the rest of the night."

"When's he coming?"

"Any time, I hope. I asked him to come straight away but he said he had to do something first."

"I'll interview him with you," said Bob. "I'll find myself a job until he comes. Give me a bell."

* * *

While he was waiting, Dave Smart went in search of Jenny Wren.

"Have you time to do something for me?" he asked with his best smile.

"Anything," she replied in an exaggerated fashion.

"You remember Patricia Feltame's letter files? I made a list of her correspondents. This morning her father went round her social contacts — mostly by phone I expect — and made this list of those he reached. None of them could help at all, needless to say. Could you just collate these two lists for me? You might have some thoughts on the matter generally?"

"All right."

She is a pleasant, helpful sort of girl, Dave decided, good to have about.

Jenny was thinking, I wish that smile had been for me and not because he wanted something doing. Not that it will take long. He could have done it himself in five minutes. What is it about him I like? Height, build, colouring, yes, they are all acceptable. He's got that dependable air, yes. But it is the intangible, isn't it? I feel happy when he's there. Oh dear, career girl, this isn't the way to be reacting!

She went in search of him when she had done the task and found him leaning against the window and whistling softly.

"It was a very small job," she said. "Here — these are the people not contacted by Mr Feltame. Only three, actually, I'll ring them for you if you like."

"Thank you, Jenny. I hoped you'd say that."

"There is a funny thing." She hesitated.

"Yes?"

"I've been thinking. The twins were separated for long periods of time, weren't they?"

"Boarding school — university — recently his work — I suppose they were."

"They were bound to write to each other."

208

"They seem to have been very close. I would expect it, yes."

"But you didn't find a single letter from Sebastian."

"No. Funny when you come to think of it. Perhaps they rang one another up. We know they did that."

"I think they wrote, too. Is it all right if I go out and have another talk to Mrs Briggs? She will know what letters come into the house."

Dave looked intently at Jenny. She could see now that his eyes were grey. Kindly eyes.

"Good girl," was all he said.

* * *

Harry Brate walked into the police station as if he owned the place. He responded to Bob and Dave's questioning by being helpful and courteous. No, he had no alibi whatever for Saturday night once he had left the Black Mamba at eleven o'clock. He had walked home. That was why he had a flat in the city centre, he liked being in the thick of things and able to walk wherever he wished. Yes, he had used his car to drive out to the hotel where Dave and Charles had met him. He'd been going out that way on business, often did, and stopped to eat *en route*.

They asked what kind of business ventures he had, but he was rather evasive on that. So wide and general were his interests, they gathered, so much in a perpetual state of flux, that it was hard to say at any one moment. They'd have to have a word with his accountant if the information was important, he tried to keep track of things.

He signed the statement and they let him go.

Bob and Dave both felt rather flat. Brate had been unperturbed by their obvious suspicion of him.

"Nasty piece of work," was Bob's comment.

"I'm glad you agree with me."

"You say Charles Feltame's a friend of his?"

"Longstanding. They both grew up here, Feltame said, were in the same youth club, began the upwardly-mobile path together. Maybe Brate has changed and Charles hasn't noticed — that's possible, I think."

"You said Brate wouldn't do his own dirty work, and you are right, of course. He'd be the puppet master, pulling strings."

For a minute or two they sat thinking. Dave was whistling again. Then he said, "Charles Feltame was going down to London — he'll be there now — to enquire into his boy's dismissal. I think we had better ask the Met about the drug habits of Sebastian's circle."

"Right. Look, I'll do that, Dave, and I think we ought to have a talk to our own drug squad. Do you know you're beginning to look all in? What's wrong with going and getting a bit of sleep? You'll solve this thing all the sooner if your brain's working properly."

Dave turned to look him full in the face. "Do you think I can rest?"

"You're a police officer, or have you forgotten that? This is a job, or have you forgotten that too? Are you leading a one-man vigilante mission, as foolish as Patricia's, or are you detecting a crime? Incidentally, I'm sure social workers aren't meant to get mad ideas like that, or do such daft things. Your body is a machine, Dave Smart, as much as your car. If you have three hours' sleep your brain might begin to function again. Then you can roam about the back streets, trying to guess where she went after the Black Mamba."

Dave wondered how on earth the DCI knew what he meant to do. Seeing the look in Bob's eye he thought he'd better behave as he was told.

"I'll go home for three hours," he said.

"Right. That'll take you up to eight o'clock. Soon enough. And spend that three hours sleeping. I'll put a memo on your desk if I come up with anything on crack. I'll stay on for a bit."

"I won't be able to sleep," was Dave's parting shot.

He did, though. He threw himself on his bed just as he was, apart from taking off his shoes, thinking he'd practise relaxation for a few minutes and then get up again and spend the three hours meditating on the case. But no sooner had he begun to relax one group of muscles after another beginning with his toes than he was deep into a dreamless sleep, as if he had fallen into it from a great height. It was one of those sleeps which imitates death. Dave's body did not move nor his eyelids flicker. Not once in the three hours did he make the slightest alteration in his position. He did not snore, or even breathe heavily. No dream, remembered or not, idled across his mind.

When the alarm rang he opened his eyes as simply as a child and looked at the clock in surprise. He automatically swung his legs off the edge of the bed and sat up, rubbing the nape of his neck as he came to. "I've been asleep!" It surprised him. He could hardly believe the clock-face, telling him that it was past eight o'clock.

Before lying down he had drawn the curtains against the night, and now he parted them a little and looked out. The street lamps shone on wet roads and rain was falling, but not fast. It was one of those clean, clear wet evenings which would not be unpleasant if rain was warm. As it was, the very sight of it made Dave shiver, remembering all the nights such as this when rain had made its way insidiously down his neck, into his boots, through the seams of his waterproofs, into the cuffs of his gloves. There had been many times when he had had to be on duty throughout a wet night. On the beat, when he was a young man, it had not been too bad. He remembered with gratitude the waterproof cape and strong helmet which together did a good job. Once out of the uniformed branch and into mufti, things hadn't been so good. Really waterproof waterproofs made you too conspicuous altogether and even the best of them . . .

Dave dropped the curtain. He couldn't be really awake yet, or he wouldn't be drifting into long reveries about rain. He yawned enormously and shook his head to clear it. He ought to go back to the station and see what messages Bob had left for him, if any, but he didn't want to. He felt as though he was on automatic pilot and his body would decide what to do without him telling it.

After a coffee and a snack from the fridge it was half-past eight when Dave left his flat. It was fortunate that after six a lot of the 'foot streets' could be used. He cruised quietly into the city in his car, grateful for the warmth of the heater, wondering if he was altogether awake yet. What could he do? Enter the places he might find a drug pusher and show his photo of Patricia, asking if they'd seen her the previous Saturday night? Fat chance. Anyway the uniformed team had already done what could be done in that direction and were still pursuing enquiries. He brought the car to a stop in a side street where he had a view of one of the suspect pubs. There had to be some way of finding out.

The pub door opened and a group of young people came on to the street. They all seemed to be in black which was gleaming in the wetness of the night. One girl whose mini skirt barely covered her behind had blonde hair which stuck up in a great shrub of stiffness. A car door banged shut, a motor bike revved away, there was the explosion of sound and then the street was empty again.

Dave whistled softly, *"Et ma jolie colombe qui chante jour et nuit, qui chante pour les filles qui n'ont point de mari* . . . and my pretty dove, which sings day and night, which sings for the girls who have no husbands . . . " The rain drummed on the roof of the car. It drummed persistently, without rhythm, as if it was boring into his head.

★ ★ ★

Patricia had begun her desperate search the Friday before.

It had been midday when she had gone to Pete's Hotel and found him missing, and her heart had jumped into her throat with fear. All afternoon she'd had to carry out her work, unable to think straight or see anything in her mind's eye but an empty hotel room. She'd even gone home at half-past four and eaten an early meal with her mother, trying all the time to appear normal. No need to divulge what she had been keeping secret so painstakingly, no need at all. Seb must be somewhere, somewhere near.

She searched for him. She searched down the side alleys and the back streets. She peered into doorways and behind dustbins and startled prowling cats.

It was time to do what she dreaded — go into pubs and bars and try to contact people who bought and sold the white powder, or the yellow powder or whatever . . .

She stood for a while on Lendal Bridge and looked upstream. Black night with lights reflected in the water, a few houseboats moored at the riverside, a few street lamps, the moon now also breaking the blackness. A nocturne by Whistler.

Going into a bar. Looking round. Approaching a likely person. Asking.

"Snort? Not here, mate. You need to be over in Bradford for that kind of stuff." She hadn't mentioned crack. If she once found someone, some lead, that was soon enough.

The wind was rising. All day it had been practising for a good equinoctial blow. During the summer they'd been free of it, since the damaging gales in March. But now the wind twanged the city, experimentally, as if the thick buildings were an Aeolian harp. It howled playfully through the great covered tunnels of the station and rushed up the hill to dash against the fretted West Front of the Minster, spraying against the high Heart of Yorkshire window a random selection of fine twigs and small leaves. It canyoned through the narrow space between the Minster and St Michael le Belfrey.

The rain began, driving on the wings of the wind. Curtains of it changed from vertical to horizontal in the varying gusts. Sheets of it were slapped insultingly into the faces of the buildings. A band of rain swept up the street passing over Patricia as she ran before the wind. It soaked her stockings and covered her hat and coat with a layer of water. She put up a hand to grasp the brim of her hat and ran harder than ever for the car-park.

Once inside the car she gasped for breath.

"It's no use," she said aloud. "I'm getting nowhere like this. I need someone, some contact . . . "

★ ★ ★

Dave had stayed out until the last of the late-night revellers had left the streets.

"Useless," he decided. "Bloody useless."

He was parked in a good place for observations but there had been nothing to observe. A good police officer wasting time, fretting himself silly, drawing with his forefinger on the steamed-up car window letters of the alphabet, spelling out 'Patricia' . . .

10

THE second post-mortem took place the next morning, Wednesday, at the York District Hospital mortuary.

Martin Smith had arrived there early and made everyone's life a misery, fussing round until he was sure that things were in apple pie order.

Bob Southwell had decided to be present himself as the police observer. He parked the police car next to Smith's Granada a few seconds before Dr Banarjee arrived in a silver-grey BMW as elegant as himself. The two men shook hands formally and walked on together shoulder to shoulder, then had an elaborate parley as to who was to enter the door of the mortuary first.

In the sterile white glimmer of shining white ceramic tiles and white paint and undimmed lighting the body of Patricia Feltame had become an academic exercise.

"You found nothing abnormal, Dr Smith?" asked the forensic pathologist.

Martin Smith explained what he had done, and what he had found.

"Um-ha. The clothes bagged — excellent. You removed the brain — ah, yes. Not dissected, I see. Very good. I am very pleased about that, Dr Smith. I can examine those later, if you will allow me. I see that you made the routine hospital incisions. Just as you would normally do, and as I expected. Very good."

Smith could not have been at his ease anyway. It made it worse having this foreign personage, who seemed so aloof and regal. No rapport possible here, he thought. Dr Banarjee was hardly the sort of person you slapped on the back or gossiped to over a pint. Mint tea in a marble hall would have seemed more appropriate.

Bob Southwell watched impassively as Banarjee slowly and carefully examined the body and everything that Martin Smith had done. The thin shapely brown hands in translucent gloves seemed to touch too lightly to wake the living, let

221

alone the dead, but they had strength in plenty.

"You see, Dr Smith, while your incision down the midline of the neck is perfectly all right . . . perfectly all right for a normal PM and in the usual position for hospital deaths, I think for our purposes it would be helpful to have a look at an angle, making a wide Y shape, and we can see what has been happening under these neck muscles here . . . "

There was the glitter of stainless steel tools aiding the delicate, precise work of a master craftsman in progress.

"That side is perfectly all right, you see here, Dr Smith. Quite normal. Yes. Absolutely. Let us have a look at the other side."

Dr Banarjee worked rapidly but with complete concentration.

"Aaaah," he said.

"I thought so."

"It seemed the logical explanation."

No one else had dared to say a word. They waited.

Dr Banarjee straightened his slender back.

"If you would care to come closer, gentlemen . . . "

They gathered round, trying not to get in each other's way.

"In the muscles on the side of the neck here there is evidence of bruising. Not extensive."

How did I manage to miss it? thought Martin Smith; but "It isn't noticeable, even now," he excused himself. "You wouldn't see it at all except in such a wide Y-shaped incision."

"This looks like a rare condition. Only when you've been doing as many of these as I do are you at all likely to think of it. Just so. On looking inside we uncover the vertebral artery. At this place it is very vulnerable; it passes over the bone. There has been bleeding around the artery. And here . . . "

Dr Banarjee stood back so that Bob Southwell and Martin Smith should not have the least problem in seeing what he was showing them. "We will have to take out the whole of the cervical spine and X-ray it, but it is pretty certain we will find a tear . . . Ah, yes, look here — the transverse process of the Atlas and this 'sticky-out bit' is involved as well . . . let us have some photographs, Detective Chief Inspector. So that has caused the bleeding around the artery which you, Dr Smith, very reasonably, believed to be attributable to another cause."

Bob Southwell blinked at the evidence he was being shown. He knew what that tear in the artery meant. He was only waiting for Dr Banarjee to tell him.

"There is no doubt," the forensic pathologist remarked, "no doubt at all, that this girl died as a result of a karate-type chop to the side of the neck."

Bless you, thought Bob Southwell, bless you, Dave Smart me old darlin', bless your intuition, bless wretched interfering Charles Feltame, bless the pair of you for your obstinate belief that this girl did not die a natural death when she had so much to offer to the world.

Aloud he said with feeling, "I'd like to nail the man who did this."

"Such a blow could be delivered by a woman," said Banarjee.

"All right. I'd like to nail the person who did this."

"Who does a thing?" asked Dr Banarjee. "The person who orders it or the person who carries it out?"

Bob Southwell looked at him in surprise, but the capped head was already bent once more over his work.

★ ★ ★

Dave Smart had been sitting around in his car at various places in the streets of the city for nearly the whole of the previous night without a thought in his head, and without seeing anything in the least useful.

This morning he stayed in the police station on Clifford Street.

Jenny had left him a memo. She had been to Murtwick the previous evening and talked to Mrs Briggs, who had confirmed that the brother and sister were always writing to one another, and that Patricia had come down and personally burnt letters in the Aga from time to time, and Mrs Briggs guessed they were Sebastian's, because she'd noticed the writing looked like his.

"It only confirms the relationship,"

Dave decided. "As if they were constantly nearing one another and as constantly shying away. As if it was something they dare not even look at, this closeness."

Of course, Jenny was on two till ten. He'd have a word with her later. Now, he remembered that at the very beginning of this case he had spent night hours checking through records in search of any mention of Patricia. He got out his notes again. There was something he remembered. Hadn't she — at one point — cropped up in regard to a drug enquiry? The cases she dealt with were mostly to do with children but — yes, here it was. Someone had been up for possession of drugs, suspected dealing, yes. James Gotobedde. Released on probation. That was the craftsman whose shop he'd called at — no wonder the bloke had been so antagonistic, hadn't wanted any contact with the police. Dave sat drumming his fingers on his notes.

At that moment the phone rang.

"Someone to see you, Dave. Steve Watson, the probation officer. Said he'd seen you in the social security office. You applying for assistance?" came a voice.

"You'll apply for assistance in a minute, James Jester. Try to get your facts straight. Bring him up."

Steve lounged into the office which was home base for several detectives. Dave got up to greet him. They were all three of a height — Dave, Steve, and James Jester; and Steve was as slim as James. But there was an essential difference between the three men. Steve came over as gentler, more casual, in many ways more approachable, though not as much so as the social workers. He considered himself a cut above them, and occupied a place somehow half-way between them and the police force.

"Jesus, that place," Steve said afterwards to Frances, wanting to impress her and show off a little. "It would give you the willies. You couldn't work in a place like that." Frances looked interested. "Too — too — " He shook his head. "There is a feeling of the armed forces somehow, in the middle of a campaign." "They are, I suppose," responded Frances. She retained his words, lingering over them, remembering Dave Smart, relishing while disapproving of macho men.

Steve said hello and sat down but said nothing until James had left and as it happened he and Dave were alone. The other staff were out.

"It's Patricia Feltame," he brought out at last.

"Yes, I thought so."

"Since you came in yesterday morning I've not been able to forget it; and it came to my mind that when she first came back to York she was with me for a while, volunteer probation officer, until she decided she'd be happier with social work. She attended court with me on one of my cases connected with drugs."

"James Gotobedde?" asked Dave.

"Yes." Steve looked annoyed. "If you knew, why all that appeal yesterday morning?"

"I didn't know. Right at the beginning I checked through records of court cases." Dave held up his page of notes. "It seemed a waste of time — none of it relevant, but I've just been checking through again in the light of what we now know, and come across this case you mention. Tell me more. I've only got the bare essentials."

"There's not much to tell." Steve stretched himself more comfortably in the chair, establishing his territory.

"He seems a bit old for a drug addict," said Dave.

"Forty?"

"He looks older."

"No, he's only forty, and he wasn't an addict, though a good few people of his age are. You mustn't think they're all teenagers."

"I didn't."

"Mind, he might have been an addict once. No. He was in possession, suspected of dealing, but it was a first offence, and there was the suggestion that he might have been framed, so we managed to get probation. I was his probation officer."

"Is it right for you to be here, then?"

"I discussed it with my boss. Since the whole business is so serious. Since it's the only contact we or the social work team know of Pat having with the drug scene."

"He's kept his nose clean?"

"Oh yes. Whiter than white."

Dave always suspected people who were whiter than white. They made him think of sepulchres. He wondered whether to tell Steve Watson that Pat had had contact with James Gotobedde in his craftsman capacity. He decided against it. Steve had to do his job without prejudice; the less he knew the better.

"In possession of what?"

"Only cannabis."

"Right." Dave thought Steve might have sounded more disgusted if Gotobedde had been in possession of tobacco. Only cannabis, as though cannabis was nothing and had no deleterious effects. "Anything else you can tell me about this client of yours? You think he's learnt his lesson?"

"Yes. In his business he can't afford to do anything illegal. He says you people are always checking on him for licences etcetera."

"Does seem unfair, doesn't it? It's not that we're picking on him, it's the trade he's in. Why did he want the cannabis? You say he's not an addict."

"For a party, he told us. That seems likely."

"Surely does. Any other ideas?"

"Not at present."

"Anything you hear . . . "

"All right. I'll go now, then."

When Steve Watson had gone Dave sat gazing into space. He began to whistle softly, '*Pour moi ne chante guère Car j'en ai un joli — Dites moi donc, la belle, Où donc est votre mari?* For me the pretty dove doesn't sing often, for I already have a handsome husband. Tell me then, lovely one, where is he? . . . Near my blonde sweetheart, it's so good, so good, so good . . . ' Dave's whistling gradually died away and he sat silently. Tell me then, lovely one, where is he?

He'd been trying to forget the second PM was this morning. There was plenty to keep him occupied in the station. Detectives detected sitting at their desks these days and talking on telephones or reading reports from people who'd been out and done the leg work. Bob would be back eventually, and he'd let him know, he wouldn't keep him in suspense. Dave decided to go out and buy fish and chips.

★ ★ ★

231

The general office downstairs was busy with the change-over of shift. The six-till-two foot patrol men were coming in and signing off and the two-till-ten men were signing on.

As Dave walked through, returning from his brief lunch break, a pleasant-faced young constable looked up and saw him, then put the pen down quickly and caught Dave as he was about to mount the stairs.

"Sir! Can I have a word with you?"

"You surely can," said Dave. Bother. He'd meant to stop and have a word with Jenny Wren. He could see her signing on now. She'd been into the locker room to leave her outdoor things, and she'd just come back into the office.

"It's like this . . . "

"Come upstairs."

"Are you going off or on?" asked Dave as he went over to the office kettle, weighed it in his hand, and plugged it in. There would be enough water in it for two mugs.

"On, sir, but thanks, I don't want anything."

"I do." Dave was curt. He measured

232

a heaped teaspoonful of powdered coffee into a mug he took from a drawer in his desk. "Now, what is it?"

"Monday, sir, I was on the search for the dead girl — we were asking in the cafés if anyone had seen her last Saturday night. So I had this photograph."

He took the photo of Patricia from his pocket. Dave flinched. He could hardly bear anyone to look at that photo. What sort of husband would he have made? Pathologically jealous? He hoped not. If she hadn't died, if he could have looked at the living girl, he would have been proud to have her admired. Now it was a stab of pain every time.

"Yes?"

"Well, on my way home last night I just had time to have a drink at my local. The barman had the *Evening Press* on the counter with the article in about her. The picture was a bit muzzy. 'I've got a better one than that,' I said, and pulled this out to show him. He looked at it, and then he said, 'I thought so. That's the girl that was in here Saturday night last thing.' So when I got home I rang in and left a message for you, sir. I only wondered if you'd got it and if it was helpful. That's all. Don't want to be a nuisance, I just wondered."

Of course he'd wondered. A dead girl was more exciting than routine drunks and traffic duty.

"I haven't had that message," said Dave. He looked down at his desk. Perhaps there was something in the clutter of papers? Probably the message had landed on the wrong desk or not been written down at all. "Which is your local?"

"I live at Acaster Malbis, sir. I drink at the Ship."

"And it was at the Ship that . . ."

"Yes, sir."

Dave looked at his watch.

Wednesday afternoon. Five past two o'clock.

"Have they started opening all day?"

"Not yet, sir. I think they're planning to in the summer. They'll be closing now, I expect."

"Do they live on the premises?"

"The landlord does."

"Thanks." Dave grasped the constable's shoulder for a moment and shook it cordially. "You've moved the whole enquiry on a bit, do you know that? Good man. Now you'd better go if you're due on."

The constable was still young enough to blush with pleasure at the praise.

★ ★ ★

Before Dave could shoot off to Acaster Malbis Bob Southwell rang him.

"Dave? I'm with the Superintendent. Can you come up?"

"Right away."

Dave was pleased that he'd just had this breakthrough. He'd been dreading meeting Bob with nothing new to report. He walked into the Superintendent's room looking more cheerful than he had for a while.

No one else was looking cheerful at all.

Dave felt as though he'd walked into a room where everyone was talking about him. He looked around and wondered what was the matter. The Super's face was as long as a fiddle.

"Sir," said Dave.

"Sit down, Dave," said Detective Superintendent Birch. "This is the beginnings of a conference. We've asked drug squad to send someone along."

Dave sat down and shut up.

Looking at his blank face, Bob took pity on him. "You remember it was the second PM this morning," he said.

"Yes?"

For the last four hours Dave had been trying to stop his mind running on that PM. Once had been bad enough.

"I'm going to talk about the result in a minute. When we're all here."

It wasn't long before someone from drug squad arrived. The young man looked half asleep and certainly hadn't shaved that morning. He was wearing a T-shirt of lurid pattern under an old-looking jersey and a black leather bomber jacket which had seen better days, and jeans, naturally.

Altogether there were now half a dozen men in the room, a couple from the uniformed branch.

"Gentlemen, we've come to hear the latest developments in the case you've no doubt all heard about — the body found by DI Smart here by the river on Sunday morning. It was assumed at first that this was a normal accidental type of death. However, sufficient doubt arose for us to authorize a second post-mortem, which took place this morning, carried out by Dr Banarjee, and attended by DCI Southwell. Perhaps you'd report, please, Bob."

"The second post-mortem, carried out this morning as you've heard, revealed that the death of this young girl was not an accidental one. On examination of the tissues of the neck, Dr Banarjee discovered slight bruising, and a tear in the vertebral artery. From his experience he was able to tell us quite positively that the girl's death was caused by a karate chop to the side of the neck."

Everyone in the room changed position, shuffling in their chairs.

"Yes. So instead of an unavoidable death we are faced, gentlemen, with a murder enquiry. We are now setting up a murder team, which is why you are all here. Superintendent Birch will head it. I and DI Smart, who has so far been the Officer in the Case, will be working under him. We will also need the co-operation of the lads in blue and of drug squad." He paused to let his words sink in.

"Unfortunately time and opportunities have been lost, but with the co-operation of the uniformed branch we've already been pursuing enquiries and have made some progress. Dave, would you like to give the meeting a run-down on progress so far?"

Dave wasn't really prepared for this, but he stood up. He felt he'd be more comfortable on his feet. When what you've believed turns out to be true it somehow becomes unbelievable. He could give this report automatically, though.

"We've been pursuing several lines of enquiry. First, we've been trying to find out what the girl was doing in the hours immediately preceding — just before — her death. I would like to announce that we've had a breakthrough there, thanks to a bright young constable on the beat, who has been able to tell me that she turned up at the Ship Inn at Acaster Malbis shortly before closing time last Saturday night. We already knew that she had had dinner at the Black Mamba and left there between half-nine and ten. She is believed to have died at about six on the Sunday morning, so we have narrowed the gap considerably. The Ship closes at eleven, so the gap is now about seven hours. I haven't been out there yet — I was just about to go when this meeting was called — but the barman recognized her photograph and will probably be able to tell us whether she actually stayed until closing time, which I would expect she did as it seems to have been only a short while." He cleared his throat, then went on.

"That was the first point. The second line of enquiry was her previous life and activities. She had been very distressed recently by the fact that her brother has become a drug addict. We understand from a family friend that he was on crack, which as you know is a form of cocaine which can be almost incurably addictive in sometimes as little as one dose."

"Can I just butt in there a minute,

Dave," said Bob. "We have been in touch with the Met, who have been checking for us on the brother's contacts. He worked in the City. They are aware that in the brother's circle of friends coke-sniffing has been going on for some time, but the girl's brother is the only person known to have become addicted by crack. In fact they didn't know there had been any crack about in that particular set-up, and are investigating further for us. Do go on, Dave."

"As I said, the girl — Patricia Feltame — had been very distressed by her brother's drug addiction, and after he vanished from where he was staying last week, she apparently tried to meet drug pushers and anyone on the dope scene, partly in order to trace her brother and partly with some idea, we are told, of trying to stamp drug abuse out in York."

"Join the club," put in the representative of drug squad.

"I don't think I have anything further to add at this point," said Dave, and sat down.

"I'd like to add something, if I may,"

said the man from drug squad.

"Go ahead, Mark," said the Superintendent.

"We'd rather dismissed this as a false alarm. We received a phone call last Sunday night about five a.m. — I can check the time for you. The call was from a young girl judging by the sound of the voice. When I say young, not teenage. Perhaps early twenties."

"Right."

"She sounded distressed. Breathy. Agitated. She told us that a quantity of crack had been brought to York, and that it was intended to distribute it to a network of agents who were to come to the city for the ostensible purpose of attending York Races. It would then be distributed over the whole North of England. You can imagine the number of addicts we would then have on our hands in a very short time indeed."

"Yes."

"Naturally we tried to hold the girl in conversation but she was anxious to get off the line, which was a bad one. We did not get her name. We tried to persuade her to meet us but she would not make an appointment to do so."

"What steps did you take?" asked the Super.

"Of course we have arranged to be at the races in force. You will know, I am sure, that the last meeting for the season was scheduled to take place today, tomorrow, and Saturday. The going is too soft today, so the meeting has been cancelled. They have hopes for tomorrow. We were rather inclined to dismiss the phone call as a hoax, and wonder what was due to happen elsewhere in the city while our attention was distracted."

"Was the message recorded?"

"Yes, sir."

"Good. We'll get the voice identified. I'd like drug squad to see if through your contacts, Mark, you can learn anything of the girl's movements last Saturday night."

"It would be worth asking about Friday night as well, I think, if I can suggest that," said Dave Smart.

"Friday?"

"Her brother left his hotel either late Thursday night or Friday morning. She was going to see him every day, often in her lunch hour. She would have found out that he had skipped off at the latest by Friday lunch time, and almost certainly started to look for him right away. If she was asking around for the drug pushers a certain section of the population is going to be very aware indeed of her actions and progress."

"The trouble is . . . " said Bob.

"Yes?"

"The trouble is . . . a karate chop . . . there was no sign of a struggle or fight on the girl's body. It seemed as if she was just dropped by that single blow. No evidence of another person's contact with her, as far as we know — I suppose Dr Banarjee might turn something up but it doesn't seem likely, and the scene has been trodden over by a thousand feet since then, even if there had been any trace at all of the assailant."

"How are we to bring home the murder," said Dave.

"Exactly."

* * *

It was later that afternoon when Dr Banarjee telephoned Bob Southwell at the police station.

"Goodness, you've been quick," said Bob. "Reporting already?"

"My dear Detective Chief Inspector," said Dr Banarjee, "reports take time, as you know. I will of course be as speedy as I can on that. I have just made the most cursory examination possible of the girl's clothing; it was bagged, if you remember; and there was one tiny point I thought I would mention."

"Just a moment, Dr Banarjee . . . " Bob called through to Dave Smart to come and pick up the extension.

"I was just going out," objected Dave, but Bob's beckoning wave was peremptory.

Then, "Yes, Dr Banarjee."

"The very elegant dress she was wearing . . . "

"A black one, yes."

"Which had a collar of coarse white lace, which fastened on to the neckline with a number of very small pearl buttons."

"Collar?"

"I didn't see one," said Dave, putting his hand over the mouthpiece.

"The officer who found the body did not see the collar, Dr Banarjee."

"That is why I am ringing you, Detective Chief Inspector. The collar of the dress would have been very visible at the lady's throat. You would have seen it even though she was wearing a coat, because of the cut of that garment. There are traces of it having been in place, attached to the dress, recently. But it was folded up, in the pocket of the coat. I thought you would want to know."

"Oh," said Bob.

"I just thought I would let you know, in case this has any significance."

"Thank you very much, Dr Banarjee."

Bob put down the phone.

"Why should she take off her collar and put it in her pocket?"

"There might be a lot of explanations," Bob said. "She might have decided she liked the dress better without the collar. She might have put it in her pocket in case she changed her mind and wanted to wear it later."

"A white lace collar?"

"That's what Dr Banarjee said."

"She would have looked more dressy with it on. We can find out if she did wear it, from Harry Brate. It would be more festive — more suited to a meal out at the Black Mamba."

"Dr Banarjee said it had been on the dress at some time."

"Fibres left?"

"He would hardly have had time yet to have the clothes gone over for fibres."

"He might just have looked quickly, even with a handglass before ringing you, and seen a white fibre; it would show up easily enough on black."

"True."

"She was wearing nothing but black on top," said Dave. "The collar."

He tried to visualize it. "It would have shown up in the darkness. It would be the only visible thing. The only thing, apart from her face and hands, which would have been seen on a dark night."

"If she was watching something — "

"Or someone — "

"And didn't want to be spotted . . ."

"She could push her hands up her sleeves . . ."

Dave drew a deep breath. "What a difference," he said, "between working with Dr Banarjee and with that Martin Smith."

* * *

It had been late on the Saturday evening that Patricia had at last run across someone she recognized and someone who could tell her something.

In a group settled in a corner of one of the extended bar areas common in the city, where a lot of old small rooms have been thrown together, was James Gotobedde, the restorer of antique guns. She didn't like seeing him there. It was more comfortable when people stayed in their compartments. In his niche as craftsman she knew and respected James Gotobedde. Drinking with a set of youngsters in one of the more dubious pubs he seemed out of place, but it was the place where she had expected to find him, where she had been sent.

Yet she felt relief too, because she could speak more openly, though she must be careful. He might not want his companions to know that he'd once been up in court suspected of dealing in illegal substances. Surely, though, they'd know.

"I need your help," she said quietly. "Seb's gone missing. He was looking for a dealer." As she glanced round the group several of them looked vaguely familiar.

"He's not on anything, is he?" asked someone chipping in perkily. She can't have spoken as quietly as she had intended to.

"I'm afraid he is." She was beginning to get used to admitting it. She would give them time to think before pressing the matter. So far she had hardly drunk anything. She went over to the bar to buy a glass of wine.

"Interfering bitch," said James Gotobedde. He bent over towards one of the circle. "Think of something to tell her," he hissed. "She'll spoil the party. I want her sidetracked — sent off on a false trail somewhere."

When Patricia returned to the group they looked a little more friendly. One of them had risen and gone off presumably to the loo and she took his seat for a minute.

"I must find him," she said to James. "If I can find the supply I can find Seb."

James appealed to the group. "Anybody got any ideas?"

They looked as if they hadn't a thought between them.

"You'd better try Bradford," someone said. "Or Halifax or Leeds. Anyone wants a supply they go over there."

"We'll let you know if we hear anything," volunteered James Gotobedde.

Patricia drank her wine slowly, listening and trying to pick up a lead from the chat. Someone knew, she sensed it. They were not talking freely because she was there. There was something behind all this. This was the most cohesive group she'd met and she couldn't make out what they had in common. She was reluctant to believe that James was still involved in the drug scene. But he seemed knowing. If he was, he wasn't telling her, that was obvious.

At last she gave up and finished her drink before standing to go. As she neared the exit the young man whose stool she had taken spoke to her. He'd been lounging there for long enough, waiting.

"Shitty for you," he said sympathetically.

"Yes."

"I heard a whisper about Seb."

"You did?"

"Yes. You needn't worry. There's been a boat down river wanting an extra hand. I heard he'd signed on. Trip to Holland."

"When was this?" Patricia was convinced instantly. Seb was good on the water.

"They were wanting someone yesterday. I was asking earlier if they'd found anyone. They said yes, Seb Feltame."

Holland said drugs to Patricia. Of course he'd jump at it.

"They'll be back next week." The young man was reassuring. "It's only a short cruise. I was interested but I hardly thought it was worth bothering."

She hadn't liked the look of him, earlier. Now she was grateful and smiled her relief. She remembered seeing him at a party she had been to with her brother, a party of rowing and sailing mates, where the talk was all of currents and draughts and hidden hazards like the clay humps on the bed of the Ouse.

"Stay and have another," he said with a warm look in his eyes.

"Thanks, but no thanks," she said. "I'll go and see if I can find out anything else. Were they above the lock?"

"They were yesterday. I guess they'll have gone now, though."

Later, he said, "I've sent her on a wild-goose chase. We won't see her for a day or two."

* * *

Above the downriver lock yesterday but gone today. The lock was Naburn, and you could only pass through it when the tide was up. At half-past seven the lock-keeper would have finished for the night. Patricia began to run to where she had left her car, in the car-park near the river Foss. There was no need to run. If Seb had signed on and they'd left on the last tide he was out of her reach and there was nothing she could do.

She felt brightened and exhilarated by

the elements. The heavy feeling of dinner and drink had passed off a bit. The thought of Seb on a small ship slipping down the Humber to the open sea did not worry her in the least.

She thought of going to Naburn, then decided that she could get better information at the Ship Inn at Acaster Malbis, if she was quick enough. They were bound to close at eleven and it was half-past ten already. But someone there would have heard about this boat wanting an extra crew member and she started the car engine.

Patricia had been sent on this wild-goose chase the night before she died, at half-past ten.

11

THE early winter dark was already drawing in by the time Dave drove out to the Ship Inn at Acaster Malbis. He wished he had not stayed up most of the previous night. It wasn't as if he had gained anything from it, and now he knew the lack of sleep during the last few days was going to catch up with him again.

He was so affected by tiredness that he went the wrong way from Clifford Street and instead of going via Bishopthorpe he took the A64, the Leeds road, and turned off at the traffic lights into Copmanthorpe. He turned again at the signpost to Acaster Malbis. The country road was black and he didn't know the area very well. His windscreen wipers were working overtime.

He reached what he supposed was Acaster Malbis. The village houses loomed up at him out of the wet darkness, one by one. This wasn't a compact village, he realized. There was no street lighting. Many of the houses were off the road and he hadn't found a pub so far. Whatever made that young copper want to live in a benighted spot like this?

He saw a signpost to a caravan park, then some kind of country club. No Ship Inn. Suddenly he realized he'd been driving a long time since reaching the village, and there were no longer houses beside the streaming lane. A T-junction was coming up; no other traffic was about. Acaster Malbis was half a mile back the way he had come. Cursing he swung the car round, spraying the hedgerows with rainwater. At this rate he wouldn't find the place before closing time.

He went back past the country club and past the caravan park. The dark roads seemed to wind all ways and run into one another. He couldn't find anything remotely resembling a village street as such. Aha, there was the post office. That didn't help but at least he was still in the place. Now one of the last houses in the village was coming up; he recognized its outline and the bend in the road from entering minutes earlier, even though he was now approaching it from the opposite direction. He'd be out of the place again in two shakes.

Just in time he saw the big squarish notice on the corner. No wonder he hadn't seen it before — there was no light shining on to it as he would have expected. He turned sharp right down the narrow lane. Here it was. The Ship Inn. Opposite, a carpark, roomy and well surfaced. He parked and got out.

In front of him was the river, almost at his feet, great breadths of it reflecting distant lights. The surface was pitted all over by rain. Shivering, Dave turned away and walked to the Ship.

The pub stood by the road from Bishopthorpe, with its back to the lane and its frontage to the river. It looked warm and welcoming, with strings of coloured electric bulbs along the fascia boards.

It was an attractive pub. There was a restaurant, but Dave turned into the bar which was long and low. At the end, a step up from the rest of it, were tables where people were sitting, ready to eat evening meals. In the centre was the bar itself. On the left was an area with the original stone-flagged floor and a coal fire blazing away in an efficient though antiquated grate, low down in a kind of inglenook.

Everything was enlivened by the gleam of shining brass: horse brasses hung up for decoration and other brass objects here and there. Dave looked round in appreciation. The old comfortable windsor chairs and settles were the kind which, he remembered, had once been common in country pubs. As a little boy in short trousers he had been allowed in very briefly, just long enough for his father to pass him a glass of lemonade, then he had had to take it outside and drink it on a bench in the open. Not here, but in a similar kind of pub, for in those days there had been many similar pubs. It was nice to know that the breed was still in existence.

★ ★ ★

At about the same time, his superior officer was on his way home.

"Golly gum drops," said Bob Southwell as he walked into the kitchen. "What a day." He hung up his damp coat on the back of the door.

"Don't swear in front of the children," teased Linda. She reached inside the oven and produced a casserole.

"We had ours at dinner time, Daddy," said Susan. She was in her nightdress and ready for bed. "We only stopped up to see you. Mummy says we're to have an early night."

Susan and Paul gave their father hugs and kisses and disappeared upstairs.

"They're going to sit up in bed and watch a video on the portable telly," explained Linda. "You needn't think you've got deprived children. They were out late last night at that party and overexcited, so I wanted them settled down early. With any luck they'll be asleep before the video ends."

"What's wrong with reading them to sleep like you used to do?"

"They nearly always get a bedtime story. You know that."

"A video seems a bit of a cop-out."

"It is. But I wanted a quiet evening with you."

"Oh well . . . " Bob pulled her down on to his knee.

"Bob, you've not had your meal yet."

After a minute Bob released her. He was hungry, and the casserole smelt good.

"There's treacle tart for afters."

"You're buttering me up. Now what are you after, Lindy-lou?"

"Nothing. What should I be after?"

"Something." Bob tucked into his casserole.

Linda sat down opposite and quietly watched him for a while. The radio was producing gentle music. The kitchen where Bob was eating on his own at the white table was bathed in friendly light; it was pleasant to know that the darkness was shut out; that on the other side of the window pane was the night.

"Nasty day?" she asked.

"You can say that again. Post-mortem this morning, on a lovely young girl."

"Ugh."

"I don't want to think about it," said Bob.

Linda was silent for a while, then, "I was lucky," she said.

"In what way?"

"I found a professor and his wife for our dinner party."

Bob groaned.

"I knew I wasn't getting treacle tart for nothing."

"Hartley Danes and his wife Lilias."

"We don't know them very well."

"If you don't make the effort you never get to know people."

"How nice."

"Do you want a piece of treacle tart or don't you?"

"They're not too bad, I suppose."

"I've arranged it for Saturday night."

"Isn't that rather short notice? Aren't people usually busy on Saturday nights?"

"Luckily they can all come."

Bob, who had just been handed a wide slice of treacle tart, said nothing.

"So I've been planning the menu. Avocados are good at this time of year."

Bob had had a bright idea. "What

about Yorkshire pud?"

"Avocados, followed by Yorkshire pud, followed by roast beef . . . "

Bob wondered how Linda managed to get her treacle tarts crispy on top and moist and luscious underneath. He'd watched her grating breadcrumbs for them, but still felt there was something magic about it.

"Good Yorkshire fare," he said, talking about the dinner party.

"Yes. I haven't thought about the rest of it yet. But I'm going to go and talk to David tomorrow about the joint of beef."

David was the butcher Linda had found who saw eye to eye with her on the kind of meat which was worth buying.

"I don't know how it is that you always stay like a yard of pump water, as my granny used to say," remarked Linda, passing Bob his third piece of treacle tart. He had helped himself to the second one.

"Slim and elegant, with muscles like whipcord, is what I think you mean, Lindy-lou. I stay thin because I don't get enough treacle tarts."

For the time at least work was forgotten. Dave could be relied on; he was out there, doing something.

* * *

Dave went up to the bar in the Ship Inn and ordered a pint. The barman gave him a bright intelligent glance.

"Will there be anything else, sir?" The space behind the bar was buzzing with young members of the staff dashing to and fro, yet Dave was sure that this slightly older man was the one the young constable had referred to.

"Some of those garlicky bread things in a packet."

When he had them, Dave showed his police card, and the barman knew why he was there.

"I guessed," he said, rather proud of his ability to notice things. "As soon as you came in I guessed."

"Can you join me in a pint?"

The barman got a half and they sat at a small table near the fire. Dave showed him once more the photograph of Patricia.

"Yes, that's her. She came in about a quarter to eleven, too late really for anything. A few people were still eating over there, but we take last orders for meals at nine thirty."

"Can you tell me as exactly as you can everything you remember?"

"She came straight up to the bar like you did and asked for a white wine. 'There isn't much time to drink it,' I said. 'I'll manage,' she said. Then she asked me if I knew what boats there were on the river. There's so many I can't keep track of them all, as I told her. This was bigger than usual, she said, and was off to Holland, and wanted an extra crew member. I told her I did remember that, because they'd asked us behind the bar if we knew of anyone, just the night before. They'd come up river from Hull."

"Had they found anyone?"

"Yes, so I heard. They'd set off on the last tide, she was too late to contact them."

"Was she disappointed?"

"Very." The barman sipped his drink. "She wanted to know the name of the

262

hand they'd taken on, but no one could remember."

"She asked more than you, then?"

"Oh yes, she asked all round. There can't have been anyone in the pub last Saturday night who didn't hear her asking."

"No one told her anything?"

"No one seemed to know anything. One young chap said he'd heard they wanted a crew member but he didn't know either who they'd got. She thought it was her brother."

"Oh! That was it!"

"Yes. Said he's slipped off without telling anyone. Of course half the people in here didn't believe it was a brother at all. Lover more like."

"She was looking for her brother," said Dave.

"Well! Sorry."

"It's all right."

"The young chap said he thought they'd be back the next week . . . this coming Saturday."

"What did she do after this?"

"Well, it really was getting late. She looked very disappointed. She went and

263

sat at that table over there."

"To finish her wine?"

"Yes. She'd been too busy asking questions to drink. I reminded her of the time."

Dave turned round to look down the length of the pub and the barman explained where Patricia had been sitting.

"Would you show me exactly?"

The pub was not as full as it would be later, and the table the barman indicated was empty. Dave sat down where Patricia had been, shuffled his shoulders and looked about him.

"You'd be able to see everything she did," he said to the barman.

"Yes. We were busy, thronged, but she was a very pretty girl. You couldn't help looking at her."

"Can you remember anything else? This seat is very close to the tables where people eat, isn't it?"

"Folks seem to like to be squashed close together. They don't object, any road."

Dave sat and thought for a minute. The people at the table next to him were being served with their meal. He couldn't help hearing everything they said. When the bar was fuller, he was sure the general noise would drown individual conversations, but he wondered who had been sitting near Patricia on that Saturday night.

"Did she seem to enjoy sitting here?"

"She looked a bit down in the mouth."

"Do you remember who was sitting at this table next to her?"

"No. That's impossible."

"Nothing's impossible," Dave encouraged him. "You were glancing over at her, you could hardly avoid seeing the people near her."

The barman screwed up his eyes as if it helped him to concentrate.

"Two blokes," he said at last. Strangers. I think they were tied up at the mooring. They'd been in all evening, first drinking and then they decided to eat, just when we were taking last orders for meals."

"So you'd plenty of time to have a good look at them."

"Do me a favour! How many customers do we get on a night? And you're talking about last week!"

"What sort of boat did they have?"

"Jeff!" shouted the barman. "Last Saturday. There was a boat tied up at our mooring. Two blokes were in here all night. Did you notice the boat?"

"Yes. Motor boat. The *Susie Ann*."

"Seen it before?"

"Don't think so. Rough types."

"Well, a bit unwashed," the barman amended as he turned back to Dave. "Cleanliness might be next to godliness but you can soon look scruffy if you've spent a few days on a small boat."

"How long were they moored here?"

"When did they go, Jeff?"

"That night. They weren't there when I looked next morning."

"They must have gone upstream, then," said the barman.

"Why?"

"Don't you know anything about the river?"

"Not much."

"Well, it depends on what time Jeff looked, but to go downstream they have to go through Naburn Lock and it's shut from seven thirty at night to — I think it's seven next morning. Are they important?" the barman asked with his eyes gleaming. After all, the girl had been found dead.

"Probably not at all. What did she do next?"

"Finished her wine and went out."

"Were these two men from the *Susie Ann* after her or did they leave before?"

"Now then." The barman paused to consider. He shut his eyes to think better, and there was a pause. "I've got it," he said at last. "I noticed her get up to go, because as we've said she was a good-looker, there was no doubt about that, and I watched her go out of the door, and, yes, do you know I'm sure of it now, the more I think about it the more sure I am, I can just see her walking out, because I was looking at her legs, she'd got shoes on with a bit of a heel, a nice thin heel, and she was walking out just after those two from the *Susie Ann*, close after them, you'd have thought she was with them really."

There was nothing else to be dredged up from the minds of the staff at the Ship, except that Jeff confirmed that he always woke up early and took his dog for a walk and that last Sunday morning

267

he'd been earlier than usual.

He'd slipped out of the house without waking his family and walked the river bank along Cobbler's Trod. They'd walked as far as the Ship, through the car-park, then turned and gone back and he'd made himself a coffee. No, he hadn't seen the *Susie Ann* at the mooring. Yes, he thought he would have seen her, he was sure he would have seen her. Time? He got back to the house at about seven o'clock. No, he didn't need much sleep. He was like Margaret Thatcher in that, four hours a night did him. Although it had been Saturday the night before and they always finished late he'd woken up before six like he always did.

"So the *Susie Ann* can't have gone down river? Naburn Lock wouldn't be open?"

"Unless they were waiting at Naburn outside the lock gates."

"And if they weren't, they must have gone up river, towards York?"

"Must have done."

"Thank you very much," said Dave.

"Do you think they're implicated, then?" asked the barman.

"The two men from the *Susie Ann*? I've no reason to think so, but if Patricia left more or less with them, they might have noticed where she went. They could take us the next step in discovering her movements during the night. Certainly if you see them again, I'd be grateful if you'd let me know. That includes you, Jeff. If you see the *Susie Ann*, or the crew, let me know instantly."

The lock-keeper at Naburn confirmed that when he had opened the lock gates the previous Sunday morning there had been no boats waiting on the river.

"It's not like summer," he said. "You might get them then, sitting cooking their breakfasts and waiting for me to get cracking. But not this time of year."

No, he hadn't noticed the *Susie Ann* particularly, there were that many boats he couldn't notice them all, could he? But he thought the first traffic that Sunday had been a barge laden with paper for the *Yorkshire Evening* Press. He remembered that.

Dave was amazed to discover how close by water Naburn Lock was to the Ship. If the *Susie Ann* had been on that stretch of water someone would almost certainly have seen her on Sunday. It did appear likely that she had headed up river towards York. Dave wished he knew more about boats and things to do with boats. After all, the two men on the *Susie Ann* were probably a red herring. Probably they had never noticed Patricia in the pub, never noticed her leaving when they did, never seen which way she went. Was it worth spending more police time on them?

Patience, thought Dave Smart. All right, he was no nearer finding the man who had raised his hand and killed Patricia Feltame than he had been on Sunday morning, in spite of the thinking, the leg work, the all-night vigils, the questions, the police conferences, the dead girl's father. Where was Charles Feltame now, anyway, he wondered? There'd been nothing from him since he set off for London, and Charles was not a man to let grass grow under his feet.

Dave got back into his car and sat wondering what to do next. He fingered Patricia's perfumed key-ring, which was still in his pocket, rubbing it round and round in his palm. He thought of her, long thoughts. He whistled 'Auprès de ma Blonde'; suddenly it had become very appropriate. *Dites moi donc, la belle, Où donc est votre mari? Il est dans la Hollande, les Hollandais l'ont pris. Que donneriez-vous, belle, Pour avoir votre ami?* Tell me, lovely one, where is your husband? He is in Holland, the Dutch have taken him. What would you give, beauty, to have him back again?

He remembered that the next clue they had was the recording of the phone call to drug squad. If that had been Patricia, at about five in the morning, it needed a lot of explanation. He had better return to the station to listen to the recording. So far it had been taken to Murtwick to be played to Mrs Feltame and her housekeeper, Mrs Briggs, for their opinion as to whether the voice was or was not Patricia's. At the thought of hearing her speak he found himself breaking out in a sweat in spite of the coldness of the night.

The radio crackled.

"Smart?"

He recognized the Superintendent's voice.

"Sir?"

"Where are you?"

"Naburn, sir."

"Can you come back here? We've fetched in one of the social workers to listen to the tape of the call to drug squad and you might like to talk to her."

Frances! It must be Frances. Dave didn't want to talk to her. But he answered, "I haven't heard that tape yet myself, sir. I'll be with you in ten minutes at the most."

The dark wet night was ideal for driving round York because most people had stayed at home. Clifford Street was deserted when he reached it and it was easy to park.

It was almost with dread that Dave anticipated hearing the voice that might be Patricia's, but he had not realized that he would not be alone at that moment, that — to make everything worse — Frances would be there. He let himself into his Superintendent's office in the Clifford Street nick as he had been requested.

Although it was by now quite late in the evening Superintendent Birch was presiding behind his desk, and a couple of uniformed men were in the room. Frances was sitting with her back to the door and looked round at his entry. Her face was pale between the curtains of brown hair and she looked as strained as he felt. Today she was wearing soft dull blue; a long cardigan with pockets, over a cotton top and skirt. He nodded at her and tried to look friendly.

"Any progress, Dave?" asked the Super.

"A little." Dave sat down in obedience to a gesture.

"Yes?"

Dave glanced at the Super and then at Frances, as if he was saying, "Do you want me to go into it with her here?" The Super, his eyes fixed on Dave, nodded in reply.

"Patricia Feltame arrived at the Ship about ten forty, bought a glass of white wine, and made general enquiries about the boat on which she believed her brother had gone to Holland. No one could help her by confirming that he had in fact gone on that voyage. She sat to drink her wine close to where two men from a small motor boat, the *Susie Ann*, were finishing a meal. When they left she followed them out close on their heels. The *Susie Ann* was berthed at the Ship but had gone by about six forty-five next morning. It does not appear to have gone down river, therefore it must have come up towards York. We don't know where it is now and it may have no connection with the case at all, but the two men may have seen where Patricia went after the Ship; if they only saw her drive off it would be something."

"At least we have extended the time of her known movements and that can only be to the good. The phone call to which you are about to listen was recorded at five forty-five a.m."

"Ah," said Dave. "Mark wasn't quite sure of the time before. When he mentioned it to us." He shivered when he thought of the implications of the time.

"From memory he wasn't sure. Right then."

The recording machine was switched on. The Super moved the tape on and stopped it a couple of times, taking a few seconds, before he found the right place.

"Here we are."

The recording was not good at all. There was a lot of crackling on the line, and Dave remembered the heavy rain they had had recently, which crept into the underground telephone ducts and cables and tended to cause this. The voice seemed to come and go in between the crackles. From what could be heard, it was a clear warm soprano and Dave felt his pulses throbbing. It was an agitated voice, rather out of breath, but the quality came over, even through the emotion of the speaker, the crackling, and the poor reproduction of the recording. He looked at Frances. She had clenched her hands together and looked paler than ever.

"Drug squad," said the voice urgently over low crackles, "there is a shipment of drugs on the river. Just arrived in York. Crack it is. It's to be distributed under cover of the race meeting to dealers from all over the North."

"Will you give your name, caller?"

A burst of crackling was the only answer to this, although Dave thought the voice was replying, in the background. Then some more words came clearly.

"I'm watching them now."

"Your name, caller? Where are you?"

"It's crack they've got."

"Where can we reach you?"

Again there was a burst of louder crackling than the level which was normal on this call.

"What did you say?" asked the caller.

Drug squad asked again where they could reach her.

Crackles . . . Then "I must go. I'll try to stop them leaving. Get here soon," said the soprano voice hurriedly, and the tape recording ended with the police voice, "Hello? Hello? Get back to us, caller . . . " as the phone clicked down.

"That's Patricia," said Frances. "I've never heard her anything but calm before but that's her all right."

The Superintendent breathed out a long sigh. "Good," he said. "Her mother and Mrs Briggs weren't absolutely sure — they both became very upset — although they thought it was her and her father is still in London. We take this warning seriously, then, Mark." He turned to the man from the drug squad.

"No sign of a thing so far. All informers quiet. No whispers at all."

"Did you get BT to trace the call?" asked Dave.

"They didn't manage it."

"I can't understand why they should move drugs on the river," said Frances. "It's stupid. They could put them in a car and have them anywhere at all, faster than you could find them. Why choose such a silly and slow method of transport?"

The police present exchanged looks.

"It's been very good of you to come in and help us," Superintendent Birch said courteously to the girl.

Dave turned towards Frances. He was not surprised to see crystal tears welling up in her eyes. It was amazing that they had not been there before. The two round drops apparently about to fall were curiously touching.

"Have you eaten yet?" he said to her. Any distraction to stop those tears spilling over and rolling down her cheeks.

"No, I haven't." She blinked the tears away.

"Can we go?" Dave asked Superintendent Birch.

"Certainly. I only hung on myself until we had a definite yes or no on this tape. You drug boys can take it from here, can't you?"

"Don't forget," Dave could not resist saying to Mark from drug squad, "that this is a murder enquiry and the drug aspect takes second place."

"Each to his own," said Mark, but his smile was comradely.

"May I take the witness out to a meal?" Dave asked the Super as the three of them went down the stairs.

"I'm sure that will be in order."

"I'll look on my desk as we go by. There should be a message from Patricia's father. He said he'd keep in touch. Yes." Dave stood for a minute reading the message. "That's very helpful," he said.

"Can you tell me?"

"It's not a secret. Information about where Sebastian was living. His father's company have a flat in their London office block which they use for hospitality,

278

or for the directors to stay in when they're in the city, or for clients visiting from abroad. Sebastian had the use of it temporarily as no one else was needing it for a while. He was supposed to be looking for his own place."

In fact Charles had said much more than that. He had said that he had persuaded the Metropolitan police to search the flat, that they had fingerprinted it, and that the results were on their way — he thought York might find them significant. Luckily the regular cleaner had been off sick and no one had been in the flat since Sebastian had locked it and gone to the clinic to take his cure. The memo also said that Charles was on his way back, as he had done all he could in London. Dave felt that Charles Feltame was a powerful ally.

"Come on," he said, escorting Frances out of the building. "Where do you want to eat?"

The tears were forgotten and Frances glowed. She was surprised to find herself being taken out by Dave Smart. He seemed extra pleasant and friendly and there was about him that strength, that air of machismo, which excited her. In spite of her grief there had been something rather thrilling in her visit to the police station.

"You did say you hadn't eaten?" Dave was puzzled by her long silence.

"I haven't."

"Is there anywhere you would like to go?"

"There's a new vegetarian place opened I haven't tried yet."

"Let's go there, then." Dave liked vegetarian food. He took her by the elbow. "Where did you say it was?"

The soup was excellent and they followed it with vegetable lasagne and jacket potatoes. The trifle was superb and the coffee reasonable. There wasn't much conversation at first. Both of them were more hungry than they had realized, and they were also a little shy with one another.

It was not until they reached the trifle that they ate more slowly and began to talk between mouthfuls.

"I can't believe that Pat did the things you say she did," said Frances. "It's against all her training. She just wouldn't behave like that."

"What would she have done?"

Dave found Frances's eyes were rather appealing when she was gazing earnestly at him and trying to make her point.

"Certainly not what you say."

"Explain to me."

"How did she find out he was on drugs in the first place?"

"Perhaps he contacted her? Asked her to help him?"

"If he did that she'd ask for time off work and go to stay with him and sort it out. Now I come to think of it, Pat did ask for time off not long ago. She said someone in trouble needed her."

"There you are, then."

"That ties in," said Frances thoughtfully. "So she went down and told him he ought to get away from the contacts he had who were taking cocaine. She tried to get him to take up a new life in a different area — to lead a new life with a new circle."

"He went into a nursing home."

"That would be with his agreement. But drug addicts unfortunately can be tricky. They agree and say they want to be cured when underneath they don't."

"That's what I would have imagined," said Dave. "He ran away from the place after about a fortnight, anyway."

"He did?"

"Surely did. Came to York, to Pete's Hotel, as I told you."

"He didn't go back to London, you see that's significant. The fact that he came to York instead means that he was asking for help. But Pat would have felt very frustrated and sad that he hadn't been honest with her. She would want to talk things through and make him realize that his health and his lifestyle are his responsibility and not hers."

"She would?"

"Oh, yes. We can none of us take the responsibility for someone else's life. She would try to get him to think it through and decide what he wanted. A lot of his sports achievements were a young man's achievements. He'd be past his peak in most of them already. Probably that's why he met this crisis, changing his goals and ambitions."

"I can't see her as detached at all."

Dave spoke slowly through a mouthful of trifle.

"She would try to keep her own emotions out of it and try to think of it from his point of view. Really," Frances sat back and sipped her coffee slowly, "it's better not to be involved with your clients, as a social worker. Suppose you allow yourself to hate a man who has been abusing his children, for instance, and then later you've got to reintegrate him with his family. No, you've got to stay detached."

"I see that point."

"If Sebastian was really depressed about growing past his peak in some ways, well, if you have nothing else in life drugs are a way of feeling good about yourself."

"It was a pretty desperate remedy."

"What I can't understand," said Frances, "is why he didn't go home."

"They were afraid of the effect on his mother."

"That's nonsense. They shouldn't have kept it secret. It is an illusion that a drug addict can be cured quickly. First they get better, then they relapse, and so on."

"And so in the long run they would have been found out?"

"Pat was taking on too much responsibility for other people's feelings and not doing her brother any good. Pat should have told their mother. It created more problems than it solved. The family had a right to know and try to pull together. Pat should have given her mother the right to react for herself."

Frances finished her coffee and looked down at her dish of trifle. She was surprised to find there was some left. She ate it.

For a while they were both quiet and thoughtful.

"Look, Frances," Dave said at last, "I want to ask someone a couple of questions, and I want to visit the Black Mamba, where he might well be. Will you come with me, as though we were just dropping in casually for a drink?"

"Isn't it a night club? Don't people have to be members?"

The girl looked slightly shocked, a little reluctant.

"It isn't a night club as such. It's

a restaurant which tries to give the impression of forbidden naughtiness, as I understand it. I haven't been there myself. I'm sure you've more to tell me," he added.

"All right, then."

Dave's car was still parked at the police station and it was raining again, but it wasn't far to the Black Mamba so they dashed there through the rain.

12

SOMEHOW once down the steps and into the darkness of the restaurant Dave Smart and Frances felt very conspicuous as they handed their wet coats to the white-jacketed doorman. Frances thought Dave's sports jacket and hand-woven tie were far too square. He looked almost with disgust at the fringed hem of her embroidered dull blue skirt. They had both felt perfectly all right in the vegetarian restaurant.

The Black Mamba was long and narrow with odd unexpected lighting here and there and curls of tobacco smoke. Frances began to cough.

"Just a drink, we thought," Dave said to the waiter.

"The bar is at the far end, sir."

They made their way between the tables until they reached a wider part, with the small circular dance floor, a ring of tables, a curved bar, a couple of musicians playing idly.

At one side was a recess with an extra table and there in the shadows sat Harry Brate. Dave pretended not to notice him. He took Frances to the bar and bought her a lime juice, which was all she would have. He got himself a beer. They took two chrome and orange stools at the bar and looked at the musicians and the dancers and back down the alley-way between the tables.

Frances kept choking periodically and Dave was irritated. They made their drinks last a quarter of an hour and it felt like an age.

Renewing their previous discussion Dave said, "In fact they didn't keep the secret such a long time. Sebastian was in the nursing home a fortnight and in Pete's Hotel for only a matter of days. There may have been reasons we don't know about for the secrecy."

"What did she do when she found he had gone?"

"She spent Friday evening searching for him, as we understand it. She told someone so, and drug squad have picked up various sightings in pubs and clubs. I don't know if you saw Superintendent

Birch pass me a brief report."

"On her own?" Frances sounded horrified through her coughs. "She should have told me or someone else in the team and gone in a pair. We never go anywhere as dangerous singly, never."

"She must have panicked."

"I can't understand her behaving in that foolhardy way. The whole thing is dead against all our training. Even you asked me to come here with you."

Not as protection, thought Dave, and couldn't help smiling. You're excellent cover, though, Frances.

He saw that she had finished her lime juice and quickly drank the rest of his beer.

"Come on," he said.

Turning as he rose he appeared to notice Harry Brate for the first time, and waved. Then they walked over to Harry's table.

"DI Smart." Harry rose to shake hands. "You're new to our little dive."

"I thought it would be interesting to see it," Dave replied, "since Patricia spent her last evening here. Very elegant."

Harry did not appear to be taken in

by the casual manner. "Look around," he said.

"We have . . . enough . . . thanks."

Harry smiled, suggested they joined him and offered them another drink, but a fresh outbreak of coughing from Frances averted that.

"You can't wait to get out — I do see."

"I'm a bit asthmatic," explained the girl.

"Tell me," Dave spoke as though the thought had just occurred to him, "how did you know Sebastian Feltame was on crack, as opposed to any other type of drug?"

"Did I know?"

"You mentioned it."

The large pale hands sketched in a movement. "You must excuse me. I am wool-gathering. Of course I knew, because Pat told me."

"When you met her in the street, or when you were dining here?"

"Here. Yes, I'm sure. She did not go into such detail in Coney Street."

"And she sat . . . "

"On the chair you're leaning on."

Dave looked down at his hands clenched over the back of the chair and made an effort to relax them.

"Of course . . . And one other thing, while we're talking . . . "

"Yes?"

"She was wearing a black dress that night. Did it by any chance have a white collar?"

"Yes, and very pretty it was. A white fluffy sort of thing framing her neck. Most attractive. A round one — what are they called . . . " His hands drew a curved line.

"Peter Pan shaped?" coughed Frances. "I remember that dress."

"That's the word. Why do you ask?"

"Just a point we're checking on."

"It brings it home, rather." Harry Brate grimaced at the sudden thought of Patricia's death.

Casually, Dave asked, "Have you come up with any corroboration yet, Mr Brate, of your movements later that Saturday night?"

"Still the old cry," said Harry Brate, with a wry smile. "The last person to see the murder victim alive, eh?"

"We would be pleased to have confirmation. Only routine, you understand."

"Surely, Detective Inspector, a guilty man would have arranged an alibi?"

Frances began to cough again.

"We'll have to get you out of here," Dave said to the apparently suffocating girl in a concerned manner. He put his arm round her shoulders affectionately.

"You'll excuse us, Mr Brate. Frances is much affected by tobacco smoke. It's been very interesting. You won't forget the corroboration?"

The restaurant was beginning to fill up. As they edged their way between the tables Dave took in, without appearing to, the type and appearance of the clientele. More money than sense, he thought to himself. They were an elegant lot, many of them with the tall slim build, the aristocratic features, which reminded him of Patricia. They looked well off, young, upper middle class. Dave had no doubt that they were going through a phase — part of growing up. They would come through. There was a sprinkling of older people, exclusively men; Harry Brate was not unrepresentative of this type. They tended to be with women much younger than themselves.

Both Dave and Frances felt a good deal more at home outside in the wet, although Frances doubled up against the wall with a bout of coughing.

"I just can't take cigarette smoke," she gasped out at last.

"Does it always affect you as badly as this?"

"No. I think it's a combination of things." She coughed again. "The confinement — I'm a bit claustrophobic. The smoke, of course, that always bothers me — but I think it's partly emotional, the thought that Pat came here that evening and ate with that awful man after she'd had lunch and shopped with me in town."

"It is a complete contrast," agreed Dave. "You disliked Harry Brate, then?"

"Disliked him? I detested him. I wouldn't trust him as far as I could throw him."

After a pause, when the girl had fully recovered, Dave Smart said, "The only effect the smoke had on me was to make me long for a cigarette."

"Do you smoke?"

"I did until last week. Frances, I'll run you home. It's only a short way to the car. The rain's eased off a good bit."

They walked quickly and once they were driving it only took a few minutes to reach Sycamore Terrace where Frances had her flat.

As the engine died Frances said, the thought still obsessing her, "On Saturday she met me as if nothing in the world was wrong and all the time the night before she'd been raking round York in the most dangerous way, and she never said a word about the whole thing, not a word. Would you like a coffee?" she then asked.

"I won't, thanks. I'd better go back to Clifford Street."

"Wouldn't you like to dry yourself a bit?"

"No, no. I'll be fine. Thanks for coming to the Black Mamba with me."

"We've talked about this on the team, you know," Frances said suddenly when Dave was expecting her to get out of the car. "We're all agreed that there is no way we would rush in there and take the matter into our own hands as you say Pat did. She was holding the wrong attitude. She set herself up as a victim."

"If I'd said a woman was setting herself up as a victim you would have been down on me like a ton of bricks."

"Man or woman, that's what she was doing. You have to keep your boundaries, keep your distance, and not get involved. If it had not been the person who did kill her it would have been someone else. You have to keep your personal beliefs intact but to yourself, and be aware when it is appropriate to show them. Being emotional doesn't help anyone. It's easier to run in than to sit back and think things through."

Dave felt more friendly towards Frances than he ever had before. Sympathy, even at times fellow-feeling, had existed between them during the last couple of hours.

"I'm sorry," she jerked out. "Hearing that tape seems to have got me going. I haven't been keeping my beliefs to myself, have I? It's hearing her — not giving her name or where she was — out there in the middle of the night by herself, not waiting for drug squad to reach her and provide reinforcements . . . . "

Dave found himself putting his arm round her again and giving her a hug, he believed of the brotherly variety.

"You've been very helpful," he said. "Good-night."

She exploded out of the car and into the house she lived in.

After a few seconds Dave drove away. The theories she had expounded to him about the way a social worker ought to tackle the problem of a brother who was a drug addict made a good deal of sense. If Patricia had followed those theories she would still be alive.

Frances had been close to Patricia, and the unease her personality gave him wasn't Frances's fault — she was just herself.

★ ★ ★

When he reached his desk once more there was another message from Charles Feltame. He was back in York himself and where the hell was Dave?

Dave whistled quietly to himself, '*Il est dans la Hollande, les Hollandais l'ont pris. Que donneriez-vous, belle, Pour avoir votre ami?* He is in Holland, the Dutch have taken him, what would you give, beauty, to have your friend back?'

★ ★ ★

Patricia Feltame had not met Harry Brate by chance.

When she took in Seb's antique firearm for restoration something in her conversation then with James Gotobedde had sparked her memory. Since that day, off and on, she had been thinking about the time when for a year both Harry Brate and Sebastian were part of the same shooting syndicate.

After the one season Sebastian had decided that shooting was not his kind of thing, but it had been during that season that the older man had gained some ascendancy over the younger one.

She had never liked Harry Brate, but in spite of dislike and distrust she had to admit that he was the sort of man who knew everyone, who could always fix everything. There ought to be goodwill there, because he was a longstanding family friend. A strange man. He had more power than anyone else she knew — power and money — and yet he appeared rooted here in York and liked to seem no more than an ordinary businessman.

Seb owed his job in the City to Harry's influence, although he had shown his unexpected flair for the work immediately. Patricia almost hated Harry for getting Seb that job, which had taken him away from her more than anything had previously done, and which had led to this present situation. She disliked him also for his attitude to herself.

Yet before meeting Frances for lunch that Saturday she had deliberately gone looking for Harry Brate, and had managed to bump into him in the street in a convincingly casual manner.

He was one of the few men she knew who still wore hats, and he swept it off in a flattering salute.

"Patricia, my dear," he said. "How are you?"

"Harassed."

"But you don't look in the least harassed."

She came to the point.

"Harry, I want you to help me find Sebastian. He's . . . he's . . . gone missing. Here in York somewhere."

A look swept over Harry's face, hardly there before it was gone. Patricia felt that what she told him was already known.

"He's on drugs," she added.

"Aha," Harry nodded. He didn't even look surprised. "Anything I can do . . ."

"I'd like to talk to you."

There was no doubt about it, Harry was relishing this approach. She'd been the ice maiden long enough, he considered. Many a time he'd tried to do just that — to talk to her, but he'd always got the frozen mitt. He'd only to let his eyes wander a bit and she'd freeze up on him. Barbeques, dinners, hunt balls, private party or public function, whenever he saw her he'd tried.

"Delighted."

It stood to reason that with that slender figure, adorned by curves like that, over that narrow waist, then coming out to hips like — what — melons? No, they weren't large, and melons sounded large — some sort of smooth fruit, anyway . . .

298

Patricia could feel the blood rising under her skin already. Take your time, damn you, she thought. I might as well stand here in Coney Street with no clothes on.

"Would you have dinner with me tonight?"

She smiled. "Thank you."

"We can talk over the meal. At the moment I sort of have an interest in the Black Mamba . . . and the food is good. Why not enjoy it — I shall be selling out in a few weeks . . . "

* * *

What would you give, beauty, to have him back again?

* * *

Harry Brate smiled his thin smile and waved one of his large white hands in the air. In goodbye? In triumph? It contrasted oddly with the stolid weather-beaten appearance of his inexpressive face.

The coming meeting was in her

thoughts for the rest of the day. She bought a dress for the bridge party and met Frances for lunch, but she hardly heard what Frances was saying to her. In a kind of daze she went with Frances to Habitat and helped her choose curtains. "I'll have to go home to change," she heard herself saying. "I'm going out this evening."

★ ★ ★

Patricia stood in her bedroom and hesitated over what to wear. She had never been alone with Harry Brate before. They wouldn't be alone, of course, they'd be in a restaurant. Harry's restaurant. The waiters would be his staff.

What was wrong with her? Nothing untoward was going to happen. She was dining with an old family friend who might be able to help her. That was all. End of story.

She was damned if she was dressing up for Harry.

* * *

What would you give, beauty, to have him back again?

* * *

There was something about their meeting in the morning — the knowledgeable look on Harry Brate's face. He knows who is behind this drug traffic in York, she thought. He knows a good deal. And if I don't play my cards right he'll hold out on me.

* * *

What would you give, beauty, to have him back again?

Je donnerais Versailles, Paris et St Denis, Les tours de Notre-Dame Et le clocher de mon pays.

I would give Versailles, Paris and St Denis, the towers of Notre Dame and the clocktower of my homeland . . .

My homeland.

* * *

301

She was standing naked by the chest; opening the drawers; turning over the piles of pure silk underwear, laced, embroidered, gathered, threaded with ribbon. She enjoyed her pretty under-clothes, but they weren't meant for this.

How far would she need to go to ensure Harry's co-operation?

Purple grape dark satin, cream chiffon, scarlet silk, pink crepe, shadowy ecru, sapphire flower-encrusted, shoulder straps like narrow tendrils, like trails of leaves, bras and slips and teddys and suspender belts and . . .

She held up a white slip. No. Too virginal. A black lacy bra. Yes. She studied her image in the mirror, judging the effect. Panties, suspender belt, stockings . . . All black was not right. Too funereal. A dash of colour . . . The suspender belt from the red set — that was better. A flash of leg might be enough, and a promise . . .

★ ★ ★

Threading her way through the tables to the dance floor she walked erect, puritan

302

in demure black with a white collar. Harry Brate rose as she approached, and drew out a chair for her. The waiter hovered for the order. She sat, composed, cool in the dim dark heated air, the odd patchy lighting, the music which wailed high and then low and then sideways, lurching against her heart.

Harry Brate had felt a surge of triumph as he stood watching her slow approach. He was a lecherous man, a womaniser, and could usually buy anything he wanted in that direction; but she was in a different class altogether. She had always been unattainable; for several years she had either ignored him or been as cold as ice. Because he could not win her she had become an obsession. He knew that the young men who took her out and possibly made love to her were not in the running either. He had had to do something to either gain her or break her, because he could not forget her. Now, at last, he had the upper hand.

The meal went better than she had expected. They discussed things indifferent to both of them: the weather, the food.

The chef at the Black Mamba was definitely good.

Drugs came very low on the agenda. But they reached the point when the topic could be put off no longer by urbane nothings.

"Now tell me all about it."

Harry adopted a fatherly tone and leaned back in his chair, looking at her through the smoke of his cigarette.

Stumbling over the words she told him the outline. He had managed to keep those long insulting looks under control this evening, but now she began to feel the old familiar discomfort. Harry put a few questions. Once more she sensed that he knew a great deal, much more than he was telling. For the first time she began to wonder whether he himself was involved in the drug traffic. She had the feeling that it would amuse him to be behind the scenes and see people dance to his tune, to be the puppet master.

Harry said, "Well, all right, coke — everybody does it — but how did he come to be hooked on crack, my dear?"

In that one instant she knew.

304

She became alert to the backbone and as one impulse raced through her body another followed it so quickly that she did not have time to stiffen and show consciousness of the implication of what he had said before deliberately relaxing and controlling every flicker of expression in her face.

She had never mentioned the word crack.

If Harry knew Seb was on crack it was because he knew everything, already, without her telling him.

"I don't know how or when," she said with a half-smile. "It all happened in London, remember."

If you already knew, Harry, you know about the London end.

How soon could she get away? Because this wasn't a healthy place to be, no sir. Don't rush. Don't get up and make an excuse, he'll make the connection and know you know. You must behave so naturally he will think you are still taken in.

She dropped her eyelids, but slowly, very slowly, to veil her thoughts but so that it could be taken for provocation.

She moved the hand which was resting on the table a little closer to his, just a fraction of an inch — but towards, not away from that large white hand.

If she were to get out of here on her own she would have to make him believe that she would come back later, and return his amorousness. That was going to take all the acting of which she was capable.

"As it happens I do know a few people in the underworld," he said easily. "Since being involved with this place, you know. We get all types. I can tell you that you were searching the wrong spots, last night."

"Can you tell me the right ones?"

"I certainly can, but I don't know that I ought. I don't like the idea of you going round enquiring in this way."

He had to be made to believe that it was something she must do. She tried to convince him of that.

"Patricia, my dear," his voice was caressing, "I don't like to hear you talk in this way. A lovely young girl like you should have other concerns in life. This insistence on going. I was hoping you'd stay for coffee. You're really disappointing me very much, my dear. You're disappointing me very much."

Was there a threat behind the words? She didn't think she'd given herself away.

"But I'm coming back, aren't I?" She threw him a glance which was unmistakable.

"Of course," and she could feel him relax, and hear the note of triumph which came into his voice. You only had to find their Achilles heel, he was thinking. Attack them in the right place and you'd won. Soon he'd have her begging.

I'll get them, ran the pulse in her blood. For what they did to Seb. I'll find them out and get them. I'll beat you, Harry Brate.

* * *

By eleven o'clock, sitting exhausted in the Ship Inn at Acaster Malbis, she was at a dead end. There was nothing else she could think of doing.

People were getting up to leave. The fact that she walked out at the same time as the two men who had been dining at

307

the next table was the purest chance. Everyone was going, she hadn't noticed those two at all. Walking across the road to the car-park she passed them. Because she was walking faster than they were, she was well in front by the time she reached her car. She opened it briskly, grabbed her capacious old handbag and fished out her driving slippers. As she put them on the two men passed her, going towards the wooden jetty where a boat was moored.

"What time are we meeting Gotobedde?" one asked the other.

She didn't hear the words except for the last.

It had sounded like Gotobedde.

James Gotobedde? Probably she was wrong, and what the man had said was, 'Shall we go to bed,' the most obvious thing at eleven at night. Probably 'What about another drink before we . . . ' or 'What about a hand of cards before we . . . ' or any manner of things. This flashed through her mind in the split second it took her to pull her head back out of the shelter of the car door.

"He's expecting us at dawn," said the other man.

They clattered along the wooden walkway.

The boat had a curtained window, which now lit up as the men entered the compact cabin.

Patricia moved as stealthily as a cat on to the *Susie Ann*. It was a small twenty-four-foot fibreglass motor boat; there was a narrow rim of deck up the side past the cabin window. The curtains were thick. She knelt uncomfortably on the few inches of space and bent herself double to press her ear to the window and catch any murmurs she could, clinging with her fingers to stop herself sliding off into the water.

* * *

Late on Thursday night Dave had rung Charles Feltame.

Charles sounded tired, almost distraught.

"You were away longer than you expected, then, sir," said Dave.

"Not wasted, DI Smart. Not wasted." The words were jocular but Dave knew that Charles was unhappy. He waited for the other man to speak again.

"It was true that Sebastian was sacked," Charles went on abruptly after the pause. "It was because of this drug-taking, and quite right too. What no one seems to know is how he got on to a drug as addictive as crack. I think I've found out, though."

"You were away two days, sir?" asked Dave.

"Takes time to travel and not everyone is willing to work round the clock. Some of them keep office hours."

"You had his room searched, we heard? The fingerprint results haven't arrived yet."

"They should be with you in the morning. One set cannot be identified. I have great hopes of those. Apparently Seb had a visitor for a few days, an antique dealer called James, who was attending one of these important antique fairs. I reckon that visit was about the time he may have got on to this vile stuff."

"Wouldn't the prints have been cleaned away?"

"There were various stray prints from

an unidentified person. One good set was on a polythene bag in a drawer."

Dave thought he'd wait and see before getting excited.

"What time did you get back?"

"Breakfast time today. Do you remember what you said to me?"

"Sir?"

"I asked how I could help. You said, and I quote, 'Talk to your wife and to Patricia's friends. We don't know yet where she was or what she was doing in the twelve hours before her death. Look for your son.'"

"Yes. You've been very helpful. Mr Brate filled in some of the missing time for us, you talked to Patricia's friends, you've helped with the London end, and . . . "

"And today I've been looking for my son."

Dave said nothing; he waited.

"I hope to ask him soon how he got hooked on crack."

"Do you mean you've found him, sir?"

"Yes, I've found him. I've not only found him, I've got him here asleep in bed. That's progress, Dave."

"Surely is." Dave could hardly believe it. He'd been fully expecting Sebastian to be dead too. He had taken on a mythical quality. Dave found it hard to believe that he might actually see Patricia's twin, talk to him.

"He was at a refuge for down and outs. My wife's golden boy. She's taken it hard. I've had my hands full. The biggest help has been our housekeeper, Mrs Briggs. That woman is a tower of strength."

"Nice woman."

"There are some nice women about. Have you heard of someone called Lucy Grindal?"

"Yes. Canon Grindal's daughter."

"I want to meet her and thank her. She found my boy on the river bank and insisted on taking him to the refuge, where they've been doing their best with him."

"Her father spends a lot of time helping young men who are homeless or in despair."

"She enlisted the help of some canon or other — Oglethorpe, is it?"

"Canon Oglethorpe?"

"Is he also known to the police?"

Dave smiled to himself. "We had a case not long ago when all the Minster personnel were most helpful. Canon Oglethorpe has been a prison chaplain in his time. Your son could not have fallen into better hands."

"She was a brave woman, this Miss Grindal, because believe me, Sebastian is being very aggressive."

Dave rather regretted that the police hadn't found Sebastian themselves, but they had been concentrating on other issues.

"And how have you been getting on?" demanded Charles Feltame, with a change in the tone of his voice.

"We've made some progress. Can you come into the station in the morning? We'll have a chat then."

"Very well."

That's him off my back for a few hours, thought Dave. I wonder how everyone else is getting on.

Bob Southwell and Detective Superintendent Birch were presumably both at home in bed. Drug squad were probably out working. Dave went to their office to see if anyone was in.

"I've been looking for you," said Mark, as unwashed as ever.

"You can take protective coloration too far," Dave responded, looking him over.

"This telephone call. We've been making enquiries about drugs imported by water."

"Not in a tiny river motor boat, surely?"

"How do you know the size of the *Susie Ann*?"

"Two-man crew — I was guessing."

"Don't guess. We've been on to Customs, and they did have a whisper, strong enough to take them to search a ship which docked at Goole ten days ago. She was as clean as a whistle and definitely hadn't been near land."

"So?"

"So; she was in the Humber the night before she docked. They could have offloaded on to a small river craft. Usually river traffic shuts down at night like the rest of the world which is why any small boat, even a dinghy, could have slipped near enough to take the cargo and

314

most likely not be seen."

"Then proceeded in a leisurely way up river?"

"Certainly."

"So what now?"

"Customs are sending a team. They can search any craft for illegal importations without a warrant. They will be here in the morning."

"Then what are they going to do?"

"Have a meeting with us."

"Search the *Susie Ann*?"

Mark hesitated. "There isn't anything very definite on the *Susie Ann*. Because the murdered girl left a riverside pub at the same time as the crew doesn't give us an iota even of suspicion. We haven't as much as found the boat yet."

"The telephone call?"

"All right, all right. That makes us think there are drugs on the river. The only boat we have a mention of is the *Susie Ann*. It's not enough."

"Why not mount a watch on her?"

"That's what I'm going to suggest in the morning. The Ouse is one of the few open rivers left and there are no checks by British Waterways, but at this quiet time of year it shouldn't be too difficult to find her, unless they've painted out the name. Once found, we watch and lie low."

"Right."

Dave decided he might as well go to bed himself. Passing through the main office he saw Jenny Wren, still busy at her desk.

"What are you doing here at this time of night, Jenny?" he asked.

"Working," she said shortly. "Like you with that social worker," she could not help adding.

Dave realized that she had seen him at some point, possibly with his arm round Frances. Women! That was the trouble with them! Taking things personally and jumping to conclusions! Being feminine!

He answered mildly. "I thought you were on two till ten this week."

"I am. This is overtime."

"I think you ought to pack in and go home."

"Since when have you been our supervisor?" A second policewoman had come into the room and stood looking at him.

316

"Oh, sorry, Betty. I didn't realize you were working late as well."

The woman police sergeant came closer. "How's it going, Jen?"

"Just about finished."

"Your friend DI Smart is right, time to go home. We'll both go. Did you say you hadn't brought your car today? Would you like a lift?"

"Yes, please."

Dave shrugged his shoulders as the two policewomen went out to the locker room together. Much good it did trying to be concerned about people's welfare. He could have given Jenny a lift himself; it seemed to be his night for escorting the female sex.

As he got into his car the two women walked past.

"Good-night, Dave," said Jenny.

"Night."

He turned the starter in a better frame of mind.

13

FOR the first time in a week the weather was pleasant. The wind which had been so troublesome had not returned, and the rain which had persisted longer had at last faded away. A soft grey morning unfolded to show a city washed and chastened like a schoolboy who has had his face scrubbed clean.

Linda Southwell was enjoying herself. Tomorrow was her dinner party and there was nothing she liked as much as preparing for this sort of occasion. The house was shining from top to toe and would only need a quick tidy up at the last minute. Today she was doing the shopping and as much preparation as she could.

The small bright yellow van parked in Bootham caught her attention as she walked past. Yes, sure enough, there was Tom Churchyard.

"You made me jump, Linda," he said.

"A shove in the back with a shopping basket isn't the proper way to greet your nextdoor neighbour."

"You're always digging the roads up," she said.

"Not me personally. And you do like your telephone to function, don't you? Are you off shopping?"

"For the dinner party tomorrow. You haven't forgotten?"

"I'm looking forward to it very much."

"Julia Bransby's coming, and the Danes from the university, do you know them? And two of Bob's people, a young WPC and a retired Chief Constable."

Tom's face had altered at the mention of Julia Bransby, but Linda was too preoccupied to notice.

"Am I to bring a bottle?"

"Certainly not. We've selected the wine already."

"I haven't seen much of Bob this week."

"He's busy at work," said Linda.

"Anything to do with that girl Dave Smart found?"

"The investigation, yes." Linda suddenly sounded very cautious.

"It's all right. I know you can't talk about it. I'll get to know all in good time, I expect."

"I'd better dash now, Tom," said Linda.

* * *

Charles Feltame was being treated at that moment to a special interview of his own, with DI Smart, DCI Southwell, and DS Birch, and was telling them about the discovery of Sebastian right under their noses.

"The people at the refuge couldn't get his name out of him, you see, Mr Feltame," said Bob Southwell, "or they might have notified us after reading in the paper that he was missing. We haven't been looking for him intensively, because he vanished before his sister was murdered. It didn't seem as if finding him was the most important thing in this enquiry. You must remember that we have only been treating it as a murder case since the second post-mortem result, on Wednesday."

"You're too polite to say it," replied

Charles Feltame, "but what you mean is Seb's been stoned out of his mind since he found a new supply of crack, so you didn't think he'd be able to help."

"It wasn't like that — only a matter of priorities. Is he going to be any use as a witness? Can he tell us anything at all?"

"He doesn't even know his sister's dead, at the moment."

"Can you find out the source of his supply?"

"It's possible."

Everyone looked three times as alert all at once.

"I have one name."

"Can you give it to us?" Bob really wanted to say 'Cough it up' but you didn't say things like that to Charles Feltame.

"This man may not be the supplier at all. Seb just mentioned him. 'Must go to see old Gotobedde', is what he said, in an odd rambling kind of way. Most of his conversation has been a string of obscenities."

"The antique firearms man," put in Dave Smart.

"Yes. So I understand. I looked up the name in the telephone directory and then it came to mind."

"Can I say a word here?" asked Dave. "I can tell you that Sebastian's antique gun was taken in to Gotobedde for attention, by his sister, and I called and checked that. The weapon is still there. Apart from that we do have one other connection. Gotobedde was in possession of cannabis and Patricia Feltame was in court. She was a voluntary probation officer for a short time. That was some months ago."

There was a silence.

"The name may well be very significant, then," Superintendent Birch said. "Or on the other hand, your son may only have been thinking of collecting his firearm."

Charles Feltame got to his feet like an old man. "I have domestic duties," he said.

"We're very grateful to you, sir." Bob Southwell had jumped up. "I'll show you out."

The number of people Bob Southwell showed out of the building could be counted on one finger. The Super rose and shook Charles Feltame's hand. Dave Smart stood to attention.

He had never seen such a change in a man as that in Charles Feltame over the last days. Still as immaculate as ever, he seemed to have shrunk in his clothes, and his face also seemed to have lost substance. Dave could imagine him driving through some bargain about international finance, hard, imperious; but now, dealing with the matter of his own family — of his only son — he had been touchingly grateful for the help of the family housekeeper, and for the services of a passer-by, people ordinarily of no account in his world; and he was looking as if the whole drug thing was too much for him to fight.

"We'd better investigate this chap Gotobedde," said Superintendent Birch when the door had closed. "Radio the lad on the beat to call in at his premises and bring him in for questioning."

Dave went, and stayed by the radio receiver to find out the results. The bobby on the beat went to the workshop and found it locked. He asked the next-door neighbours, and they said that the door had been locked much of the week, though James Gotobedde had been in and out.

"The bloke's Christian name is James," he added to Bob.

"You're thinking of the person who stayed with Sebastian in London? Heaps of people are called James. Our own James Jester for one. We'll bear it in mind, though, Dave. I think we'd better keep a watch on his place."

Dave arranged that a young detective should stand an unobtrusive guard.

"Tell us as soon as he turns up," he instructed.

"And then what, Dave?"

"And then wait some more, and see if he goes out again."

"And then?"

"Probably follow him." Dave thought for a minute. "Follow him without him seeing you if you possibly can, letting us know what is happening as soon as you have the opportunity, and at suitable intervals."

"Right." The young detective had never

felt so important in his life.

"You're sure you know what he looks like?"

"Forty but looks older, about five feet six, thin, deeply lined face, very dark hair."

"Has a nervous look about him."

"Right."

"It might be possible for you to wait in the next premises. Tell them you're waiting to see him, you will probably be able to see him arrive."

Dave wondered if he should have sent someone older and more experienced, but there didn't seem to be such a detective available just then.

★ ★ ★

The team meeting took place when the Customs men arrived. The rooms in the police station were bright with autumn sun, and Superintendent Birch had to move his chair to keep the light out of his eyes.

"If you've all finished your drinks, gentlemen . . . "

A policewoman went round and

collected the coffee cups, then took them away.

"Early this morning we sent a police patrol out on the river. We don't have a regular patrol, or river police as such. When required we can soon send someone if there is persistent breaking of the speed limit or anything of that kind. The larger passenger pleasure boats are regulated by the Board of Trade, so we don't have to worry about those."

"How large is the boat you suspect?" asked one of the Customs men.

"Suspect is too strong a word. The evidence is practically nonexistent." Superintendent Birch went over it briefly.

"The phone message was last Sunday morning. That's the hardest evidence. The very fact that the girl was later found dead — "

"And by the river," said a Customs man.

"Yes. By the river. That did not previously seem to have any significance, do you agree, Dave?"

"When you think about it — the river is the only certain link between events at Acaster Malbis and events in York. We hadn't really thought about it that way, no, sir."

"The phone call was not linked to any particular boat, and the fact that the girl went out of a pub at the same time as the crew of a small motor boat is almost certainly pure coincidence. It has only acquired significance because it is the only vestige of a lead we have." He paused, fiddled with some papers, and then went on.

"The police patrol found that the *Susie Ann* was the only boat moored at the Ship Inn that night. The others on that stretch of water were at their own moorings and all the owners readily identifiable, either living nearby or renting moorings regularly from local people. October is a quiet period without a lot of casual river traffic. This morning we've done as thorough a check as we could, and nobody let a mooring to a stranger. The pub had a few lets this week and last but they knew all the people from previous occasions except for the *Susie Ann*. Circumstantial evidence."

"Did the police patrol manage to locate her?" asked Bob Southwell.

"We've found her all right. She's at Redby Lock, tied up there, and has been since Sunday."

"That's nearby, is it?" asked the Customs man.

"A few miles upstream. We've put a man on to watch her. He should be sitting at this moment looking cold and miserable, tied to the end of a fishing line, gazing at the water."

"Good job it's better weather for him."

"He's been there since nine o'clock. Now we've got to decide on the next step."

"There's one thing," added Superintendent Birch thoughtfully. He paused. "Our report on the *Susie Ann* says that three men have been sleeping on board."

"There were only two in the Ship," said Dave.

"Unless one has joined them since. Now — are we all going up there to check her out, is it worth that, and if so how?"

"We came up river in our own craft," said one of the Customs men.

"Has it a shallow draught?"

"There's been plenty of rain, the Ouse is high. We'll be all right. If the *Susie Ann* is clean we'll go on to do a general survey of the craft on the river, see if we can come up with anything."

"We don't want too many people along on what may well be a waste of time. If it is we've got to start thinking again, and go over everything about this murder case from the beginning."

"Suppose," said Bob Southwell, "we have a total of six — two from Customs, two from drug squad, and two other detectives, Dave and me, I suggest. These six might later form a boarding party — and some back-up in the shape of uniformed men parked nearby out of sight, with you, sir, in charge there . . . "

"You've placed me in the back-up car out of the way?"

"Yes, Super."

Superintendent Birch pulled a face, but did not object. He didn't really want to go boarding a small motor boat in search of possibly non-existent drugs. He preferred a quiet life so near to retirement. "Does everyone agree on that plan?" he said. "Six should be more than enough to tackle three."

"We could board them from the river side," said Customs.

"We will go out there, then, as soon as possible. You gentlemen don't need a search warrant, but we'd better have one in case."

James Jester tapped at the door and came in.

"Yes?"

"Radio message from detective watching for Gotobedde, sir."

"Yes?"

"He has returned to workshop. Detective maintaining watch."

"Good. Jester, get a search warrant organized for a small motor boat called the *Susie Ann*."

They gathered their things together and went downstairs in a group. As they reached the main office another radio message came through.

"Gotobedde has left workshop, has proceeded to parked car," — he gave the number — "is now driving towards Bootham Bar."

"He's on foot, he'll lose him," Dave said swiftly.

"Send a message out to patrol cars. Nearest to Bootham Bar to report."

The response came within one minute. James Gotobedde had had to wait in two sets of traffic lights, but now he was clear and heading out of the city on the A19.

"Towards Redby Lock," said Superintendent Birch. "Hurry up, everybody. But don't for heaven's sake alarm him." He turned to the radio operator. "They're not to tail him. Pass him from one to another if they can without him noticing. Think you can do that?"

* * *

Dave Smart sat idly in the police car as it drove through the traffic. He wondered if they were doing the right thing. This chasing off to Redby Lock didn't seem, somehow, the same quest on which he had set out on Sunday morning. Or was he just too exhausted to think straight? He shut his eyes. May as well rest them for two minutes.

He saw again the stone-flagged area on the riverside, the dull colours, the body of the girl. It was focused in his mind's eye as clearly as if he were still standing there. Patricia. It was the feeling that she had died in vain which was the worst, the hardest to bear. Now Sebastian had been found her sacrifice seemed even more heartrendingly unnecessary. She'd given her young life for her brother her love, and the sot didn't even know. Dave felt he could kick him.

The car was travelling steadily on the A19 through flat meadows dotted with trees and hedgerow timber. James Gotobedde was ahead of them, trundling along at a steady fifty, then turning sharp left at the junction with the road to Redby. Here he slowed to thirty-five on the narrow undulating road, driving as if he were out for a Sunday afternoon excursion.

The three police cars who were following kept out of sight. Although the cars were unmarked, their constant presence behind Gotobedde might seem suspicious. Now they had left the main road there were no patrols to tell them of his progress.

They turned left at the railway bridge

and dropped back to avoid being seen on a long straight stretch. Ahead of them rose the needle-sharp spire of a church penetrating the clouds above a red-brick village. The river lay to the left of the tree-lined road. They approached another widespread village, and turned off on to a gravelled track.

A little short of the river they drew up. Mark got out and strolled forward to see what was happening. The weather had continued clear, the moisture everywhere was drying up in the slight breeze.

Mark walked normally and gradually out of their sight. His hands were stuck into his pockets; he did not keep a straight line but wandered a little, peering into rabbit holes, picking and eating a few blackberries left on a wayside bush, kicking at a tump of grass, walking straight on the track for a while, then once more distracted, lighting a cigarette, throwing away the match. He seemed to be away for a long time.

Apart from the uniformed men who were driving there were four men sitting in the stationary cars, but they were not bored. There was a tenseness in the atmosphere which held them alert.

"Probably a mare's nest," Dave said aloud.

"I don't think so," replied Bob."

"I don't see why you don't think so." Dave sounded aggrieved.

"No quarrelling, children," said Superintendent Birch.

"Let us assume the *Susie Ann* rendezvoused with the ship importing the stuff, outside Goole. They row over under cover of night, bring the stuff back, stow it into the *Susie Ann*. We're not expecting the stuff to be cruising up river at a rate of five miles an hour, so they take their time, they're in the safest place there is. All they need to do is deliver in York for the race meeting Wednesday. By Saturday they've reached Acaster Malbis and surmounted the last obstacle in the shape of Naburn Lock. There are no more locks, no nothing, between them and the city."

"Yes. We've gone over this before," said Dave. "You know it makes sense. About a boat. We don't know which one."

"So they're relaxed — or as relaxed

as they can be. The *Susie Ann* at her mooring is as safe as she will be anywhere — the stuff's probably between the fibreglass hull and the cabin walls. They go ashore for a drink and a meal then head back to sleep on the boat."

"We know all that," said Dave impatiently.

"We know they left Acaster at the same time as the girl did — between eleven at night Saturday and, say, six on Sunday. That's suggestive in itself."

"Drug-running isn't murder," said Dave, "and what I'm after is catching a murderer."

"It's often connected with murder. Right. The *Susie Ann* is at Redby, tied up, by Sunday night. The drugs are to be distributed under cover of the race meeting which didn't take place on Wednesday — ground too soft. Didn't take place on Thursday — same thing. York October meeting is Wednesday, Thursday, and Saturday, right?"

"Right."

"So, they're still hanging round for Saturday. I don't suppose the crew mind. They'll be earning good money. They'll be playing cards, drinking but taking care not to get drunk. And they've been joined by a third man, James Gotobedde. We would like to know more about him, that's already decided. Mare's nest, Dave?"

"Maybe not, *if* they've got drugs, which we don't know. Suppose they're just innocent citizens having a quiet autumn holiday?"

"Then we apologize politely after pulling their boat to bits."

"Mark's coming back," broke in the Super.

Mark was chewing a piece of grass.

"It's all right," he said. "Gotobedde's parked and gone on board the *Susie Ann*. They must all be in the cabin, there's no one on deck. You can bring the cars closer, I'll show you where to park them."

"Where are Customs?" asked Superintendent Birch, when they had tucked the cars away out of sight.

"They said they'd hang around down river until we arrived."

"The funny thing is," said Mark, "that the *Susie Ann* is not in the lock basin where all the other motor boats are moored. It's quite convivial looking up there. No, they are moored down here, near a few caravans. Usually this mooring is only for the dinghies the caravan people have, I think."

Cautiously the four plain-clothes men walked forward. The Super and the uniformed constables remained in the cars.

"How do we get down?" asked Bob. They were standing near the road looking at the river, which stretched for quiet flat brown acres in front of them. Here it flowed slowly but sinuously into a wide bay, bare except for the filmy screen of willows further on at the waterside, behind which they could see the veiled outline of the Customs boat.

They were standing on the top of a bank which fell so sharply into the river that there was no proper path down to the water's edge. There was a kind of muddy slide nearly vertically down the bank. There was no path by the water itself, because of the sheer drop here of the banks.

They looked straight down at the little

motor boat bobbing peacefully on the calm water, autumn light brightening the white paintwork and the crisp lettering of the name. She had a tiny cabin with two berths and lockers, tucked under the bow; the living area with windows; the stern where the two seats could double at night as beds for children. The whole thing as compact and neatly planned as a caravan.

There was little deck as such. There was the rim round the edges, where Patricia Feltame had knelt, and a small space between the stern seats.

Across the river was a fisherman patiently attending to the non-movement of his rod and line.

The cabin curtains of the *Susie Ann* were closed. Seeing this, the policemen became bolder.

Bob waved to the fisherman, who moved his hand slightly in reply. Bob made a beckoning movement downriver. The fisherman made a small but decided movement, directed at the Customs boat behind its shield of scrubby willows.

Customs began to creep forward, just far enough out into mid stream to avoid butting the moored motor boat in the stern.

The sturdy little motor boat was tied to some jagged wooden stumps which stuck up a yard or more distant from the steeply sloping bank. The grey stumps had a primeval look to them, like fossil teeth, fissured and split, two feet or more thick at their tops and narrower where they entered the water.

Dave looked down the steep bank at the *Susie Ann* with horror. On the face of it it was easy — a little boat a few feet away. But the path was a near vertical slide of mud and those few feet of water would be very awkward to traverse; surprise must be out of the question, he thought.

Bob, with Dave close behind him, scrambled silently down towards the *Susie Ann*, as the Customs boat drew level on her other side.

"Someone's going to get wet," whispered Bob, hanging on to the old dead grass of the bank, his head level with Dave's boots.

He let go of the grass and slid from the bottom of the path straight down into the water, biting back the words which would otherwise have come jerking out. He felt his way out into the water with his feet, slipping downwards, his whole legs in the river, and clutched for the gunwale, then silently hoisted himself aboard.

★ ★ ★

Dave admired the way he did it, causing hardly any movement of the craft, only the slightest sigh as it moved.

Bob stealthily pushed a long piece of wood back over; it had cross pieces to stop slipping and was obviously used as a gangplank. Dave wedged it into a groove in the bank, slipping as he did so over his boot tops into the river, and crept across, clutching the splintery surface of the nearest mooring post as he crossed the few feet of water with Mark behind him.

The little motor boat made a slight but perceptible movement downwards, while the river made lapping, kissing noises against her bow. Surely the men inside must have noticed something?

Bob waved at the second drug squad man to stay on shore, clinging where he was to the muddy bank.

Then he threw open the cramped narrow door into the cabin.

14

AS the door swung open Bob with Dave peering over his shoulder could barely see into the curtained cabin. They could just pick out a table and faces round it and the glimmer of whitish packets.

"Police," said Bob, stepping forward.

A man acted as quick as light. He slammed the door fast and hard into Bob's face. Bob fell backward, his glasses knocked off and his nose streaming blood.

Dave plunged past him, and being prepared, was more successful, pushing his boot into the door first, then leaning on it, pressing it inward.

One small man had opened a window and was chucking out the packets from the table.

James Gotobedde was blocked in behind the table. The big crewman who had slammed the door was nearer to Dave and went for him, pulling out a knife and bellowing with rage. The table tipped up, falling between them. The man strode over it and reached at Dave inside the doorway. There was hardly space for him to get a blow in with the knife. Dave got hold of his arm.

Bob had recovered enough to struggle past Dave and over the table and try to save the evidence which was disappearing fast out of the window. He was snatching at the small man.

The cabin was so constricted Dave felt he could hardly breathe.

He caught tight hold of the crewman who was grabbing him, knife in hand, and tried to drag him out through the narrow doorway onto the tiny deck.

The two big men tumbled out into the open stem like corks from a bottle, then Mark walked straight over them and through the narrow door into the cabin. He began to tackle James Gotobedde, who had kept his head and was scooping packets of drugs together.

The crewman had dropped his knife as they fell through the door and now there was more room he punched Dave in the solar plexus. As he doubled up in pain Dave somehow managed to cling on to his opponent. Together they swayed dangerously on the tiny deck. The crewman saw his knife and struggled to reach it.

The men in the Customs boat looked on appalled. The little motor boat was a very stable craft but they didn't see any point in adding more weight or confusion. There was not an inch of space. She was not built to have six fighting men on board, most of them large heavy men. They had already managed to pick up some of the floating plastic packages from the water. Now they hung in the current, moving neither forward nor back, unable to help.

"Get off me!" the crewman was shouting, and landing more blows, but through his pain Dave could hardly hear him. He only knew that he had to hold on, hold on, hold on.

The other man from drug squad took a flying leap on to the stern of the *Susie Ann*. Desperately she dipped sideways towards the water. The drug squad man landed on his knees.

The crewman and Dave both fell over on top of one another again as the boat lurched. The crewman had got his knife but Dave clung so closely to him that he still couldn't get a good swing with it, and the fall had winded him.

The drug squad man looked at the two men at his feet and pulled out a pair of handcuffs. He fastened one on to a wrist from the squirming heap.

"Get up," he said viciously to his captive. "Get off this damned boat." He managed to fix the other handcuff, using a combination of kicks and blows, keeping out of the way of the knife, which was still clutched in a manacled fist.

When the second drug squad man was trying to get the big crewman to go along the piece of wood to the bank, he and his captive both fell smack into the river. Floundering and shouting they struggled there to get themselves out and up on to the grass.

Their movements and the sudden release from weight sent the *Susie Ann* out further from the bank to the length of her rope and the plank of wood fell into the water and began to float away.

Below it in the water the knife sank to the bottom.

Dave dare hardly breathe. He dare hardly move. He felt that anything might happen. Suppose they weren't tied up properly. They might shoot out into the middle of the shining water.

One of the men from the Customs boat climbed carefully on board.

He ignored Dave and looked in at the cabin door at the wrestling bodies inside. It was no longer recognizable as the neat and ordered scene it had been a few seconds before. The small plastic bags had got scattered everywhere, the table leg had been broken away and was being used as a cosh, the table leaned crazily at an angle across the middle and Mark was lying senseless as Bob tackled both James Gotobedde and the second crewman in the tiny confined space.

Dave sat up and felt his shoulder. He was sure there was something wrong with it. His hand found blood, but he seemed to be functioning.

A shot rang through the air. The bullet went into the ceiling from a gun in the hand of the crewman. Bob had him by the wrist. The Customs man went to help.

Dave got hold of Mark's legs and began to pull him out into the fresh air. Mark's head bumped helplessly along the floor of the cabin. Gotobedde kept hitting at it with the table leg.

The Customs man grasped the hand with the gun in it and tried to force open the man's grip, while Bob went for him with fists and feet. The outer edge of his boot six inches below the crewman's knee, Bob dragged his foot down the other's shin and stamped on the arch of his foot. The hand holding the gun lost its hold.

"Thank God for that," said the Customs man shoving the gun into his pocket.

Gotobedde saw his chance and thrust for the doorway, stepping on to Mark's shoulders and getting out of the cabin. Dave pulled the rest of Mark out and laid him on the seat in the stern, then whirled round and went for Gotobedde. Gotobedde had jumped for the shore and Dave was after him before he had time to think. They both landed in the river a couple of feet from the bank and laboured up the muddy near-vertical path.

Dave found himself snatching at clumps of grass to keep his footing, thinking that he would slip down again into the water below. At the top he could see two uniformed men waiting.

"Get him!" shouted Dave, indicating Gotobedde.

Gotobedde went in a wild and crazy scramble through the grass where there was no track, off to the left. Up above the two bobbies ran along keeping level with him, although he scrambled like a man possessed. They got hold of Gotobedde quite a distance away, as soon as his head came level with the top of the bank.

Dave turned to look down. He saw that the Customs boat had tied up alongside the *Susie Ann* and that a Customs man had a foot on each boat.

Bob had got the handcuffs on the man who had had the gun.

"What on earth's happening down there?" Superintendent Birch asked Dave, giving him a hand up on to the top.

"Well it's them all right," panted Dave.

"Couldn't you manage without practising to be fishes?" said Birch.

Dave looked back to see what had happened to Gotobedde. He was coming, in between the two uniformed men, who were holding his arms.

Even as Dave watched, Gotobedde seemed to sigh and slump forward slightly, as if he was giving up to the inevitable. The two PCs automatically relaxed their hold and in a flash Gotobedde drove his elbows back into their stomachs and as they doubled up he stormed forward free and running straight for Dave.

Dave did a double take before Gotobedde sprang at him with hand raised ready to deliver a vicious karate chop to the side of his neck. All Dave could see was the maddened eyes coming at him, and the hand edge flashing down. With an automatic reaction Dave threw up his left forearm and took the force of the blow on that, and in the same second thrust out his right fist to the point of

Gotobedde's jaw, with all his weight behind it.

★ ★ ★

That was the end of the fighting, but it took them some time to sort themselves out.

At last the police cars set off back for York. Mark had already gone by ambulance; he was unconscious but breathing. Customs had impounded the *Susie Ann* and her cargo.

The two handcuffed crewmen from the *Susie Ann* were in one police car with Dave Smart and the uniformed constable who was driving. Dave's arm was still feeling paralysed from Gotobedde's chop and his shoulder was aching madly. He knew that the knife had cut through his jacket and ripped into his flesh, hence the blood, but he hoped that the damage was only slight.

James Gotobedde was in another car with the other uniformed constable and Superintendent Birch. Bob Southwell, covered in blood, was driving the third car back. They moved closely in convoy

350

with Bob at the rear.

Nobody said much in front of the captives, but there was an undoubted glow of achievement.

★ ★ ★

"Well now, Dave — was that a mare's nest? Some mare!" said Bob when they were all back in the station and the prisoners were locked up in separate cells.

"All right."

"You don't sound very pleased. I thought you'd be over the moon."

"Oh, I am, I am."

"What's biting you? Have we or have we not caught Patricia Feltame's murderer?"

"I knew it was him when he came at me to deliver the same blow."

"Well then? Mission accomplished? Quest completed? Princess avenged?"

"How the hell can we prove it?" said Dave.

★ ★ ★

351

The second crewman broke down after two hours of patient tape-recorded questions and answers.

They had set off from Acaster Malbis about four in the morning, travelling extra slowly, because they did not want to attract attention. They could see perfectly well — everything was grey, but the starshine and the moonshine and the reflective quality of the water let them see as well as if it was day. The *Susie Ann* had a petrol engine and they were circulating water through the exhaust, for quietness.

They were not due to meet James Gotobedde until six, at the Tanner's Moat end of Lendal Bridge. When they got there his mate Tommy had got out, tied them up to two of the iron rings, and stayed on land to stretch his legs. He'd been standing on the side when Gotobedde arrived, and they'd had a natter. Himself? Oh, he'd been sitting on the deck and having a smoke.

Then there was this bird, see.

She'd appeared from nowhere all of a sudden, and there'd been some sort of argy-bargy. He hadn't been able to make it out, what she was shouting about. Then all he knew was that Jimmy had hit her and she was lying there, and Tommy had untied them fast and then both Tommy and Jimmy had come scrambling on board and Jimmy had said, 'Get us out of here'.

So he had. And they'd gone up river to Redby, and decided to lay low for a bit, and that was all he knew about it.

★ ★ ★

On the previous Saturday night it had taken some time for Patricia, crouched uncomfortably on the *Susie Ann*, to hear enough to realize what she had come across.

Then she had begun to edge her way back towards the landing stage. She went slowly and quietly along and to her car and because her driving slippers were muddy and she liked her car to be immaculate she changed back into her heeled shoes, leaving the slippers side by side on the ground outside, ultimately forgetting them. (They were picked up the next day by children.)

Then she sat in the car in the darkness. She remembered that she had taken her big old handbag with her when she boarded the *Susie Ann*, and that it had been in the way, and that she had stuffed it under one of the stern seats; but she didn't feel like going back for it now. She sat immobile for hour after hour, watching while the men slept on the *Susie Ann*. At last there were signs of life. When the boat pulled away from the bank and headed stealthily up river she had waited five minutes and then started her car and driven into York.

Once parked at the Esplanade she had not known what to do next. There was nothing in sight on road or river. She stood in deep shadow, watching, watching, as the time crawled by. There was time to meditate on what she was doing, but she was not capable of that. Her whole being was possessed by the elemental feelings of love and hatred; the cool calm intelligent Patricia was overridden completely.

At last she had seen the motor boat. Hidden by shadows she had seen Gotobedde's arrival and heard the beginning of his conversation with the big crewman, and it was then that she had gone quickly to the telephone kiosk on Rougier Street and raised the alarm.

Not realizing the inadequacy of her side of the conversation, sure that drug squad would be rushing to her aid, afraid that the drug-runners would get away before aid came, overcome by the emotions she had been bottling up for so long, she had rushed out at last and challenged them . . .

* * *

"She didn't die in vain, Dave," said Bob. "They were frightened by the incident, or they would have been distributing some of the stuff earlier in the week. There can be no doubt that was their intention. As well as meeting dealers from other parts, there was the local network of pushers who would certainly have been supplied straight away if they hadn't been scared out of their skins. She saved goodness knows how many new users from becoming hopelessly addicted, do you realize that?"

James Gotobedde refused to admit he had done anything wrong. It appeared that the whole problem was a little technical difficulty.

"Is Detective Inspector Rollo about?" he'd asked the constable guarding the cells. "Can I have a word with him? I want to know if anything can be done."

The constable passed the message on.

"What's this?" asked Bob. Rollo of course was on holiday. "Who's been working with Rollo lately? Jester. Fetch him up. Bring Dave Smart as well."

Bob frowned at James Jester.

"We've got your namesake in the cells, Jamie boy, wants to see Rollo. One James Gotobedde. Can you tell me what this is about?"

"Yes, sir. James Gotobedde was up for possession of cannabis some months ago."

Bob and Dave looked speechlessly at James Jester. He obviously hadn't heard about the day's events.

"What time did you come on, James?"

"Two, sir."

"And nobody in the station has talked to you?"

"Talked to me? It's been a bit hectic, actually, sir . . . "

"OK. You were telling me about this man who had possessed cannabis."

"After he was put on probation he came to John Rollo and offered to be a police informer."

"I see. Has he been useful?"

"Oh yes, fairly useful, sir. Well, that is, not very, but we have hopes."

"Your hopes are blighted, boy, blighted," said Bob.

★ ★ ★

Bob Southwell and Dave Smart were interviewing James Gotobedde.

"You wanted to talk to DI Rollo."

"I wanted to know if anything could be done."

Dave wanted to smash in his cocky face.

"Nothing can be done," said Bob. "You'd better contact a solicitor."

"You've got nothing on me."

"I think we might have something."

"I've been blackmailed, that's all. Because I've been in court about that grass. This man's been blackmailing me. He's wanted this doing and that doing. Then there's been the police as well. Give us the dirt on other people, there's a good chap, and we'll see you're all right. Now where is John Rollo when I need something done?"

"Small-scale informing isn't going to help you on this kind of rap. And as for blackmail, who's been doing it? Give us a name. Now that might help mitigate your sentence a bit."

"You must be joking."

"I'm not joking at all," said Bob passively.

Dave wished he could be alone with James Gotobedde for a short while on a dark night.

"Look, the sort of people who've been blackmailing me — you don't get to know their names. It's a voice, and he talks about the boss. I don't know who the voice is and I don't know who the boss is, and if I knew I wouldn't tell you because it's as much as my life's worth. You can send me to prison but I'd rather serve twenty years than face what they'd do to me. Besides, they'll see me right. I'll be a king in the nick and set up for life when I get out — as long as I don't squeal, that is. So if you think you're going to get them through me you've another think coming."

"You're up for murder, do you know that? Murder and drug-running."

"Murder? It was an accident. That girl would butt in where she wasn't wanted. She deserved all she got. I only meant to knock her out. She must have had a thin skull."

"And are you telling us as well that you didn't know what you were dealing in? That you thought the packets contained ecological washing powder? Pull the other one, it's got bells on," said Bob Southwell.

"Look here mate . . . I don't want no concrete overcoat," replied Gotobedde. "You can do what you like to me, I'm saying nothing else."

And they could progress no further with him.

"I'm going home," said Bob, when he and Dave were back in the detectives' office. "It's dark already. If I were you, I'd go home too."

"I'm going to see Charles Feltame," said Dave.

He stood there looking sullen and obstinate. Bob scrutinized him.

"Good idea." Bob whistled through his teeth, very faintly. For some reason he fell into the tune he had noticed Dave whistling lately, '*Auprès de ma blonde . . . Qu'il fait bon, fait bon, fait bon . . .*'

"Don't," Dave snapped irritably.

"I know what's wrong with you. It's that answerphone message we found at Gotobedde's workshop, isn't it?"

"Yes."

"There is nothing else we can do, Dave."

"We could try, at least."

"We will keep a look-out. We can't devote a special enquiry to this at the moment. There are too many other law and order offences taking place throughout the city. Tomorrow the race traffic will take every man we've got apart from the most basic work. This case has been satisfactorily completed. It is very rare we can catch the Mister Big."

"We ought to try," answered Dave.

"See you in the morning," said Bob.

"Look, this isn't good enough," shouted Dave all of a sudden. "I want to take this further. I want to see the Super."

"I'm sorry?"

"You can't shut me up like this. I want to take this to a higher authority," shouted Dave, going red in the face.

Bob went over to the telephone. "Superintendent? Southwell here. Can DI Smart and I have a word with you, please? . . . Right away if that's convenient . . . Yes, sir." He put down the phone and turned to Dave. "We can go up now," he said.

They mounted the stairs in silence.

"Yes?" said Superintendent Birch. He was looking pleased with himself.

"DI Smart would like to say something to you, sir." Bob sounded serene. He stood to one side and left the field to Dave.

361

"I'm not satisfied, sir." Dave was still loud and angry. "We're putting this case on one side as all over bar the shouting and the man really responsible goes free. I demand that we go after Harry Brate and investigate him and bring him to justice."

"You're demanding, Dave?"

"Yes, Detective Superintendent Birch. I'm demanding that we try for a conviction of Harry Brate whose money was behind all this and who was really responsible for the girl's death and for the drug addiction of God knows how many human beings and directly for Sebastian getting on crack and for the ruination of the family of his friend Charles Feltame. I'm demanding that we smash this man, sir."

"Look, Detective Inspector . . . On what do you base this charge?"

Dave blinked. "He was responsible, sir."

"Evidence?"

"He got Sebastian this job in London. He took Patricia out to dinner the night before she was killed. He told us she was on a vigilante mission to clean up the

362

York drug trade. I don't believe it. We didn't get that from anyone else. I think she was only out to save her brother. He was the most important thing in the world to her — it's sometimes like that with twins. James Gotobedde didn't have the money to finance a big operation like this drug-running. Harry Brate did. Gotobedde is terrified of someone. It's got to be him."

Dave's voice throughout had been loud and hectoring. Superintendent Birch was beginning to get a little tired of it. He looked at Bob, who looked expressionlessly back at him.

"You haven't enough evidence to hang a cat," said Superintendent Birch.

"We didn't have any evidence to go after the *Susie Ann*, sir."

"We can't do anything to Harry Brate."

"A search warrant for his flat, sir."

"On what charge? As if he'd keep anything incriminating in it!"

"A voice profile on that answerphone call and on all his office staff, sir."

"You think the bona-fide staff of Brate's company would be involved in anything shady? Be your age, Dave."

"I want to take this to a higher authority, sir!" shouted Dave.

"Permission not granted."

"Do you want to get back into uniform, Dave?" asked Bob, dangerously.

Dave stared at him.

For a very long minute there was complete silence in the room.

"We know how you feel, Dave," Superintendent Birch said calmly. "You've been very involved in this case and that has produced good results. You've made your feelings known on the subject of Mr Brate and they will be noted. Although at present we can do nothing, we will not forget your suspicions of this man. That ought to satisfy you, DI Smart. Now you have my permission to go, and to take a week's sick leave. What did they think to your shoulder at the hospital?"

"Light flesh wounds, sir. Clean. Stitched up and bandaged," responded Dave in a toneless voice.

"If I hear no more of this outburst we will consider that it never happened," said Superintendent Birch, standing up.

Dave turned and left.

364

"Phew! What was all that about?" the Superintendent asked Bob Southwell.

Bob shrugged. "Strain," he said.

"Better keep an eye on him."

"Yes."

"Tell me how you sum up this murderer. He seems a bit odd to me."

"James Gotobedde. Well. He strikes me as having no moral sense whatever. He's a respected craftsman. Why he got into drugs in the first place I don't know, but it was probably as harmless as alcohol to start with. Then after he got probation he was leaned on by the heavy mob, according to him, although he must have done something he's not telling us about, for them to use as a lever. His work as a grass for us was very small-scale indeed, and seems to have been a kind of insurance or cover-up."

"I can follow that, but what happened next?"

"The Met found his finger-prints in Sebastian Feltame's London flat. It seems, though I'm not sure if we can prove it, that he was sent down there on a mission to hook Seb on crack. He was on friendly terms with

365

the lad. The next thing seems to be that someone financed this big-scale drug importation and Gotobedde was to act as distributing agent. Usually it's more the market economy — big boy buys and sells on to group of littler boys who sell on again who sell on again — as you know, sir."

"Why the murder?"

"I think quite simply that he's got a hair-trigger temper and an interest in the martial arts and, as I said before, no moral sense."

"And he'd already sold the brother down the river."

"Exactly. If he has a conscience, it would make him uneasy and all the more likely to strike out."

★ ★ ★

Dave Smart had taken some time to cool down. Now he was determined to carry out his programme as he had planned it.

"Job for Jenny, if you can spare her," he said to Jenny's supervisor. "She dealt very well with Mrs Feltame. Could she come out to The Grange with me to help break the news of Gotobedde's arrest?"

Jenny found Dave very quiet. She sat beside him as they drove out of the city and felt concerned. She had expected him to be jubiliant, bubbling over; although she had never seen him like that, she knew in her bones just how he would be, how his eyes would crinkle up even more than usual, how the whole of life would please him and he would find fun in a thousand small things. Contrary to expectation he wasn't like that at all. He was heavy and brooding and silent.

He turned to her as they drew up outside the modern repro porch which, like the repro windows, seemed incongruous with the old building of The Grange. They would need several decades before they had blended in.

"Good girl, Jenny," he murmured, touching her hand gently.

Good girl? She was suprised. What had she done? Nothing. What had she said? Nothing.

Their reception by Charles Feltame was very different to their previous treatment by Mrs Feltame. He threw open the door himself, welcomed them in, yelled to Mrs Briggs for a pot of tea for four, and drew them into the sitting-room.

Dave was again shocked by his appearance. Charles was as immaculate as ever, as much the tycoon, but his face was unbelievably haggard and his manner nervous.

"How is Sebastian?" asked Dave.

"Not good, I'm afraid." Charles poured himself a stiff whisky, offering one to Dave and Jenny with a gesture, a lift of the eyebrow; they shook their heads.

"Not good at all." He moved to a chair and sipped the whisky. "I'm going to curtail my commitments," he said, "and devote myself to him. It's time I was slacking off, anyway. Together — he and I — we might make something of his life yet."

Dave could think of nothing to say. Even if he was in trouble now, such an athlete had achieved a great deal already in his life; but somehow he knew that to Charles Feltame sport was merely playing, and real life something quite different. He doubted if Charles knew one end of a golf club from the other.

"We've come with good news," he said rather diffidently. "The man we believe to be the murderer was apprehended this morning."

The change in Charles Feltame was instantaneous. He sat up straight, looked five years younger, and put down his glass. Mrs Briggs came in with the tray of tea, and Mrs Feltame followed her.

Jenny got up and went to the older woman, who received her with a softer manner than usual, and allowed Jenny's little caring movements when she helped her to a chair as though she were just recovering from a long illness. Jenny poured a cup of tea and took it to her, and Mrs Feltame said, "Thank you, my dear."

"They've arrested the murderer, Margaret," said Charles, and she looked relieved, and nodded.

"Tell me all about it," he said to Dave Smart, and Dave explained what had happened.

"It's all over then."

"Well, not quite," Dave replied.

"Not quite? Not all over?"

"Not really."

When he showed them out Charles said to Dave, "I'll come down to the station presently."

Again Dave and Jenny drove in silence, as they returned to the station.

He left her in the general office and went upstairs, saying as he went, "You're a good mate, Jenny."

She sat at her desk and gazed after him, wondering.

★ ★ ★

Charles Feltame arrived half an hour later. He was still looking cheerful.

"Your news has done me more good than anything else in this ghastly week," he said. "Not that I'm surprised."

"You're not surprised?"

"I was at first, but when I thought about it, I wasn't any more. Finding Sebastian drove it out of my head, but one of his colleagues said that Seb had had a visitor not so long ago, he'd brought him along to a party. A thin dark man with pronounced wrinkles, called James, he thought."

"Gotobedde?"

"Must be."

"And hooked him on crack while he was in London?"

"Certainly."

"Yes."

"But why is it you aren't satisfied, Dave?"

"Because Gotobedde is only a little man in this organization. We haven't caught the big boys, and in a way catching these three has stopped us catching the others. Our men have been over Gotobedde's workshop and they tape-recorded this message from his answering machine. Listen."

It was a man's voice, rather toneless, not very distinctive. "The boss says it doesn't matter about the girl, she wasn't interesting any more. He wants the delivery finished tomorrow at the latest."

There was no identification, no preliminary clearing of the throat or name and telephone number given, just the bare statement.

"There's a bit of carelessness on the part of a criminal, leaving messages on

371

one of those machines," commented Charles. He had gone white.

"You see what I mean. Gotobedde is far more frightened of them than he is of us."

"Have you any idea who it is?"

"The voice is only a henchman. It's the big boy I want. The one who sends a message, 'It doesn't matter about the girl.' Yes. I have an idea I'd like to investigate, but doubt if it will be possible."

"Tell me."

"You might be upset. I can't help wondering about your friend Harry Brate."

"Old Harry? You've got to be joking."

"No. Now, sir, I ask you to be very careful not to let him have any inkling of this."

"Harry and that silly restaurant of his?"

"Good cover."

"But why should you think it is anything to do with Harry?"

Dave hesitated.

"Go on."

"His business dealings are often only just on the right side of the law."

Charles Feltame shrugged his shoulders. In the kind of multinational corporate business he was involved in local laws tended to appear unimportant. You set up a deal with a country, you found out how its particular laws affected you, saw if you could swing them if they didn't fit . . .

"He was the only person who told us that Patricia was leading a one-woman vigilante crusade against drugs. I don't believe she was. She was going against her training in her actions but I believe she was motivated only by her love of her brother, a strong emotional reaction she couldn't control."

"He may have misunderstood something she said."

"I remember an old retired detective telling me once — before I even joined the force — that you can tell a real criminal by the atmosphere of evil they have around them."

"Like my old friend?"

"I want you to be on your guard, sir. If I'm right he is completely heartless and has no loyalty to you or to anyone else. I've said this more to put you on your guard than anything. The forensic pathologist said something to my boss which he repeated to me. He said, Who is guilty, the man who strikes the blow, or the man who causes it to be struck? Or words to that effect."

Charles Feltame walked about the tired, shabby office. As always he looked spruce and immaculate. He drummed his fingers on the top of the desks.

At last he turned to Dave. "Look, Dave — we've got on well together — "

"Yes, sir."

"You know what losing my daughter means to me. There's a saying, 'the apple of his eye' — Patricia was the apple of my eye, the best thing in my world, my hope for the future. Your idea seems incredible. I don't think you ought to have said what you have said to me."

"I ought not, sir."

"I will tell you this, Dave. I'm not without power in this world. I can probably find things out about Harry better than you can. I'm sure you're mistaken, you know. They won't let you pursue it, eh?"

"That's it."

"No one can stop me pursuing it."

"You must be careful. You have Sebastian and Mrs Feltame to think of."

"I will be careful. Time shall go by. Seb shall be put on the right track and kept on it and his mother made happy. Then, Dave, then . . . Look, you aren't the only one with a recording. I want to leave you with a good feeling. Listen to this."

He produced a miniature tape recorder and set it on the desk. At the flick of a switch the office was filled with a golden voice, a rich warm soprano, singing.

"It's Patricia," whispered Charles, and his eyes filled with tears. She was singing a folk-song, something about young women being like the hares on the mountain. There could have been no happier sound. It seemed to come from a different world. They listened until the song ended.

Charles picked up the recorder and his raincoat and walked to the door. He turned for a last word.

"Dave, I say to you, this case is not a closed case."

15

THE Southwells' guests began arriving soon after seven on the Saturday evening. Linda had been feeling nervous. Would it go all right? But with the first knock on the door she decided that it was going to be fun.

Earlier in the week Paul had said, "Ugh, you're not going to have a dinner party?"

"Yes, we are. Why not?"

"Because you always push us off to bed early and we have to be quiet."

"You can say hello to the guests before you go, if you like."

"They're boring."

"I like saying hello to them," put in Susan, who scented a chance to wear her new party frock.

"It's not even Halloween or Guy Fawkes night."

"Look, Paul, if you are good for my party, I'll have one for you on Bonfire Night."

376

"You will?"

"Is it a bargain?"

"Oh, yes, then!"

All day the weather had been calm and genial. This might only be a lull, before they went back to tearing winds and soaking rain; but Linda was glad that the lull had come when it did.

Jenny Wren arrived early and felt self-conscious when she was deposited by DCI Bob Southwell in his sitting-room, with two men she didn't know and two children.

There was telephone engineer Tom Churchyard, who was the Southwells' next door neighbour, and Richard Sugden, as well as a bright-eyed Paul and a party-frocked Susan.

Jenny stood there with a glass in her hand and tried to make conversation and was glad when she heard another woman arriving.

Julia Bransby lived so close that she had been able to walk round to the Southwells' house. In the small hallway she slid off her neat grey coat and handed it to Bob with a smile.

"You look very attractive," said Bob.

"I almost wish I was unattached."

"Flattery will get you everywhere," said Julia. "Do you hear your husband, Lindy?"

The kitchen door was open next to them and she could see Linda replenishing little bowls of nibbles.

"He gets like that," said Linda, looking up. "Have a cheese straw. I made them. That is a lovely dress, Julia. Where did you find it?"

"I have my sources." Julia smiled like the cat with the cream. It was a genuine New Look cocktail dress, with a pretty bit of beading on one shoulder, which had been given to her by an old lady.

"It's got the forties look," said Linda. "Come and meet everyone."

She led the way into the long through sitting-room.

"Tom you know. I'd like you to meet Richard Sugden who has come to live in York, he's a retired Chief Constable, you don't mind admitting to that, do you, Richard, and this is Jenny Wren, one of our WPCs. We're just waiting for Professor Hartley Danes and his wife from the university, I don't know if you've ever met them. Now what would you like to drink?"

"Can I have some more orange juice, Mummy?" asked Paul.

"Auntie Julia I like your frock because it's velvet but I like Jenny's better because hers is pink," announced Susan.

"Yours is pretty, too, Susan."

Susan twirled around.

"Time you two went to bed," put in Bob.

"Dad, Mummy said we could meet everybody and . . . "

"Five minutes longer then."

"Susan, you go round with the cheese straws and Paul, you go round with the peanuts," said Linda.

Julia accepted a glass of the white wine everyone was drinking. She might have known Thomas would be here, as he lived next door. She had got to know him and the Southwells during the last production of the York Mystery Plays — the production in which a murder had taken place. Since then she and Tom had met sometimes for lunch or coffee. Then, earlier this year, they had felt very passionate about one another for a time. Then things had happened . . .

Julia nodded and smiled at Tom and he nodded and smiled back. Neither of them wanted the other to think they were being chased.

They said simultaneously, "Hello! I didn't know you'd be here."

When they had stopped laughing Julia went to stand next to Jenny Wren, who was looking shy.

"You've moved to York recently?" She included both Jenny and Richard in her glance. "How do you find the housing market?"

"I'm renting a few rooms," said Jenny. "It's beyond me at present to buy my own place." She took a cheese straw from Susan.

"How young people are ever going to get on the housing ladder I don't know," said Tom.

"I'm lucky of course," Richard remarked. "I had a house to sell, although York is more expensive than the West Riding."

"Prices are coming up there fast now, though, aren't they?"

"In the last twelve months they certainly have."

"They seem to be slackening off down south, no one's buying," put in Tom. "No thanks, Paul. I've had enough peanuts for now, look, I've still got some."

At that moment in the hall the telephone rang.

"Southwell." They could all hear Bob answering it. "Oh, I'm so sorry . . . You will? Oh, that is good of you . . . Would he? Splendid."

Going into the kitchen, he said to Linda, "That's torn it."

"What's the matter?"

"Hartley Danes has been in a shunt on the M1 on his way home to pick up what's her name? Lilias?"

"Hurt?" Linda looked aghast.

"Fortunately not, and the cars only slightly dented and quite drivable. But you know how long it takes if something like this happens. There were a lot of cars involved in a patch of mist. He could have driven home straight away but there are investigations to be done and some cars are more damaged. She's been wondering where the heck he was and he's only just managed to get to the phone."

"So they're not coming."

"She's coming on her own by taxi and he'll come along later to pick her up. I said that would be all right."

"Yes, of course. I'll have to rearrange the dinner table."

"No, I'll tell you what. I'll give Dave Smart a ring and see if he's free."

"Oh!" Linda looked at the wall clock. "It's quarter past seven already!"

"He's looking hag-ridden over this case he's on. I've never seen him in such a state before. And yesterday afternoon we had a bit of a do with him. I'd like to have him here for a bit, reassure myself."

"Well, if he won't be too long . . . "

"It's an order, Dave," Bob was saying a minute later. "Get yourself over quickly." There was no nonsense in Bob's voice and it wasn't a tone Dave could disobey: he felt forced to agree — most unwillingly. Turning from the phone, Bob was the sunny and genial host once more. Dave arrived, rather sullen, a quarter of an hour afterwards.

"Now, you go to bed," Linda had said firmly to Susan and Paul, and they went meekly after an elaborate goodbye to everyone. As they left the room Paul took Susan's hand.

"How sweet," said Julia. "They do seem fond of one another."

"You wouldn't have said so last Sunday, when they were fighting over the colour supplement."

"But siblings have a special relationship, don't they? I was reading about George the Fifth, how he and his unmarried sister used to ring one another up every day of their lives, and how affected he was when she died."

"I hope they do grow up to be a support to one another."

"I agree with you," Richard Sugden said to Julia. "There's something special about a brother and sister relationship. It seems to transcend the usual self-seeking element. If there is a pure love, it is among children."

When Lilias Danes arrived they all went in to the dining-room and seated themselves at the long table of pale ash. The wine stood ready on the matching dresser. It was an airy, pastel-shaded room, much loved, often used.

Linda felt a deep satisfaction. The lighted pink candles set sparkling reflections dancing on glasses and cutlery. She felt as though she had created an iridescent bubble whirling on the surface of the everyday.

Richard Sugden gazed around him with interest, as Linda passed the avocados stuffed with prawns. He was the new boy at this gathering, though he was older than any of them.

He had the feeling that Julia Bransby had been asked for his sake. A pleasing, mature, intelligent woman. A pity she kept glancing at Tom, that big dependable looking fellow across the table. A little younger than she was, Richard guessed.

His host and hostess he already knew and liked. Bob was sparkling now, full of wisecracks as he poured wine, the candlelight glinting in the large lenses of his spectacles. A good keen able police officer. Linda was looking very attractive.

His consideration passed to Lilias Danes, whose taxi had brought her at twenty-five to eight, the same time that DI Smart had arrived in his own car.

Lilias had created a sensation. She had walked in talking and had never stopped yet. She gave an overall impression of beige, except for her flashing white teeth. She was lively, chatty, sociable, and quite wrapped up in her own concerns. Although she was so slim, she had worked her way solidly through the avocados and the Yorkshire pudding, and now was gleefully accepting the roast beef.

Richard Sugden's survey of his fellow diners left only Detective Inspector David Smart and Woman Police Constable Gladys (Jenny) Wren to consider.

It was obvious that she was in love with him. She had trembled slightly when he had walked in at the door: she was always aware of him. She was a nice no-nonsense girl and Richard Sugden thought it must be good to have someone feeling like that about you.

Was Dave Smart responding, that was the question?

At last Richard came to consider Dave.

A big, solid, red-faced man, with blackish slightly curled hair. Crinkled up eyes which could be brown, or might be grey. Age — between thirty and thirty-five. Having been summoned peremptorily to this social occasion he was doing his best not to damp it, but he looked — what was Bob's expression? Hag-ridden? Not the right word, Richard felt. Haunted would have expressed it better.

Dave's hands shook as he used his knife and fork and he looked as though he had lost weight recently. His face showed it.

As an ex-Chief Constable Richard Sugden appraised Dave professionally, wondering if he could help. Here was a darn good detective — Bob's concern alone would have told him that — looking on the verge of some sort of breakdown. Was it only exhaustion?

The housing market gave them plenty to talk about, then there was a discussion of wine and Tom told them an exaggerated story about the time he made it at home and the date wine exploded when it was fermenting on the hearth and put bits of date all over his sitting-room ceiling.

As he had considered them, in their turn the other members of the dinner party were considering Richard Sugden.

Julia had decided that she liked him. He looked intelligent, reserved, and whimsical.

Bob Southwell and Linda were grateful for the way he helped to keep conversation flowing.

Dave Smart who didn't want to be present anyway found that the older man made the whole thing easier. He and Jenny Wren. Jenny was a soothing, emollient presence. Dave felt as though prickles were sticking into him all over. He had been pacing the floor of the flat when Bob phoned and insisted on his coming.

I suppose he meant to do me good, Dave thought. He knew that Bob knew roughly what he was going through. Now he felt that Richard Sugden and Jenny Wren also understood. Jenny had been a good mate during the investigation, even though sometimes he'd noticed a purely female reaction to things. Still, there wasn't a policewoman he'd rather have worked with.

The meal was good. He'd probably not have bothered, at home by himself. He hadn't been interested in eating lately, but he'd shoved food into himself just to keep going. Even here he didn't feel hungry but good manners made him eat a reasonable amount. He accepted a second glass of wine.

"Cheers," said Jenny, and clinked her glass with his.

"Cheers", he responded. "Thank goodness the case is over. Now you can relax a bit?"

"Over?" he snapped at her. "Over, with the man who really murdered her going free?"

"No shop," put in Bob quickly.

Everyone at the table had heard Dave and he had broken Linda's floating bubble like a stone breaking reflections in a pool.

"Sorry," he said now, and tried to smile, and clinked his glass with other people's.

"This sounds fascinating," gushed Lilias Danes. "Do tell us all about it."

"I'm afraid he can't," put in Bob

again. "I couldn't allow him to." He spoke and smiled with such charm that no one could have taken offence, but he kicked Dave's ankle, under the table.

Dave tried to concentrate on general conversation and keep his thoughts under control. He was sorry he'd been sharp with Jenny. For a moment he'd seen tears shining in those honest friendly hazel eyes. He looked at her now, hesitantly.

"It's all right," she said as though she'd read his thoughts. Then she smiled and passed the lemon souffle. They finished with cheeses, grapes and celery, but Dave had done all he could by then in the eating line.

Back in the sitting-room for coffee, Dave sat next to Jenny. This was the first time he had seen her out of uniform. He registered her pretty arms, firm and rounded without being too plump. She had nice hands too, but he'd seen those before. She's a good kid, he thought.

Richard Sugden sat on Dave's other side.

"One shouldn't talk shop, of course," he said in his quiet cultured voice. "But occasionally, you know, they do get away, even when we know they're guilty. You must have had such cases before, Dave."

"I'd like to nail the bastard," Dave said, then wished he'd expressed himself differently. But that was how he felt.

"And we can't allow ourselves the luxury of becoming too personally involved, either. Like nurses who must always remain detached from their patients, however sorry they feel."

"You've got to care," responded Dave.

"If you care too much it takes it out of you and you can't give of your best to the other cases — who deserve your attention just as much."

Dave was silent. It was elementary really. Just that it had never seemed to apply to his emotions about Patricia Feltame.

Lilias Danes was joined by the professor, very late indeed. He told them, at too much length, all about the accident. The Danes certainly added something different to the party. Linda found the professor's arm circling her before he had been in the house ten minutes and when they took their leave he kissed every woman in the place.

This signalled the end of the evening.

Julia shook hands with Tom Churchyard and they looked intently at one another.

"I'll be seeing you," he said at last.

"Of course," she replied brightly, too brightly.

Richard Sugden had been standing waiting, watching them. She was silent as they left the house, but he enjoyed the walk, for its own sake, enjoyed passing in and out of the pools of light shed by the street lamps, and looking at the gleams which came from curtained windows and fell in a random way on the gardens of the modern semis. They soon reached the flats where Julia lived.

His newly adopted home town had been feeling a little lonely. Now he was beginning to know people: Julia had suggested one or two organizations he might like to join, and he was seeing her the following day.

Jenny Wren was not walked home, because both she and Dave Smart had come in their own cars.

He had turned to her at the end of the evening, and asked her, rather diffidently, how she was fixed about transport. "Oh. I was going to offer you a lift," he said when she explained, and Jenny was annoyed with herself for having told the truth. Why hadn't she said that she'd come on foot?

"It would have been nice," she said. "Although I'm in rooms, I would have offered you a coffee."

"Your landlady wouldn't mind, then? You're allowed gentlemen visitors?" and the hint of a teasing smile awoke in Dave's eyes.

"I could always have said you were a long-lost cousin," she replied gravely. Taking her courage in both hands she went on, "Why don't you come all the same? It seems a shame to break the party up so early."

"All right."

She told him where she lived, and they set off together, with him trailing her car.

★ ★ ★

When everyone had gone except Tom, the party really started. Linda and Bob began to clear away and Tom put on Linda's apron and washed up. They all talked and laughed and nibbled left-over bits of things and drank up the bottles of wine. The others had been careful how much they drank but Tom only had to walk next door and Bob and Linda only had to get themselves upstairs.

"Leave the rest, Tom," said Linda. "You've done marvellously. All the pans and things can soak until tomorrow. Come into the sitting-room. Let's finish off the petit fours."

The three of them made as much noise as the whole eight had earlier. "The next door neighbour might complain," said Bob.

"He might, and quite right too," said Tom.

"You two are hopelessly squiffy," said Linda.

When he finally went home and was on his own Tom felt a little down. There hadn't been a special girl for him at the party. Lilias and Linda were both very married, that nice policewoman Jenny only had eyes for Dave Smart, and even Julia — who he'd thought was still his if he should stretch out his hand — Julia had walked off with someone she'd only just met . . .

"Dammit," thought Tom.

Somewhere, wasn't there the right person for him?

"Are you pleased then?" Bob Southwell murmured to Linda.

"Yes, it was super," she murmured back.

"Wasn't it a bit ironic?"

"In what way?"

"Well, we asked Jenny as company for Tom, and she never looked at him."

"She was too busy looking at Dave. And we asked her because she's new, so that was all right. I'll tell you something," Linda said in his sleepy ear.

"You're always telling me something."

"Dave's changed."

"He's hag-ridden, I told you."

"No. It's not that. He's back in the market."

Bob tried to wake up a bit.

"What do you mean?"

"Well, he lost his wife tragically, didn't he, five years ago, right?"

"Right. What is it about giving dinner

parties that makes you talkative? What's wrong with a bit of kip?"

"Well, he went around wearing 'out of bounds' notices for all the women he met."

"Did he?"

"Very much the widower. I would have said that it was on the cards that he might never take an interest in women again."

"You mean that now he is?"

"I mean something's got rid of those 'Keep off' notices. He's available."

"Oh. Something women can tell, is it?"

"Oh yes."

"Well," Bob reached out an arm to pull her close so that he could feel the warmth of her against him. "As long as it's other women, not you. You're spoken for."

"Booked solid," said Linda.

"Didn't we ask Julia for Richard Sugden?"

"How was I supposed to know that she and Tom have got a thing going?"

"I don't think they have."

"There was something."

"At the end Richard Sugden was making headway, didn't he take her home?"

"And Tom looked out of it?"

"Exactly."

"Mm. Well, I don't think she'd suit Tom."

"Why ever not? Don't you want Julia living next door? Perhaps you think Tom's your exclusive property," teased Bob.

"I've enough to cope with, with *you*, thanks very much, without taking Tom on. But let's face it, Julia *is* older."

"That doesn't matter these days."

"She has a teenage son."

"What a lot of undercurrents! Crime's straightforward compared to dinner parties. I never realised there'd be all these hidden meanings. Did you, Lindy-Lou? I expect you did. I think you are a bit of a witch."

"If Tom married Julia he would have to be a step-father. And she's a career woman. Would she want to stop work and have more children? I doubt it. No. I'd rather see him marry someone younger who would make him the centre of her world and give him a nice little family of his own."

Perhaps these thoughts of Linda's were Tom's too. Perhaps that was why he and Julia — all through the summer of surreptitious passion — had never really made progress.

"I'll have to find someone for Tom," finished Linda decidedly, after a pause.

"Look out Tom," replied Bob, nearly asleep.

16

JENNY WREN had most of the first floor in a house in Vyner Street. Her landlady, who had split the house into three, had the ground floor; a student nurse had the converted roof space and part of the first-floor back extension.

Jenny wished, as she approached the house with Dave Smart in his car behind hers, that the street was a bit better for parking. She wished this every single time she went home.

Had she made a mistake, asking him back for a coffee? Would he think she was being unduly forward? Would he misunderstand her?

She wondered this as she jockeyed her car into a short space. Goodness knows where he's going to put his car, she thought. One thing she was sure of. He would not take advantage or make unwelcome advances. With Dave Smart anything like that would have to be mutual — he wasn't one of those men who automatically make a pass at every female they're in contact with in life. The trouble was — she didn't mind admitting to herself — she had fallen in love with the great mutt, and even the thought of his entering her flat made her tremble.

She got out of the car and locked it. Further along the narrow street with the line of cars on either side she could see Dave going through the same kind of performance she'd just gone through. He was lucky there'd been any space at all.

She watched him as he walked back to her.

He looks all in, she thought. He had looked pretty rough at the dinner party, as if he was having a job to hold himself together, but as he came towards her in the patchy orange light of the street lamps he looked worse. She decided she'd have to do what she could to be soothing company and not expect anything of him in the way of conversation.

"Phew!" she said as he reached her. "This street is really hell. With the City General Hospital at the end and a constant stream of traffic up and down you wonder how people manage. But during the day most of the cars are away, and when there's a lot parked and it's only single-line traffic people just wait at the end if they see another car on its way down. It's a nice little street otherwise. I like these modest sedate kind of terraces."

This stream of low-voiced comment had eased them through the low gate and up the couple of yards of path to the front door.

Jenny put her key in the lock as she went chattering on, like Tennyson's brook.

"They were built for a time when people really lived in their town, going to work on foot or bicycle, walking into town to shop or at best going by bus. The time when there really were communities."

"You don't think there are now?" Dave's tone was dead, flat. They began to go up the stairs.

"I think they're surviving, yes. You can't change human nature and that's the way it's natural for us to live, all hugger-mugger. But society is being fragmented.

Every day in every way. We're being made to live as individuals and not as the groups which are natural to us."

Jenny trudged before him up the stairs. The last thing she'd expected to be doing was giving a lecture on the changing nature of society.

Jenny's living room was a typical rented room. There was a fitted carpet of aggressive design, a cheap three-piece suite, a coffee table on spindly legs and, under the window, an old dining-table with three uncomfortable upright chairs. She drew the curtains more closely, trying to make them meet in the middle. The curtain rail had no overlap and the flimsy material was not wide enough.

Dave dimly thought it looked homely and pleasant. He saw the soft glow from the lamps which Jenny had dotted about the place and smelt the fragrance of the bowls of flowers. He felt the warmth of the gas fire which she had turned on as she moved past it to the window. Without being asked he chose a chair next to the fire and sat down.

"Percolated all right?" she asked.

"I don't mind powdered."

"Real is nicer."

Jenny vanished into the tiny kitchen and he could hear the little noises of cupboard doors and pottery, the tap being turned on and off again, the hiss of gas.

"There are some magazines on the side," she called.

"I'm all right."

He knew that he was happy to be there, in that happiness can often be only a cessation of pain. He dreaded going back to his lonely flat where the thought that after all he was not going to be able to really avenge Patricia would come and torment him and torment him and there would be nothing at all he could do to defend himself from going raving mad.

It had been only a different kind of purgatory to take part in the dinner party. The effort of not showing what he was feeling had been almost too great. The bright social chatter, the good food, the pleasant company had been wasted on him.

At least what had gone before had made him able to appreciate this. He had never — apart from one or two small instances when Jenny was being what he called feminine — felt uncomfortable in her presence. She did not give him the uneasy feeling Frances gave him. With Jenny he felt on firm ground. He liked to hear her fiddling about in the kitchen making coffee. He liked the way she had instantly provided warmth and soft lights on entering the room, and drawn the curtains more closely, as if tucking him up into a homelike atmosphere.

"Potty really," said Jenny, coming back into the room with a trolley on which were cups and saucers, coffee pot, milk and sugar, a plate of home-made cake and some biscuits. "Drinking coffee at this time of night. We'll never get to sleep and then it will be impossible to wake up in the morning."

"I'm off duty so it doesn't matter," said Dave.

"Well, I'm on afternoons. So it won't matter for me either, too much. But there's all sorts I was going to do."

Dave didn't bother to answer.

"I didn't know a soul tonight except you and DCI Southwell," said Jenny.

"You'll get to know Tom Churchyard

and Julia Bransby, they're always turning up, particularly if there is a murder." Dave sounded sardonic. "I hadn't met the others before, myself."

"You know Linda and the children quite well, I expect."

"Yes."

They sat opposite one another and drank the coffee. Although they'd eaten well not long before, they both took a piece of cake.

"Home-made?" asked Dave.

"It's only one of those quick packet ones," replied Jenny.

He didn't trouble to ask what she meant.

There was silence between them for some time. Jenny thought it would never end, but she didn't mind if it didn't.

Dave put down his cup and saucer on the trolley and brushed some crumbs of cake from his jacket.

He never knew why it was that he suddenly reached breaking point.

"Oh my God," he said abruptly, sinking his face into his cupped hands.

"What is it?" Jenny was alarmed.

He did not answer her. He began to

shake all over. He shook so much that it was visible to Jenny. His hands trembled over his face.

"Oh my God," he said again, and a sob was wrenched from him as if he was being torn apart in order to release it.

"Whatever is it?" Jenny hastily put down her own cup.

"It's . . . it's . . . this case . . . "

Jenny had fallen on her knees on the hearthrug in front of the gas fire.

"Dave, Dave, the case is over — you've locked up the man who murdered her . . . "

"No." He shook his head violently. "We only locked up the man who dealt the blow."

"That is the murderer!"

"*No!*"

He sobbed.

"Oh God," said Jenny in her turn. She sat on her heels and looked at him. She'd never been confronted with a sobbing man before. Not one she loved. He wasn't weeping, just this awful heart-rending sobbing.

"I didn't do it," he jerked out.

"What?"

"I didn't avenge her."

"What more could you have done?"

The time stretched out second by second.

At last Jenny could stand it no longer. She shuffled on her knees the few inches which divided her from Dave Smart and put her arms around him.

"It's all right, Dave," she said softly. "It's all right."

He did not answer.

She drew closer still, until his bent head buried in his cupped hands was resting on her shoulder. She gathered him in and rested her cheek on his ear. Almost she rocked him, bending very very slightly to and fro.

The next hour was one neither of them ever referred to again.

There was one point in which he wrenched away from her and felt desperately in his pocket for his handkerchief.

"I'm all right," he said. "Perfectly all right."

He was all right for the two seconds it took him to blow his nose.

He felt afterwards as if he went down into the pit in that hour. There were things he'd never understood about human nature, but he learned them then. Things about how one can suffer, can put oneself unsparingly on the rack. Things about the end of one's personal world.

He remembered much later how he had felt when his wife died, and it had not been quite the same. It had not been the same because when she died he had frozen inside, frozen tight up as if arctic permafrost had got into his heart. That arctic frost had stayed there, until it cracked right open one Sunday morning in October by the river Ouse.

He'd been going through emotional hell all week, but this was the worst time.

* * *

Dave Smart woke next morning in Jenny Wren's bed.

It would be strange for a woman to wake in an unknown place. Perhaps for a big, powerful, macho male it wouldn't seem strange at all — just something perfectly normal he would take in his stride, then get up whistling and go in search of a shave and a cup of tea.

When Dave Smart opened his eyes, he couldn't think for the life of him where he was. It was a very warm and comfortable place, and there was someone else with him. Looking up at the cream-washed ceiling and not daring to move, he tried to remember. He felt that someone else's arms and legs were somehow twined up with his own. That person was asleep, and breathing gently.

Turning his head away, he looked out into the room. Grey light came through the curtains and he could hear the sound of persistent rain. On a chair were his clothes, neatly folded, and on a bedside table were his watch and handkerchief and other contents of his pockets. He could see the glint of Patricia Feltame's key-ring and its golden bauble and for a moment could not think what they were.

I should have handed those in, he thought. It was as though the camera of his mind had been turned on one — as though the key-ring had been clicked decisively into a photograph of yesterday, and the eye of the camera lens had opened on a different scene, today, ready to discover something new.

He moved his head by degrees, and looked at the head beside him on the pillow. It was half on his shoulder, so he had to squint sideways and down. The knowledge of who it was grew within him, as if he'd known in the first second.

His left arm was free of restriction apart from the duvet so he brought his hand over and touched Jenny's hair. It was very short and a pleasant nut brown, shining and straight. He played with the bits of it he could see. Then he relaxed again and let his head flop back on the pillow and tried to think and work out what exactly had happened.

His mind flinched away from the crisis he'd gone through. Neither now nor at any other time would he be able to admit to it.

But he did remember Jenny's firm voice. "You're in no fit state to go home," she had said, and she'd taken him and insisted on him removing his clothes and sliding into a bed which had been beautifully warmed by an electric blanket, and he remembered her bringing him a hot drink with a good measure of whisky in it.

Then he didn't remember any more.

Yes he did, though.

He'd fallen asleep like a log — yes, he was sure of that. But then after a number of hours he'd woken again. Woken to find that he was not alone in the bed. It's lucky it's a double one, he thought, or there wouldn't have been much room.

Somehow, in the night, their arms had gone round one another, and one thing had led to another, and . . .

Yes, he remembered that very well, very well indeed.

He'd forgotten how good it could be.

He'd forgotten how great you felt the next morning when it had been really good.

He moved a little away from Jenny so that he could look down at her properly. All week he'd wanted cake. But if you couldn't have cake, home-made bread was very good. It was something you never got tired of, something that would go on and on for the rest of your life.

TO FIGHT THE WILD
Rod Ansell and Rachel Percy

Lost in uncharted Australian bush, Rod Ansell survived by hunting and trapping wild animals, improvising shelter and using all the bushman's skills he knew.

COROMANDEL
Pat Barr

India in the 1830s is a hot, uncomfortable place, where the East India Company still rules. Amelia and her new husband find themselves caught up in the animosities which seethe between the old order and the new.

THE SMALL PARTY
Lillian Beckwith

A frightening journey to safety begins for Ruth and her small party as their island is caught up in the dangers of armed insurrection.

THE WILDERNESS WALK
Sheila Bishop

Stifling unpleasant memories of a misbegotten romance in Cleave with Lord Francis Aubrey, Lavinia goes on holiday there with her sister. The two women are thrust into a romantic intrigue involving none other than Lord Francis.

THE RELUCTANT GUEST
Rosalind Brett

Ann Calvert went to spend a month on a South African farm with Theo Borland and his sister. They both proved to be different from her first idea of them, and there was Storr Peterson — the most disturbing man she had ever met.

ONE ENCHANTED SUMMER
Anne Tedlock Brooks

A tale of mystery and romance and a girl who found both during one enchanted summer.

CLOUD OVER MALVERTON
Nancy Buckingham

Dulcie soon realises that something is seriously wrong at Malverton, and when violence strikes she is horrified to find herself under suspicion of murder.

AFTER THOUGHTS
Max Bygraves

The Cockney entertainer tells stories of his East End childhood, of his RAF days, and his post-war showbusiness successes and friendships with fellow comedians.

MOONLIGHT
AND MARCH ROSES
D. Y. Cameron

Lynn's search to trace a missing girl takes her to Spain, where she meets Clive Hendon. While untangling the situation, she untangles her emotions and decides on her own future.

NURSE ALICE IN LOVE
Theresa Charles

Accepting the post of nurse to little Fernie Sherrod, Alice Everton could not guess at the romance, suspense and danger which lay ahead at the Sherrod's isolated estate.

POIROT INVESTIGATES
Agatha Christie

Two things bind these eleven stories together — the brilliance and uncanny skill of the diminutive Belgian detective, and the stupidity of his Watson-like partner, Captain Hastings.

LET LOOSE THE TIGERS
Josephine Cox

Queenie promised to find the long-lost son of the frail, elderly murderess, Hannah Jason. But her enquiries threatened to unlock the cage where crucial secrets had long been held captive.

THE TWILIGHT MAN
Frank Gruber

Jim Rand lives alone in the California desert awaiting death. Into his hermit existence comes a teenage girl who blows both his past and his brief future wide open.

DOG IN THE DARK
Gerald Hammond

Jim Cunningham breeds and trains gun dogs, and his antagonism towards the devotees of show spaniels earns him many enemies. So when one of them is found murdered, the police are on his doorstep within hours.

THE RED KNIGHT
Geoffrey Moxon

When he finds himself a pawn on the chessboard of international espionage with his family in constant danger, Guy Trent becomes embroiled in moves and countermoves which may mean life or death for Western scientists.

TIGER TIGER
Frank Ryan

A young man involved in drugs is found murdered. This is the first event which will draw Detective Inspector Sandy Woodings into a whirlpool of murder and deceit.

CAROLINE MINUSCULE
Andrew Taylor

Caroline Minuscule, a medieval script, is the first clue to the whereabouts of a cache of diamonds. The search becomes a deadly kind of fairy story in which several murders have an other-worldly quality.

LONG CHAIN OF DEATH
Sarah Wolf

During the Second World War four American teenagers from the same town join the Army together. Forty-two years later, the son of one of the soldiers realises that someone is systematically wiping out the families of the four men.

THE LISTERDALE MYSTERY
Agatha Christie

Twelve short stories ranging from the light-hearted to the macabre, diverse mysteries ingeniously and plausibly contrived and convincingly unravelled.

TO BE LOVED
Lynne Collins

Andrew married the woman he had always loved despite the knowledge that Sarah married him for reasons of her own. So much heartache could have been avoided if only he had known how vital it was to be loved.

ACCUSED NURSE
Jane Converse

Paula found herself accused of a crime which could cost her her job, her nurse's reputation, and even the man she loved, unless the truth came to light.

CHATEAU OF FLOWERS
Margaret Rome

Alain, Comte de Treville needed a wife to look after him, and Fleur went into marriage on a business basis only, hoping that eventually he would come to trust and care for her.

CRISS-CROSS
Alan Scholefield

As her ex-husband had succeeded in kidnapping their young daughter once, Jane was determined to take her safely back to England. But all too soon Jane is caught up in a new web of intrigue.

DEAD BY MORNING
Dorothy Simpson

Leo Martindale's body was discovered outside the gates of his ancestral home. Is it, as Inspector Thanet begins to suspect, murder?

A GREAT DELIVERANCE
Elizabeth George

Into the web of old houses and secrets of Keldale Valley comes Scotland Yard Inspector Thomas Lynley and his assistant to solve a particularly savage murder.

'E' IS FOR EVIDENCE
Sue Grafton

Kinsey Millhone was bogged down on a warehouse fire claim. It came as something of a shock when she was accused of being on the take. She'd been set up. Now she had a new client — herself.

A FAMILY OUTING IN AFRICA
Charles Hampton and Janie Hampton

A tale of a young family's journey through Central Africa by bus, train, river boat, lorry, wooden bicycle and foot.

THE PLEASURES OF AGE
Robert Morley

The author, British stage and screen star, now eighty, is enjoying the pleasures of age. He has drawn on his experiences to write this witty, entertaining and informative book.

THE VINEGAR SEED
Maureen Peters

The first book in a trilogy which follows the exploits of two sisters who leave Ireland in 1861 to seek their fortune in England.

A VERY PAROCHIAL MURDER
John Wainwright

A mugging in the genteel seaside town turned to murder when the victim died. Then the body of a young tearaway is washed ashore and Detective Inspector Lyle is determined that a second killing will not go unpunished.

DEATH ON A HOT SUMMER NIGHT
Anne Infante

Micky Douglas is either accident-prone or someone is trying to kill him. He finds himself caught in a desperate race to save his ex-wife and others from a ruthless gang.

HOLD DOWN A SHADOW
Geoffrey Jenkins

Maluti Rider, with the help of four of the world's most wanted men, is determined to destroy the Katse Dam and release a killer flood.

THAT NICE MISS SMITH
Nigel Morland

A reconstruction and reassessment of the trial in 1857 of Madeleine Smith, who was acquitted by a verdict of Not Proven of poisoning her lover, Emile L'Angelier.

SEASONS OF MY LIFE
Hannah Hauxwell
and Barry Cockcroft

The story of Hannah Hauxwell's struggle to survive on a desolate farm in the Yorkshire Dales with little money, no electricity and no running water.

TAKING OVER
Shirley Lowe and Angela Ince

A witty insight into what happens when women take over in the boardroom and their husbands take over chores, children and chickenpox.

AFTER MIDNIGHT STORIES,
The Fourth Book Of

A collection of sixteen of the best of today's ghost stories, all different in style and approach but all combining to give the reader that special midnight shiver.